THE EHRICH WEISZ

CHRONICLES

INFINITY COIL

THE EHRICH WEISZ

CHRONICLES

INFINITY COIL

MARTY CHAN

Fitzhenry & Whiteside

Published in Canada in 2015 by Fitzhenry & Whiteside, 195 Allstate Parkway, Markham, ON, L3R 4T8
Published in the U.S. in 2015 by Fitzhenry & Whiteside, 311 Washington Street, Brighton, Massachusetts 02135

www.fitzhenry.ca godwit@fitzhenry.ca

10 9 8 7 6 5 4 3 2 1

We acknowledge with thanks the Canada Council for the Arts, and the Ontario Arts Council for their support of our publishing program. We acknowledge the financial support of the Government of Canada through the Canada Book Fund (CBF) for our publishing activities.

Library and Archives Canada Cataloguing in Publication
The Ehrich Weisz Chronicles: Infinity Coil
ISBN 978-1-55455-345-7 (paperback)
Data available on file

Publisher Cataloging-in-Publication Data (U.S.)
The Ehrich Weisz Chronicles: Infinity Coil
ISBN 978-1-55455-345-7 (paperback)
Data available on file

Text design by Daniel Choi
Cover design by Tanya Montini
Cover image courtesy of Shutterstock
Cover art courtesy of Suzanne Del Rizzo

Printed in Canada

ACKNOWLEDGEMENTS

I'd like to give a standing ovation to the generous and talented people who helped me realize this story. Thanks to Christie Harkin, Cheryl Chen, Michelle Chan, Brad Smilanich, Wei Wong and Tanya Montini. Also, a special thank you to Billy Kid and Sheldon Casavant for the peek inside the magician's hat.

RAID ON MUSEUM

New York, June 3 – Demon Watch hunters raided the Museum of Curiosities late Monday night. Three Dimensionals were arrested, but Mr. Serenity, the owner of the establishment, is still at large.

Under the new leadership of Thomas Edison, Demon Watch has shut down forty-seven suspected hideouts for illegal Dimensionals. The Wizard of Menlo Park was appointed Commissioner of Demon Watch after a brazen attack on Devil's Island, the immigration facility for inter-dimensional beings immigrating to New York. The former commissioner, George Farrier, has not been seen since the attack and is presumed to be deceased.

Mr. Edison supervised the raid on the Museum of Curiosities. He declared the raids to be the most effective means to find the culprits behind the attack on Devil's Island: "We are interrogating the illegal Dimensionals and we are certain one of them knows something. We will not stop until we apprehend those responsible."

To date, 146 Dimensionals have been detained.

THE HUNT IS ON

The street urchin huddled against the brick wall, pulling her undersized woollen reefer jacket close around her body to ward off the spring night's chill. She fluffed her sack of rags and papers but froze at the sound of a sharp whistle. She curled into a ball, trying to blend into the heap of garbage.

Shadowy figures prowled the street outside the tenements. They flitted from one side of the cobblestone road to the other. One advanced, then stopped and waited for another to come ahead. The eerie blue glow from their bowler top hats bobbed like will-o'-the-wisps in the narrow lane.

A teenager stopped in front of the ragamuffin and leaned down to inspect her grimy face. "You live here?"

She shook her head.

"Then scram," ordered the lanky boy as he lifted the green-tinted goggles over his eyes.

She scrambled over the pile of trash and bolted around the

corner of the brick tenement building.

Wilhelm signalled the other hunters to join him. "The street is clear."

The four members of his Demon Watch squad approached, their teslatrons raised. A dull blue aura glowed from the doughnut-shaped ends of their black blunderbuss rifles.

Margaret, a snub-nosed bruiser with crooked teeth, took a position in front of the wooden entrance to the tenement. She gently nudged the butt of her rifle against the door and it creaked open. She peered inside and waved to her squad leader.

"Dear lord, the place reeks."

The pungent stench of human waste mixed with rotting garbage and mould assaulted Wilhelm's nostrils. He strapped his teslatron over his back and drew his dynatron pistol from the holster under his leather duster. The weapon's barrel glowed from the electro-dart inside. Atop the pistol was a clip of six needle-sharp darts with glass tube bodies. "Small quarters. Switch over to dynatrons."

The squad drew their pistols. Margaret checked her clip, jamming it into place so that one dart entered the main chamber.

Wilhelm tapped one of the male hunters on the shoulder. The freckled boy jumped. The others snickered.

"Gino, stand watch. Any of the demons try to run, give them the business end of your pistol."

Gino glanced around the dark street. "You sure you want me down here? Why don't you make Albert keep watch? He's the new guy."

A lanky boy with round spectacles spit on the cobblestone street. The spittle landed inches away from Gino's boot. "That's because I'm handy in a fight."

"Ehrich never pretended to be better than me," Gino mumbled.

Wilhelm's nostrils flared. "No, he didn't. He just betrayed us."

"Okay, there is that, but I still don't think I should be left down here while Albert gets to see the action," Gino whined.

Margaret quipped. "I don't want you accidentally shooting me in the back again."

"I make one mistake, and I never live it down," Gino complained.

"One? Try more like a dozen," a pimply-faced hunter said.

"James, I saved your hide more times than I can count."

"Since when could you count," Margaret joked.

"Cut the gab," Wilhelm hissed. "We're going up."

The group of young hunters slipped into the narrow corridor with the precision of seasoned veterans. Up the creaking stairs, Margaret led the charge while James covered her ascent with his dynatron. She took a position at the top to cover the others as they climbed the stairs. Amid the filth, she detected the strong scent of cigars.

Wilhelm noticed it as well when he arrived at the top of the stairs. "Cigar makers are here," he said. "Must be a few Bohemians among the demons. Careful you don't mix the two up."

"What's the difference?" Margaret asked.

"Bohemians will complain to the newspapers," Albert quipped. "Demons won't."

Wilhelm counted six doors on each side of the corridor. He signalled Albert to take a position past the first two doors and cover the hall. Then he motioned James to watch the one opposite the apartment he was about to enter.

He lifted his foot and kicked open the flimsy wooden door. He and Margaret tried to charge in, but there wasn't enough room for both of them in what appeared to be a closet. Margaret provided cover from the doorway as Wilhelm stepped in. He nearly recoiled from the stench of mould and body odour, but he bit his lip and surveyed the room. A wobbly table and two lopsided chairs hemmed in a pair of bodies, who had been sleeping on either side of a black valise but now were wide awake. An old man with a handlebar moustache and bulbous nose glanced from the hunters to the closed door at the other end of the closet. On the other side of the valise, a rotund bald man propped himself up on his elbows.

"Who are you? What is going on?" the old man demanded.

"Demon Watch business," Wilhelm explained. "Show me your documents."

The man had smooth hands for someone so old. He reached into the pocket of his grey sack-styled jacket. Wilhelm trained the barrel of his dynatron at him.

"We're not travellers," he said. "We're as human as you are."

"Are you the only ones living here? Who's in the other room?" Wilhelm pointed the barrel of his gun at the closed door.

"You have some nerve barging in here. What gives you the right?" the bald man argued.

"This gives me the right," Wilhelm said, waving his dynatron pistol in the bald man's face.

The two men backed themselves along the filthy floor.

"Check the other room," Wilhelm barked at Margaret.

"Yes, sir." She hesitated as she surveyed the cramped area.

"Clear a path," Wilhelm ordered the two men. "On your feet."

"Who is your superior? I want to talk to him," the bald man said.

The German teen shrugged. "Tell it to the wind."

"Lower your voices," the big-nosed man pleaded. "You'll wake the baby."

The two men climbed to their feet and blocked the hunter's path to the closed door.

"She'll wail until she wakes the entire tenement."

"Wilhelm?" Margaret asked, searching for direction.

"You want to alert everyone to your presence?" the old man said.

Wilhelm eyed the pair, then gave the order: "Margaret, move them out of the way and check that room."

Before she could take one step, shouts erupted from the hallway.

"Halt!" Margaret yelled. "Stand down."

Wilhelm whirled around and peered out of the room. A mammoth creature stood in the corridor. A rhinoceros horn jutted out of his wide forehead. He dwarfed all the hunters, filling the entire width of the corridor with his thick, muscular body. His black trousers and white shirt nearly popped at the seams. The grey-skinned Dimensional lumbered toward Albert and James who raised their pistols.

Albert shouted, "Do you understand English? I said stand down."

The titan stopped.

"Where are your documents?" Wilhelm asked, stepping into the hallway.

"I have them," he said, reaching into his back pocket.

"Slowly," James said, his finger twitching on the trigger of his dynatron.

The Dimensional gingerly retrieved a folded yellow paper from his trouser pocket and snapped it open. Wilhelm approached the man, flashing his bowler lamp on the paper.

"Divesh Mintari..." Wilhelm slowly sounded out the name.

"How long have you been in this dimension?"

"Two years."

"We have reason to believe illegals are hiding in this tenement. Is there anyone else in your apartment, Divesh?"

"I live alone."

Margaret elbowed her squad leader. "You sure about that name?"

"Why?"

"There was a newspaper article about a guy who jumped off the Brooklyn Bridge. Remember? The reporter tried to pin it on the hunters."

"Yeah. So?"

"Well the victim's name was Divesh Mintari."

Wilhelm narrowed his gaze at the big man. "You sure, Margaret?"

"Yup."

"Hold your horses! Looks like we uncovered a miracle," Wilhelm said as he stepped right behind James and Albert. "A genuine, bona fide, resurrected man."

"We seem to be finding a lot of them these days," James said.

"You're coming with us," Albert ordered.

"I swear, the papers are mine!"

Wilhelm glared at the big man from the other end of the corridor. "How is it that you're in possession of a dead man's papers?"

"It is a common name in my sector."

"You expect us to fall for that flam?" Margaret said.

Divesh pleaded, "The newspapers never get our names right. How do you know the reporter didn't make a mistake?"

Wilhelm raised his dynatron. "Because you're acting like a demon who's bitten off more than he can chew."

"I came to your sector to find a better life, and instead your kind treats me like a criminal. I'm an honest man trying to make a living so I can bring my family across. Why won't you leave me alone?"

Wilhelm waved the pistol in the air. "Because one of your kind attacked Devil's Island. Come along."

"What are you going to do?"

"Take you in for questioning."

The giant charged the group. Though massive, the Dimensional was nimble. Albert fired. The energy bolt struck the Dimensional's abdomen. His body lit up with electrical charges. He roared in pain but remained upright. James took a shot, but to no effect. Wilhelm fired his pistol. The Dimensional howled and ran headlong at the group, lowering his horn to impale Wilhelm.

Margaret grabbed Wilhelm by the collar and hauled him back into the closet as the behemoth tackled Albert and James. He drove the two hunters down the flight of stairs. Divesh lumbered down the steps after their tumbling bodies.

"Stop him," Wilhelm ordered.

"On it," Margaret holstered her dynatron, unslung her teslatron rifle, and pursued the titan down the stairs. Wilhelm followed after her.

Arcs of electricity filled the air as she shot three times into the man's broad back. Her two fellow squad members lay limp on the bottom of the stairs. James' leg was bent at an awkward angle while Albert's arm was covered in scrapes and bloody cuts. Only Gino stood between Divesh and freedom. Gino fired, but the Dimensional didn't stop. He slammed Gino into the wooden door and shattered it into a thousand splinters. The unconscious boy slid into the street.

"Enough!" barked Margaret as she stepped out of the tenement. "Surrender!" She raised her teslatron and took aim at the back of the titan's head.

Divesh spun around. He assessed the situation and raised his hands.

"Your choice, demon. I can fry you right here and now, or you can go down on your knees and live to tell your kids about tonight."

"I'd do what she says," Wilhelm said, emerging from the building with his rifle aimed at the horned man. "She doesn't like repeating herself."

Divesh complied, lacing his fingers behind his head and shifting himself onto one knee and then the other. As Margaret covered her prisoner, Wilhelm bent over to check on Gino.

"He's okay," the teen said.

Margaret said, "What about Albert and James?"

Wilhelm shook his head. "Albert looks a little banged up, and James won't be dancing any Irish jigs in the near future."

"We need medics," she said.

"Cuff the gorilla first. I'll cover you."

Margaret reached behind her back and pulled out a set of Darby leg irons and Irish 8 handcuffs. The D-shaped cuffs barely wrapped around Divesh's thick fingers let alone his massive wrists.

"He's too big," she called back. "They won't fit."

Wilhelm waved his rifle in Divesh's face. "Then he's going to have to be on his best behaviour."

"Where are you taking me?"

"Devil's Island with the rest of the demons," Wilhelm spat. "Move."

The giant refused to budge. He crossed his legs and sat on the cobblestone road.

"You want another zap?"

The titan gritted his teeth. "Help! They're going to torture me!"

Wilhelm shoved the man, but he didn't budge. Margaret joined him. They pushed to no avail. After several moments, they gave up. A crowd of gawkers had started to gather, brought out by the sounds of the Dimensional's shouts.

Wilhelm glanced around the narrow street. "We're going to need some backup."

She grimaced. "You think you can hold the fort?"

"No other choice. Don't dawdle."

She grunted. "I'll be back faster than a fly can blink."

She ran off as more residents of the nearby tenements filtered into the street. Among them were the big-nosed man and his bald companion. He swept the teslatron back and forth in front of the crowd.

"This does not concern you. Go back into your homes."

No one complied. The cries of the titan had piqued their interest, and they weren't about to walk away before seeing how this incident played out. Wilhelm began to break into a sweat as he paced around the Dimensional. He checked over his shoulder in case someone tried to slip behind him.

"What are you going to do with him?" the old man with the bulbous nose asked.

"Demon Watch business," Wilhelm said. "Now all of you, move along."

The German boy backed against the wall of a nearby tenement so that he could keep the suspect in sight and ward off the crowd. The standoff stretched on forever. Wilhelm's finger twitched on the trigger. He wanted to shoot, but he elected not to—at least not until he had some backup.

"Back to your homes," Wilhelm ordered.

The crowd advanced on him. He had no choice. He fired into Divesh's thick neck. Electricity danced up the man's face as he howled in pain and collapsed.

"You didn't have to do that!" the big-nosed man shouted. "He wasn't a threat."

Divesh moaned on the ground and rolled around, his horn scraping against the cobblestones. The crowd surged ahead. Wilhelm walked up to the big man and pointed the barrel of his rifle at the man's face.

"You are all responsible for what happens next," he yelled. "We intend to bring this demon in for questioning, but if you make that difficult for us, then I will have to take more forceful action. It's all on your shoulders."

His threat quieted the mob. A few people began to back away. Only the old man and his companion were defiant.

"This is beyond your scope," the old man said. "What good is all this violence against an innocent traveller?"

"We're seeking the ones responsible for the attack on Devil's Island a few months ago. A young man, Ehrich Weisz, is a human who would be among them. Short fellow. Curly brown hair. If anyone of you know where that traitor is, give him up, and I won't have to make this demon suffer any longer."

"He's a hero if he stands up to your tyranny," Divesh said.

Wilhelm pressed the barrel of his rifle into the Dimensional's temple. The bald man waved everyone back.

"Son, these people are scared. You don't want to frighten them anymore. No telling what they might do out of fear."

"Want to take his place?" Wilhelm threatened.

The bald man fell silent, but his big-nosed companion spoke

up. "There are many eyes here and half as many mouths. I'm sure one of them might whisper in the ear of a newspaper reporter that the Demon Watch is now willing to torture New Yorkers."

Wilhelm raised an eyebrow. "We have ourselves a high-falutin' Bohemian in our midst."

"We are better than this, young man. You can set an example for others."

"Do you see what he did to my hunters?" Wilhelm shot back.

"Easy there, young fella," a new voice said. "You poke the bear, sometimes it swats back."

A thin gentleman with a charismatic smile and intense gaze approached the group, flanked by Margaret and two squads of hunters. Thomas Edison had arrived. He wore a top hat, a frumpy tweed suit, and an opened Norfolk jacket that hung down to his thighs. A piece of flexible tubing extended from his ear to the hatband, where a gramophone horn stared out like a cyclops' eye.

"For heaven's sake, put the gun away," Edison said.

Wilhelm snapped to attention. "Sir, this one has papers, but we think they are forged. He might own up to knowing something about the attack on Devil's Island. He might have information about where Ehrich Weisz is hiding."

"Then we will interrogate him. Not torture. Interrogate." The commissioner then addressed the remaining gawkers. "My hunters have been overzealous in their hunt for an individual. I assure you, I will remedy this, but we cannot abide all of you on the street."

Wilhelm waved at Divesh. "Sir, what about the prisoner? I don't think he's going to cooperate."

Edison glanced at the man seated on the ground. "To

paraphrase Victor Hugo, 'If you speak, you are condemned. If you stay silent, you are damned.'"

"Then I'll be damned," Divesh said.

"We have better means of interrogation on Devil's Island. I suspect the quality of our conversation may improve under more favourable circumstances."

The squad members hauled Divesh away. He resisted every step of the way, but the hunters outnumbered and overwhelmed him.

Edison turned to the crowd, reaching into his jacket and pulling out a large rolled piece of paper. He unfurled it before everyone, revealing a sketch of a curly-haired teen with an anchor nose. "We are searching for this young man. If you come forward with any information, there is a reward. If you have information and fail to come forward, then I wouldn't want to be you."

He handed the poster to a hunter, who affixed it to a nearby brick wall.

"Now unless you want to join the big fellow on Devil's Island, I suggest you all go home and give some thought to the whereabouts of the fugitive."

This was enough to send the bystanders on their way.

Back in the tenement, the bald man knocked on the closed door at the back of the closet.

"It's safe," he announced. "Amina. Ning Shu. You can come out."

The old man took off his spectacles and rubbed his eyes. An ebony girl with a purple corset over a linen shirt emerged from the other room. Her skirt was cut up both sides of her legs to reveal thigh-high boots. Behind her followed a red-skinned woman wearing a wide-sleeved emerald robe that hid her hands.

The old man ripped off his disguise.

The bald man said. "The hunters will come back soon enough."

"We'll need to find another haven," Ning Shu declared.

"You're right." The bald man massaged his scalp. "Anyone have any ideas? Amina?"

The ebony girl stroked her chin. "Are you sure we need to move? We're running out of places to hide."

"I heard the hunters," the bald man said. "They aren't going to stop until they find Ehrich Weisz."

The old man scrubbed the spirit gum off the sides of his anchor nose. Without the disguise, the old man now appeared much younger with his mass of bushy brown hair and fresh face. He surveyed his companions with his intense brown-eyed gaze. "Then I suppose I had better not be where they are searching."

OUT ON THE STREET

Ehrich packed his disguise into a black satchel, careful to avoid tangling the hairpiece. Beside him, the bald man scratched at his scalp.

"I miss my monk's fringe," he said.

"You look handsome without hair, Mr. Serenity," Amina said. "Sometimes you're better off to let go of something that's already on the way out."

He smirked. "Perhaps we'll take the shears to your locks next time."

The ebony girl grabbed her dark hair, mocking her friend. "I'll let you wear some of mine when it's all over. I have plenty to spare."

Ehrich rubbed at his nose.

"You missed some," Ning Shu said, helping the teen rub the sticky paste from his face.

"This would be a lot easier if we still had Amina's device," Ning Shu said.

"If Ehrich's friend returns with my cameo, I'd be happy to use it to hide us all from the hunters," Amina said.

"*When* Mr. Tesla returns," Ehrich said. "Not if."

"Do you think Divesh will talk?" Ning Shu asked. She nervously fingered the jade tael pendant around her neck with her red finger.

Mr. Serenity scratched his head. "He knows what is at stake, but they aren't going to take it easy on him."

"We should have killed Wilhelm when we had the chance," Ehrich said.

"No, son, too risky. Demon Watch would have turned the tenements upside down."

Ning Shu rolled up the wide sleeves of her green robe. "Mr. Serenity, how can you be sure that's not what the hunters are going to do? They're probably waiting for reinforcements. We should leave now."

"We're running out of places to hide," Mr. Serenity said. "The hunters shut down almost all of our access points to Purgatory, and we can't risk exposing the few that are left."

"Purgatory is the safest place for us," Amina said. "They would not think to search for us underground."

Ning Shu shook her head. "If we go below, we'll be safe, but we won't find my father's soldiers. We must contact them, and the only way to do that is to stay in the city."

Ehrich leaned against the jamb of the door. "We have combed the streets for months with no luck. I think they left New York."

"We'll search harder," Ning Shu said. "We can't give up."

Ehrich fell silent, thinking how far he was from his idyllic childhood of Appleton, Wisconsin. Only three years ago, he played at being a world famous acrobat for his family's entertainment, in a dimension that bore a passing resemblance to this one; except, in his own world, he didn't need to worry about portals that opened to other worlds or invaders from those dimensions. All he had to worry about was how to keep his brother Dash and himself out of trouble. But misery seemed to follow the Weisz family like a bad penny. An inter-dimensional assassin, Kifo, had taken control of Dash's body. Ehrich pursued the possessed boy and found himself caught in this other world.

Two years of searching had led to much frustration. His only clue was the Infinity Coil, which seemed to be only a trinket until he met Amina and learned the device's true purpose. With Mr. Serenity's help, he had learned the Infinity Coil stored souls—including Dash's—and only Kifo could release those trapped within. Teaming up with Amina and Mr. Serenity, Ehrich searched for the assassin and learned he was working with Ba Tian, the warlord who was mounting an invasion of this dimension and who was also Ning Shu's father. George Farrier, the former commissioner of Demon Watch, had betrayed his own people when he allowed Ba Tian and Kifo to sneak onto his facilities and gain access to the portal that opened to multiple dimensions. Ehrich and his companions stopped the invasion, but not without paying a price. Kifo regained control of the Infinity Coil and abandoned Dash's body, leaving a blank shell behind. Now Ehrich needed the assassin to restore his brother's consciousness to his body, which now rested in suspended animation in a glass sarcophagus in Mr. Serenity's underground hideout.

"We don't know how much longer we have before my father finds a way back into this dimension," Ning Shu said.

Amina pointed out, "We stranded him in my sector without any devices to open portals. If he's going to come back, it won't be any time soon."

"He's not without allies," Ning Shu pointed out.

Mr. Serenity agreed. "True. If any of his generals learn of his fate, they will try to rescue him."

"We can't afford to waste any more time. We have to find my father's soldiers and make sure he never returns to this sector."

Though she was connected to the warlord by blood, Ning Shu had secretly rebelled against him, spiriting away Hakeem, the scientist who designed his exoskeleton soldier army under the Hudson River. As much as Ehrich needed to catch Kifo to find a way to restore his brother, Ning Shu wanted to slay Kifo. He had assassinated Hakeem, the man who was the rebels' only hope and the man who had held her heart.

"Ning Shu, what if the reason we can't find the soldiers is because he's already back?" Ehrich asked.

A tense silence fell over the group.

Amina patted Ning Shu on the shoulder, "I'm sure we would know if your father had returned. We'll leave in the morning. We'll raise more suspicion if we leave in the dead of night."

"Amina's right," Mr. Serenity added. "We go now, everyone in the tenement will wonder why. They'll remember us. I don't have enough money for another set of disguises."

"Ehrich could work the Three-Card Monte," Ning Shu suggested. "Earn enough money to pay for another room somewhere."

"Yes, but the problem is where to hide you in the meantime. You stand out in the crowd, Ning Shu," he said.

"Ehrich, I know you want to find Kifo." Ning Shu fixed her eyes on him intently. "My father's generals will be able to help us locate him."

She knew how to press his buttons. Though Ehrich had a passing interest in helping the rebels, they were only a means to an end. He needed to find Kifo and the Infinity Coil to save his brother.

"Yes, Ning Shu," he said. "I know they are our key to finding Kifo. But we have to locate them first."

"What if the generals are hiding under the Hudson River?" Amina asked. "What if they're trapped there with exoskeleton machines and are waiting for Edison to reopen the Tunnel Project?"

Ehrich disagreed. "No, when I was down there, I only saw a handful of technicians building the exoskeleton machines. Not enough to be an army. I think they were shut out with all the workers when Edison shut down the operations of the tunnel. Besides, if they had access to the machines, I think we'd know by now."

Ning Shu gripped her jade tael pendant in her fist. "We need to sneak into the tunnel and see for ourselves. At the very least, it will get us out of this tenement and away from the prying eyes of hunters and nosy neighbours."

The others relented. Her plan was foolhardy because of the sentries posted at the entrance, but staying put was worse. Ehrich sensed the truth in Ning Shu's fears. The hunters wouldn't walk away. They would come back, and Ehrich couldn't afford to be here when they returned. He pulled out a brown pork-pie hat and an eye patch from a satchel. Amina reached into the same leather bag and retrieved a veil to toss to Ning Shu. Mr. Serenity reversed his jacket. The motley crew's disguises would not hold up against close inspection, but the night would provide some cover.

To avoid attracting any attention, the group left the tenement one after the other. Ehrich slipped into the shadows and edged his way down the street until he was a few blocks away. He stopped under the elevated railway line on Sixth Avenue and waited for the others. The crowds had thinned out by now in the dead of night. There weren't even any hunter patrols.

He spotted a fresh wanted poster pasted on the iron support of the elevated train tracks. A reward was offered for any information leading to the capture of Ehrich Weisz. He ripped down the poster. Then he walked to the next support to tear down other posters.

A few minutes later, Mr. Serenity reeled toward him, posing as a drunken man. Ehrich waved him over. "They've put up my posters in the area. Now everyone's on the hunt for me."

Mr. Serenity tapped Ehrich's eye patch. "As long as you don't match the sketch, you'll be fine."

Ehrich scanned the streets. No one was around, but he couldn't relax. He pulled the hat over his eyes and angled his face toward the pillar.

Amina and Ning Shu arrived shortly after. They scurried to the muster point like two workers heading home from a late-night shift. The four then travelled west, staying to the shadows to avoid being spotted by any curious apartment dwellers. Though the windows were dark, Ehrich felt a thousand eyes boring into his back from every opening.

As they neared Morton Street, apartments gave way to warehouses and shops. The colourful awnings had been furled up, but the chalky remnants of the daily specials still clung to the boards affixed to the brick sides. The area had shut down for the night, but the life teeming on the cobblestone streets suggested otherwise. Dimensionals huddled against the walls. Some slept. Others were awake. Some were ebony skinned like Amina; others looked like Ehrich. One woman had two sets of arms: one set she wrapped around her body and the other set she used as a makeshift pillow.

"I knew many Dimensionals came here during the day, but I didn't expect them to stay through the night," Amina said.

Mr. Serenity whispered, "Where else are they going to stay? Edison shut down the tunnel months ago."

"Stay here." Ehrich broke away from the group and headed to three Dimensionals around a small fire at the end of the street.

He kept his head low as he approached the trio. They slid to one side to allow him to join them. He rubbed his hands by the fire.

"Rough night," he said. "Any word on the tunnel?"

A green-skinned titan of a man with piercings across his bottom lip shook his head. "Nothing but rumours, but if they pan out, I want to be here. Only so many job openings, and now there are more travellers seeking work. Can't afford to miss out."

A tiny man with tentacles for fingers agreed. "The humans aren't going to care who worked here before. Going to be first to come, first to work."

The conversation faded out, and Ehrich sidled to a group of former tunnel workers further down the street, closer to the gate. They didn't feel like talking, so he strolled to another group of men. He noticed an odd lack of female travellers among the groups huddled along the Hudson River.

A cold breeze blew in from the river. Two green-skinned men stamped their feet and blew into their hands. One traveller had studded piercings all over his face while the other's face was marked with magenta tattoo swirls.

Ehrich glanced at the half-dozen sentries manning the gated entrance. "I don't suppose we could rush them."

The men laughed. "Getting in would be no problem," the one with piercings said. "Getting paid, on the other hand..."

"You think they'll ever open the project up?" Ehrich asked.

No one offered an answer.

"Then they should let us go down and use the place as a shelter."

"You're not the first one to suggest that."

"Who else?"

The man with the tattoos glanced over his shoulder then leaned toward Ehrich. "Some travellers are talking about taking over the tunnel. Using it as a protest site. Might rally people to our plight."

"And get our heads bashed in," Ehrich said.

"That's my sentiment," the one with the piercings said. "I told those rabble-rousers to peddle their foolishness somewhere else. Why is it always the crimson ones that stir up trouble?"

"In their blood," the tattooed man said.

"Crimson? They were red skinned?" Ehrich asked. "Where do I find them?"

"You don't. They find you. I was at Chumley's when one of them just sat down and bought me a drink."

"When did you see them last?"

"I don't know. Maybe a couple of weeks or so."

"Well, you let me know if you do see them. I wouldn't mind getting a free drink."

The pierced one levelled a steady gaze at Ehrich. "You'd best steer clear of them. They're nothing but trouble."

Ehrich murmured thanks then walked back to his group. He deliberately walked slowly to hide his excitement. He'd had their first break in months, and he couldn't wait to share it with the others.

THREE-CARD MONTE

Once a blacksmith shop, Chumley's was now a makeshift gathering place for the travellers and anyone who did not want to be seen in the public eye. A few blocks from the Hudson River Tunnel Project, the two-storey brick tavern was nestled between taller shops on the narrow lane of Bedford Street. The inconspicuous doorway lacked a sign. If you didn't know where Chumley's was, you were not welcome inside.

Ehrich had raided the inn a few times when he was a hunter, and was well acquainted with the type of patrons who frequented the drinking establishment. Often, the raids yielded at least a dozen illegal travellers. Many of them were harmless, but every now and then they came across someone who bypassed the portal on Devil's Island to enter New York. The fugitives tried to escape through the secret passageway under the inn that was once part of the underground railroad slaves had used and now was an escape route for Dimensionals. Ehrich often flushed out the Dimensionals, driving them to hunters at the other end, until the tavern owners boarded up the tunnel.

Ehrich and Amina slipped into the crowd of weary and inebriated travellers, searching the tavern for any red-skinned soldiers from Ba Tian's army. They left Ning Shu and Mr. Serenity back at the Tunnel Project to gather more information about any other possible sightings of red-skinned rabble-rousers.

A barkeep in a filthy apron wiped the sweat from his brow as he carried a bucket of beer to fill the thirsty patrons' cups. Amina elbowed her way to the counter and surveyed the depressed faces of the men and women who had left their worlds to find a better home, and who had realized this might not be it.

"I'd like a drink," she ordered, but the bartender ignored her as he tended to the others at the bar.

"Am I invisible?" she joked to the woman with walrus tusks beside her.

The tall woman cocked her head to one side. "You need an attention getter." She pulled down her maroon tunic and pulled out a few bills from between her breasts. She slapped them on the bar.

The bartender snapped to attention and rushed over. "What'll you have?"

The tusky woman grinned. "Money. Works every time. What do you want? It's on me."

"Uh, thanks. I'll take two mugs of cider," Amina said. The woman stroked her tusk and admired Amina's form. Amina sidled away.

Ehrich found a table and sat on a chair that had not seen the clean side of a rag in quite some time. He signalled Amina to join him then scanned the crowd of drunken revellers in the corner. No sign of Ba Tian's soldiers.

Amina perched on a chair across from him and ignored the

tusky woman's leering glances. "I think this is going to be a long night."

"Where else are we going to go?"

"True. But I hate stakeouts. They go on forever." He reached into his pocket and pulled out a pair of his black Bicycle cards, named so for the twin bicycle designs on the back. He practiced his Charlier cut with his left hand, making the one-handed cut seem smooth. Since they had been on the run, Ehrich had been practicing different magic tricks he had remembered from his Robert Houdin book. He rehearsed the tricks to ease the stress of being a fugitive, but more recently, he had taken up card sleights for practical reasons. "Do you mind if I pass the time?" he asked Amina.

"They're poor travellers, Ehrich. Go easy on them."

He gave the deck an overhand shuffle, then spread the deck on the table to find the queen of spades and two jokers. "Who wants to win Three-Card Monte?" he barked.

Ehrich flashed the faces to Amina, then placed them on the table with the backs up. He switched the cards from one position to the other and stopped. "Now all you have to do is tell me where the queen of spades is."

Amina pointed to the middle. He flipped over the card. The queen appeared.

"You win. That's how easy it is."

Three men from the revellers reeled toward them from the corner. They were well into their cups and would make the perfect marks for the game of Three-Card Monte.

"Do it again," the one with buckteeth said, slurring his words.

He repeated the trick and invited the drunken man to find the queen of spades. He pointed to the middle card. Again, the queen.

"Easy," he boasted to his friends.

Ehrich suggested, "Want to put some money on it?"

The man laughed and reached into his pocket to pull out a few bills. His friends did the same.

Ehrich flashed the cards to the men, one after the other. "Keep your eye on the lady. We have the joker, the queen, and another joker. All you have to do is find the lady, and you win." He placed the cards one after the other on the table, appearing to have placed the queen in the middle. The drunken man fell for the trick. He stabbed the middle card and threw down two dollars.

Ehrich flipped over a joker. "Sorry. Bad luck."

The man's face reddened. "It was there. I know it."

The queen was on the left. "Next time, don't blink." He had reeled in his mark. More money landed on the table as new players joined in. He repeated the trick, and none of the players ever guessed right. Ehrich folded an obvious crimp in the corner of the queen of spades to make it easier to find the card, flashing it to his latest victim. When the player flipped over the card, the men groaned when they spotted the joker with a crimp in the corner.

By night's end, Ehrich had enough money that they could book a nearby hotel. Part of him felt guilty for taking the travellers' money, but he consoled himself by thinking that if they could afford to drink, they weren't as bad off as the travellers sleeping on Morton Street.

The pair left Chumley's to connect with Mr. Serenity and Ning Shu. They also found nothing about the soldiers. They would try reconnoitering Chumley's again the following night.

The next night turned into the next week, and still no one showed up. Ehrich didn't count the evenings as days. He counted them as hands played. Every now and then he deliberately lost to keep the players interested in what they perceived was an honest game and a really bad streak of luck. Amina circled the group, egging them on whenever someone lost the nerve to bet.

Then one night, a scarlet hand tossed in a bill. Ehrich followed the hand up the arm to the face of a muscular crimson man. Ehrich didn't recognize him but noted the tusks on either side of the man's nose. This had to be a soldier from Ba Tian's army. Amina slid in close. First contact.

Ehrich played, but he couldn't concentrate. He threw the cards down in the wrong order. He lost. The hulking man tucked the money into the inside pocket of his ebony silk jacket and walked away.

"Must be losing my touch," he announced as he gathered his cards. "That's enough for one night."

"Not until I win my money back," a drunken man said. He grabbed Ehrich's wrist and pulled him back down.

Ehrich tried to pull away, but the drunk had a firm grip. Amina waved at Ehrich and started to follow the red man.

"Hey, she's sending him signals," the scrawny friend yelled.

"What? No."

"She's in on it. The fix is in." He wrapped his arms around Amina.

"Let go of her!"

"I don't cotton to cheaters!"

Tempers flared as the bettors jostled one another to throttle Ehrich and Amina. Meanwhile, the man in the silk jacket disappeared into the crowd. Rough hands grabbed at Ehrich's throat and pushed him back into the rank patrons. One man grasped his shirt and reached for Ehrich's money. Bills flew out, and a few punches rained on the back of his head. He threw an elbow back and caught someone in the nose.

He jumped forward, but a hand caught his collar. Amina

fended off her attackers, but there were too many in the room, and they needed to go after the red man.

"Eighty-six!" Ehrich yelled, recalling the code word the Chumley's staff had used when they knew a raid was coming.

He wasn't the only one who knew this code. The patrons scattered, rushing toward the back door and the secret passageway. Apparently, the tunnel had proven useful again. Ehrich wondered if perhaps it led to a different exit. Only the drunken man and his friends remained to grab the rest of the money from Ehrich.

Amina threw off the last of her attackers and grabbed his hand. "There he is."

They joined the crowd going into the passageway. The back of the red man's head was just visible over the shorter patrons. He wore his long black hair in a braided queue. They followed him into the narrow corridor and eventually emerged through a small door that opened onto a street beyond the tavern. Bright sunlight blinded Ehrich. They had been in Chumley's all through the night and well into the morning.

The red man slipped away from the fleeing patrons and marched toward the Hudson River. Ehrich hooked his arm around Amina's to pose as two lovers on a morning stroll.

Their prey joined another man in a similar silk jacket and flared black pants with white cuffs. He stood on the corner facing the Hudson River. The masts of the merchant ships dotted the horizon, dwarfed by the Statue of Liberty looming over them. The pair conversed for a moment, then turned north along the river. The two men did not venture far.

Amina let out a low whistle. "They're not even in the city. That's why we haven't found them."

The soldiers had stopped at a pier where small boats were

moored. There they untied the lines holding a small craft and pushed off on the Hudson River.

Amina grabbed Ehrich's arm. "Come on. We'll need to find another boat."

"Hold on," he said. "Wait until they clear the pier. We don't want to arouse any suspicion."

Amina waited. The ship floated away from the Statue of Liberty, out of the shipping lanes and to the north.

Ehrich scanned the pier—no witnesses. He headed to the nearest skiff, hopped on board, and helped Amina board. Then he tossed the line and pushed off. He found some oars under the bench and began to row after the skiff, keeping back a healthy distance. The boat rolled against the waves of the choppy river. Under the grey sky, their boat barely seemed to move. Amina had found another set of oars under his seat and was helping him row.

"Do you think they're hiding across the river?" he asked. Ehrich's arms were aching by now, but he'd found a rhythm.

Amina grunted as she pulled the oars. "Must be the reason we haven't spotted them until now." Suddenly, she checked her stroke, staring over Ehrich's shoulder at the soldiers' boat. "Stop!" she hissed.

Ehrich cantilevered the oars out of the water. The soldiers had stopped in the middle of the river. Ehrich and Amina ducked low in their boat and peered over the prow. The men didn't seem concerned with anyone around them. Instead, they seemed to be staring up at the sky.

A low-hanging cloud appeared to be moving against the wind and was now hovering over the men's craft. Ropes dropped from the bottom of the cloud toward the boat. The crimson men grabbed the lines and looped them through the oarlocks on the sides and ends of the skiff. They then seated themselves

Marty Chan

at either end of the boat and gripped the sides as the cables began to retract up to the cloud. The men steadied their craft, maintaining balance, as water poured off the sides and the boat rose higher and higher.

Ehrich squinted at the cloud. The outline of what at first seemed like a whale soon took the shape of a massive airship. Ehrich noted the outline of the balloon and guessed the lines were coming from the gondola attached to the bottom of the giant air bag.

"They're hiding in the sky," Ehrich said.

"Great! We've found them, but how do we get up there?"

Ehrich had no idea.

ENEMY OF MY ENEMY

The floating boat brought to Ehrich's mind a grand illusion Robert Houdin might have executed. The craft disappeared into the cloud, which now began to drift north along the river, against the wind.

"They brought an airship here?" Ehrich asked. "How did they transport it through a portal?"

Amina shook her head. "I don't know."

"Hey, they're floating away." He pointed at the departing cloud.

"We can't follow them," Amina said. "They're too fast."

"Yes, but now we know where they send their scouts to the city. All that's left is to stake out the pier. Let's head back."

He rowed to the shore. As the boat rocked up and down on the water, he kept his gaze fixed on the cloud floating against the wind.

Reunited with their group near the Hudson River Tunnel Project, Ehrich and Amina informed the others of their discovery. Mr. Serenity rubbed his bald head, bewildered. "By Jovian's Anvil, how do they manage to hide the airship?"

"I don't know," Ehrich answered, "but the cloud moved with them. It was the perfect camouflage."

"My father's forces used fog machines to camouflage our troops on open battlefields," Ning Shu explained. "Wouldn't be too hard to rig a machine to hide a vessel in the sky."

"I'm worried, Ning Shu. Are you sure that if we get on the airship, the generals will listen to you?" Ehrich asked.

"Trust in me, Ehrich."

"Your father seemed intent on gaining control of Demon Gate. It's the only stable portal that connects to multiple dimensions, and I'm sure the generals will also see its value. How are we going to sway them from this mission?"

She pulled the jade tael out from under her green robes. "The generals answer to the House of Qi."

"Isn't that just a weapon?" Ehrich asked.

"No, this is the seal of the House of Qi. My ancestors bore the symbol to mark their claim to their birthright. Whoever is a member of the House of Qi rules the army. In the absence of my father, I command the forces."

Amina squinted one eye at Ning Shu. "If you come out into the open with contradictory orders, the generals will suspect you're up to something."

"They did not see me rebel against my father during his assault on Devil's Island. They have no reason to doubt me."

Ehrich argued, "But they'll question the new directive."

Ning Shu slid the jade tael under her emerald robe. "They are like one of those large ships in the harbour. They will eventually move in the direction you want, but you have to be patient."

Ehrich led the group away from nearby Dimensionals. "Do you think the generals are tired of war?"

"We are a loyal people. This flaw has cost us dearly. When my mother died, Ba Tian lost his moral compass. He led my people with him down a mad path."

"What do you mean?" Mr. Serenity asked, leaning closer.

"My father did not strike first. Marauders from another dimension wanted our realm. They sent assassins to kill my father. My mother sacrificed herself to save him. The killers fled, but he tracked them to the first portal. He realized this attack would be one of many."

"Why did he wage war on the other sectors?" Amina asked.

"To send a signal that the House of Qi was formidable. Personally, I believe he wanted to avenge my mother."

"Don't your people question his motives?"

"He tells them he seeks resources so our people will not starve. In my realm, we say, 'when your mouth is full, you cannot criticize.' As long as my father fed the people, they supported him."

"What about the soldiers who witnessed the ravages of war?"

She shook her head. "They are loyal to the House of Qi. No general or soldier would dare to speak against the House of Qi. The shame would be too great."

"A poor excuse," Amina said.

Ning Shu leaned against the brick wall. "A few generals might welcome a change in direction. Ling Po has stood by my father's side since I was a child. He served my father long before the assassination attempt. Ling Po may be our best ally."

"As long as we can find him," Ehrich pointed out.

Marty Chan

The next two days tested the group's patience. In pairs, they staked out a different pier along the Hudson River, hoping someone would luck out and catch one of the crimson scouts headed into the city. Ehrich worked with Amina at the northern end while Ning Shu and Mr. Serenity scouted the docks near the Hudson River Tunnel Project. Days wore on until a week passed with no success.

Late one night, Ehrich and the others huddled around a fire barrel the street vendors used to keep warm as they peddled their wares. He beckoned Amina closer to the fire, and the glow illuminated the high cheekbones of her ebony face. He stared at her in the orange light, but looked away when she glanced at him.

"What do you think our odds are of finding Kifo?" he asked.

"If Ning Shu is right, he will try to reconnect with the generals," Mr. Serenity said.

"Now that he's no longer in my brother's body, they won't recognize him. They'll see him as an intruder."

"Maybe they'll kill him," Amina said.

"I hope not."

An awkward silence followed. Mr. Serenity and Ning Shu walked to the river. Amina lingered. She rubbed her hands over the fire.

"If I close my eyes and shut out the buildings, I'm in the woods near my parents' home. I can almost smell the pine trees I used to climb. At night, my sister and I would start a small cooking fire in the woods while we hunted wood rats. Sometimes, we lucked out and caught a few at the start of the hunt. They are small and fast, and only come out after dark. Cooked properly, they are delicious. Other times, we'd sit by the fire and warm our hands and tell tales of the nights when we did catch the rats. When we tired of true stories, Aleira resorted to tall tales to scare me."

"You, frightened? Hard to believe."

She smirked. "My sister fuelled my fear with stories of spirits in the woods. She told me the spirits took little girls who strayed too far from the light. They ripped at the girls' souls and cast them into an abyss, where the victims would remain alive in utter agony for all of eternity."

"Sounds like the perfect older sister."

"Ehrich, she scarred me for life."

"That's what older siblings do," Ehrich said. "I remember once scaring the dickens out of my brother. We were awake far later than we should have been, and I warned Dash about the ghost in our apartment. At first, he didn't believe me, but I knew he eventually would. I spun a story about a former tenant who had been driven mad during the Civil War, and how this tenant had shut himself off from the world in the very room we slept in. He howled just like the wind blowing outside our window. When I saw my brother bundle up under his blanket, I knew he believed. I told Dash to stay near the candle because the ghost only came out at night. Without the protection of the light, we were at the mercy of the spectre. And when Dash was good and wound up, I blew out the candle. Oh, how he shrieked and squealed when I grabbed his leg in the dark. I can still hear his screams."

Amina smacked Ehrich's arm.

"Ow. What did I do?"

"That's from all the little brothers and sisters who had to put up with their older siblings' stories."

"Stay near the fire, Amina. You know what happens if you don't."

She chuckled.

"I'll take the first shift tonight, Amina," he offered. "You sleep."

"If I can after your story." She clutched the jacket closed around her body and huddled against a wall. Ehrich stayed up. He hadn't been able to sleep at all; his brain buzzed with the possibility of forcing Kifo to restore Dash to his body. He had feigned calm around the others but alone in the dark, he was consumed with his obsession to catch Kifo. He would have rather searched the streets for the man with the Infinity Coil, but he promised to help his friends. Maybe assisting them could ultimately lead to locating Kifo, but he couldn't be sure which strategy would be the most effective. Unable to still his thoughts, he let the others sleep through the night.

Dawn brought a new day and hope. As Ehrich rubbed his tired eyes, he glanced at the sky and noticed a low-hanging cloud, which lazily drifted over the Hudson River. A boat emerged from the cloud and was lowered to the water. He shook Amina awake. "They're back."

They headed to the nearest pier to meet the approaching boat. As they neared the pier, a hunter patrol emerged from one of the side streets. Amina grabbed Ehrich's arm and pulled him against the wall so they wouldn't be noticed. Wilhelm and his remaining hunters turned away from them and headed toward the pier. Albert adjusted his spectacles as he lagged behind the others, looking out of place among the seasoned hunters.

Wilhelm barked, "Albert, keep up!"

"Sorry, sir! Yes, sir."

"Save the apologies for your mother if you ever find her. I want to check the pier."

Gino whined. "Our shift's done, Wilhelm. We should head back to Devil's Island."

Margaret agreed. "If I knew you were going to push us like

this, I would have broken my own leg so I could join James in the infirmary."

"Can't we call it a night?" Gino asked.

Wilhelm shook his head. "We're done when I say we're done."

Ehrich chewed his bottom lip. Wilhelm had changed so much since the first time Ehrich had worked with him. So much anger had replaced the once innocent eyes of his former squad mate.

"Do it again," the fresh-faced Wilhelm begged.

Ehrich held the ace of spades in his right hand and a deck of cards in his left.

"Show me how you changed the card," Wilhelm said. "It's witchcraft, isn't it?"

Behind the pair, their squad leader Charlie snickered. "Yes, Ehrich Weisz comes to Demon Gate by the way of Salem. If we toss him in the East River, he'll float because he's made of wood."

Wilhelm scowled at the lanky teen with the disarming smile. "I'm sure there is some kind of sorcery at work. You can't just instantly change a card."

"You should ask Ehrich to show you his broom and black cat."

Ehrich shook his head at his friend. "Leave Wilhelm be. I like having an audience and you're going to scare him off."

"Will you perform the trick once again for me, Ehrich? Please."

"Sorry. The cardinal rule of magic is to never repeat a trick in front of the same spectator."

"Why not?"

"Seeing a trick once is magic. Twice is boring," Ehrich said. "Don't worry, I'll work on a few new ones for you."

"I will learn how you do these tricks one day," Wilhelm said. "Then we can go on the road as a magic act together. Wilhelm the Wonder of the World and his faithful assistant, Ehrich Weisz."

Charlie and Ehrich laughed.

"Why are you laughing? I'm serious." Wilhelm tried to hold a straight face, but a smirk crept across his face.

Ehrich dribbled the rest of the cards in his hands while Wilhelm watched with his eagle eyes. Charlie straightened up.

"Hey, what about me? You two would go on the road without me?"

Ehrich cocked his head to the side. "We could always use a porter to carry our trunks of money."

Wilhelm burst out laughing. "And someone to ward off our many fans."

Charlie twisted his lips into a cruel smile. "You know, as squad leader, I can make you do a few things to regret what you just said."

"Quick, Ehrich. Do you have a trick to make Charlie's ego disappear?"

More laughter.

The hunters searched the boats on the pier, flipping up tarps looking for any stowaways on the boats. Ehrich needed to distract them from the approaching crimson men. He pressed his fake moustache against his lip and pulled his bowler hat lower on his head, hoping this was enough to fool his former squad mates.

Ehrich motioned Amina back. "Stay here. If something goes wrong, we'll meet up in Gansevoort market."

She nodded and pulled a veil over her face.

He approached the group. "Fancy a game of Three-Card Monte?" He reached into his vest pocket and drew out a deck of cards.

Wilhelm couldn't be bothered with Ehrich and waved him off dismissively. "Find some other suckers. We're on official Demon Watch business."

Ehrich set up on a crate nearby and shouted, "Won't take more than a minute. Who wants to find the lady? Come one, come all. All you have to do is follow the cards and you could make some easy money." He spread the deck across the crate, drawing the squad's attention to the cards rather than his face.

Albert moved closer.

"Keep searching," Wilhelm ordered.

Margaret crossed her arms. "Our shift's done, Wilhelm."

Gino added. "Come on, we need a break."

Wilhelm stayed back while the others crowded around Ehrich. The squad leader was about to protest, but his gaze lingered on the deck of cards in Ehrich's hands. Though he was hardened, the German teen still held some fascination for magic tricks. He turned to gaze at the approaching boat when he noticed Ehrich eyeing him.

Ehrich turned his attention to the remaining hunters. "Ah, you three seem brighter than your friend."

Wilhelm stomped across the wooden planks of the pier. "What did you say?"

"Just commenting on people who walk away from easy money."

Wilhelm didn't take the bait. He gritted his teeth and stepped back.

Ehrich played to Gino. "You think your friend is bright enough to outwit me, or do you think he's as dense as a piece of wood?"

This jab seemed to rile Wilhelm but amuse his companions. If Ehrich had learned anything about his time with the German teen, it was that he loved to figure out how things worked.

"Won't take but a moment," Ehrich said. "All you need to do is find the queen. Not too hard."

He flashed the cards—two jokers and the queen of spades—

then flipped them over and spread them across the crate. Out of the corner of his eye, Ehrich spotted the crimson men's ship draw closer.

"All you have to do is bet on the right card, and you win."

Gino reached into his pocket and pulled out some coins. He bellied up to the crate and tried first. Ehrich let him win, drawing in the other two hunters. Wilhelm stared at the crimson men pulling into the dock.

"We have another winner, but let's see how keen you are this time. Follow the queen."

Margaret slapped down some money, and Ehrich scooped it up after her inevitable loss. "Guess you aren't that sharp eyed after all. What about your friend? Is he going to play, or is he going to sulk?"

The hunters laughed. Ehrich glanced over his shoulder at Amina who kept watch from the street. She shrugged. There was nothing she could do to stop the inevitable meeting. The ship docked, and the two men climbed out.

"Who else wants to play?" Ehrich asked, but the hunters now focussed their attention on the new arrivals.

"Bit early in the morning for a river outing," Wilhelm said.

"Fishing," one of the red-skinned men said, holding up a rod.

"Any luck?" Margaret asked.

"Nope," the other man answered.

"They look as if they could win a game of Three-Card Monte," Ehrich said, but no one was listening to him now.

The two red-skinned soldiers climbed onto the wooden pier and towered over Gino, the tallest of the hunters.

"Is it a crime to be on the river?" asked the crimson man with a broken tusk on the side of his nose.

"No, but it is odd," Wilhelm said. "Won't be so odd when you show us your documents."

"I left them back on shore with my family," replied the other crimson man.

"Then you won't mind if we escort you to your family," Wilhelm said.

The crimson men exchanged glances and reached into their robes. The hunters were faster, drawing their teslatron rifles and dynatron pistols. Ehrich glanced at Amina and signalled her to stay back.

"Hands where we can see them," Margaret ordered. "Nice and slow."

The two men didn't comply. The hunters advanced.

Ehrich had to act now. He ripped off his moustache and proclaimed, "Wilhelm, you really aren't all that bright, are you? Searching for me all this time, and I was right under your nose."

The German teenager spun around, his nostrils flaring almost as wide as his eyes. He sputtered, "G-g-get him!"

Ehrich jumped to his feet and spurted the deck into a blizzard of cards. The air sizzled with energy as the hunters discharged their weapons into the flurry. When the cards fell to the pier, Ehrich was gone.

Amina rushed to the scene. "Ehrich!"

"Gino, search the pier," Wilhelm ordered. "Margaret, Albert— capture his accomplice."

Amina spun on her heels and ran away from the pier, Margaret and Albert hot on her trail. As she headed further down the street, Amina slowed near the warehouse. She needed to draw the hunters away from the pier. She glanced back at her pursuers, but only Margaret was behind her. Albert must have fallen behind. Amina picked up the pace.

Margaret raised her dynatron pistol and fired. The energy dart narrowly missed Amina, and forced her to veer off down a street back to the river. As soon as she stepped into the street running parallel to the Hudson, Amina realized the hunters' scheme. Albert charged along the street. He hadn't fallen behind. He ran an intercept course, and Margaret had driven her right into his path.

She jumped back as he fired a shot. Energy crackled on the brick building beside her. She doubled back, but Margaret rounded the other corner. No escape.

The crimson men in silk jackets tried to leave the pier during the confusion, but Wilhelm raised his rifle and signalled them to sit. One of them unbuttoned the knot buttons on his jacket, flapped open the jacket to reveal his washboard abs, then sat down on a post. The other one remained standing.

"You wait until we sort this out," Wilhelm said. "Damn Ehrich. He couldn't have just disappeared."

"Guess he's still practising magic," Gino said.

"I'll bet he's hiding right under our noses. Search the boats."

Wilhelm wasn't too far off in his guess. Using the cards as distraction, Ehrich had slipped off the pier and now clung to one of the wooden support posts. As long as he heard movement above, he had to stay put. His arms ached, but he hung on to the damp post, trying to outwait Wilhelm and trying to keep from sliding into the cold water.

"If you can hear me, Ehrich, give yourself up so you can join your friend, Dr. Tesla, in prison."

Ehrich flinched. Part of him wanted to know what had happened to his friend and mentor since the battle on Devil's Island. Nikola Tesla had sacrificed his own freedom so Ehrich and the others could escape the prison. Ehrich had hoped the inventor had found another way out, but Wilhelm's barb suggested otherwise. He wondered if Tesla had been subjected to Edison's interrogation techniques. He bit his lip and stayed above the water, fighting to keep the dark thoughts out of his head.

"You think he jumped in the river?" Gino asked.

"Maybe. Gino, you ever hear the story of the workers on Devil's Island?"

"No."

"They had to blast through the rock to create the underground prison. The men weren't paid a lot to handle the dynamite. Often, they starved for days until the next pay period, but one man had enough. He grabbed some explosives and tossed them into the East River. The charge detonated, and dead fish floated up so he could scoop them up. The men ate for a week. I think we ought to try some fishing of our own."

"Wilhelm, we don't have any explosives."

"No, but this will do."

"Don't we want Ehrich alive?"

"More or less."

Ehrich could hear the hum of the teslatron rifle charging up. He inched himself up the post, pulling his feet up. A blue bolt of energy hit the water and electricity branched out across the rippling surface. He held his breath. Another shot hit the river. Then another. Ehrich's arms began to slip on the post. If he touched the surface, he was done for. Another shot. Ehrich's feet were inches from the water. He squeezed the post and willed himself to stay up.

A couple of fish floated to the surface of the water. They rolled over belly up and lifeless.

"He's not down there," Wilhelm said. "His body would have floated up by now. Let's catch up with the others."

"What about them?" Gino asked.

"Count yourself lucky," Wilhelm said. Footsteps left the pier.

Ehrich inched up the wooden post, reaching up for the deck. A red hand reached over the side and lifted him in the air. One of the flame-red men had a firm grip on his collar.

"Thanks," Ehrich said. "How did you know?"

"We watched you go over the pier."

"Why didn't you tell the hunters?" Ehrich asked.

"Why did you try to help us?"

"I needed to pass on a message from the House of Qi."

The soldiers stared at him, tensing.

"I have Ning Shu."

One of the soldiers reached under his leather bracelet and retrieved a razor-sharp tael. Ehrich instantly regretted his poor choice of phrasing.

Amina hurled herself through a door, smashing it open. The pungent odour of cured fish hit her nose as she slipped between the wooden crates and searched for another exit.

"She's in here!" Margaret's voice shouted. "Albert, cover the door."

Footsteps echoed in the warehouse. Amina had to move quickly. She aimed for the far wall. The high windows offered no escape. She needed a door. She climbed up the crates and took stock of her bearings. The tops of the boxes lined up like a maze throughout the building. She laid flat and waited for Margaret to run past her position. Her footsteps echoed as Margaret ran deeper into the warehouse.

Amina slowly worked her way back to the door she had kicked down, retracing her steps to the entrance, where Albert nervously swung his teslatron rifle to and fro, looking left and right for any intruder. Amina took advantage of his blind spot and leapt from the crate onto the ground behind the unsuspecting hunter. She wrapped her arm around the boy's throat and squeezed. He struggled to pull away but she slowly squeezed the air out until he slumped unconscious in her arms. She pulled his limp body behind a few crates. She'd be long gone by the time Albert woke up and Margaret found him.

"What have you done with General Ning Shu?" the red man with the broken tusk asked.

"She's safe. I'm working with her."

The crimson man with the broken tusk cocked his head to the side. "Who are you?"

"I'm a traveller, like you."

"You look nothing like me," he said. "What does your kind care about us?"

"I might look like the New Yorkers here, but I swear to you that I'm not. I'm trapped in this limbo where this place looks like my home, but it couldn't be farther from it. Believe me, I know what you're feeling. All I want to do is find a way back to my sector. Ning Shu said she would help me if I helped her."

"And what is the help that you have promised?"

"I told her I would find a soldier who served the House of Qi so he may send a message to the generals."

"How did you know to find us here?"

"I witnessed two of your soldiers go up into the cloud," Ehrich said. "We've been waiting for someone to come down ever since."

The men eyed each other.

"Ning Shu can confirm everything I say. I can take you to her now. Would you ignore a summons from the House of Qi?"

The two soldiers weren't willing to budge.

"How do we know you haven't set a trap for us?" the one with the broken tusk asked.

"Why would I go to the trouble of saving you only to have you captured later?" Ehrich asked.

The soldiers exchanged nods and holstered their weapons. "Show us to General Ning Shu."

HOUSE OF QI

Ehrich witnessed the transformation of the two hardened soldiers as soon as they caught sight of Ning Shu, who wore the jade tael over her emerald robe for all to see. Both men cast their eyes downward at the ground as they approached Ning Shu and Mr. Serenity.

Ehrich waved at Ning Shu, who beamed at the sight of the soldiers travelling with him.

"You found them, Ehrich! Wonderful."

"General Ning Shu, we are honoured by your presence," one of the soldiers said reverently, refusing to lift his gaze from the cobblestone street.

"At ease," she said, tucking the jade tael back inside her robe. "There is no cause for ceremony here. You are among friends, my comrades in arms."

Eventually, the soldiers peered up.

"What are your names?" she asked.

"Zhengfu Zhe," barked the one with the broken tusk as he

snapped to attention.

"Wu Bei," answered the other.

"Under whom do you serve?" she asked.

"General Ling Po."

Ning Shu beamed. "A friend to the House of Qi. You serve the best general, which must mean you are held in the highest regard among the troops."

The men grinned but did not confirm or deny.

"I would like to see my old dear friend again, and I am counting on the two of you to transport us there safely."

"General Xian has strict orders to keep the location of our whereabouts secret from any and all outsiders," Wu Bei said, eyeing Ehrich and Mr. Serenity.

"They are friends," Ning Shu explained. "Allies in the cause."

"Her orders were clear. I'm sorry."

Ehrich stepped in. "Then you will have to tell her that you failed. We know your airship is hovering over the Hudson River. If we can track it, so can others. Do you want to report that your position was compromised, and you did nothing to contain the problem?"

Zhengfu Zhe's eyes narrowed. If glares were daggers, Ehrich would have been cut to pieces.

Ning Shu addressed the crimson men. "I vouch for these two."

"Where is Amina?" Mr. Serenity asked.

"She led the hunters away from the pier just as they were trying to arrest these two men. She risked her safety for them, and they still don't trust us."

The soldiers glared at one another, murmuring. Zhengfu Zhe seemed to win. "If you already know where we are, then we best keep you near."

Ehrich cocked his head to one side. "Let's stop wasting time."

The group navigated the crowded Gansevoort market, pushing past shoppers haggling with vegetable and meat peddlers. They wanted to avoid any more demon hunters. Ehrich knew Wilhelm's squad would still be near, so he had to adopt another disguise. Using the soldiers' bodies as makeshift dressing room screens, he drew lines on his face and donned a false beard to make himself appear much older than his fifteen years. He adjusted his new facial hair, then stepped out from behind the men and surveyed the crowd of market shoppers. He waved as he saw Amina pushing her way through the crowd and searching for him.

"Took you long enough," Ehrich quipped.

"Saving your hide takes time," Amina replied. "Best be careful. The hunters have been alerted, and they are combing the streets for us."

"Good luck looking for us in this crowd," Ning Shu said, waving at the gathering of titan-sized Dimensionals in the street.

Wu Bei grunted. "Now that your party is complete, can we move on to the business at hand?"

"Yes, we need to get back to your boat," Ehrich said.

"How are we going to reach the pier?" Mr. Serenity asked. "Someone is bound to spot us."

Wu Bei had an answer. "All we need is a boat. Any boat will do."

He led the group south through the growing crowd of travellers who milled around the gate. Heated conversations sparked between the workers. Impatience was growing. The travellers needed to feed their families. The sentries stationed at the gate offered no sympathy, and Ehrich noted the ranks of the security forces had grown since the previous week.

At the entrance, a few of the travellers engaged the sentries in a pushing match. Tempers were boiling over. One sentry hauled a traveller by the hair. Two others rushed from the mob to protect the yelping green-skinned girl. Armed guards pummelled the defenseless travellers with clubs, batting them back away from the girl who was now howling in pain.

Ehrich wanted to rush over and stop the sentries, but Amina grabbed his arm. "This is not our fight, and this will give us cover to escape."

He couldn't tear his gaze away until Amina pulled him away.

Outside the gates of the Hudson River Tunnel Project, the workers surged ahead, begging for work, but the sentries repelled them. Need for employment kept the travellers from leaving the area. They pleaded their cases, some claiming they had not eaten anything for days. Others raged at the impassive sentries, blaming them for their current plight. Ehrich recognized the desperate expressions on the workers' faces.

The sweltering summer heat caused Ehrich's sore throat to grow worse. He teetered on his feet, trying to focus his gaze on something that wasn't spinning. His mother had him by the hand as she strode through the rutted streets of Appleton to find a doctor. She glanced left, then right, unsure of which way to go. Eventually, she walked forward. Ehrich's damp hand nearly slipped out of her grasp. He began to cough.

His mother waved at an onlooker. Having no command of English, she spewed Yiddish, asking the goateed man where to find the doctor's office. The man shrugged and carried on. Ehrich's mother approached a woman carrying an infant, but the woman brusquely shooed her away. "Your child is diseased. Get away from me."

One after another, the people rejected the Yiddish woman who was only seeking help for her son. Ehrich wanted to stumble after his mother and pull her away from the indifferent citizens so that she wouldn't embarrass herself any further. Waves of shame lapped against his scarlet face. His mother couldn't speak the language of the people who surrounded her. Helpless against the indifference, all she could do was ask again and again in Yiddish for help. She seemed so weak, and they seemed so cold.

Ehrich rasped, "We need a doctor."

But the man he spoke to recoiled as if Ehrich were a leper. Ehrich's face burned hot as he tried to figure out what about him set him apart. Perhaps the best thing was to keep to themselves and not invite any more cold hostility. He grabbed his mother's hand and pulled her away from the people who wouldn't even give them the time of day.

The sentries at the gate displayed the same contempt Ehrich had witnessed in the bystanders who refused to help his mother. He wanted to do something to help the workers but he didn't have what they needed. All he could do was move forward, trying to fight off the shame of ignoring the travellers' plight with the thought that if the tunnel were reopened, Ba Tian's forces would be able to access their army of exoskeletons and raze New York to the ground. Even Ning Shu couldn't stop the generals once they had the machines. Ehrich understood that much firepower would certainly spur the generals to complete Ba Tian's plans. Amina gripped his hand. He squeezed back.

Once they reached a pier near the southern end of the island, Wu Bei ushered the group down a plank to a small boat moored at the dock. Wu Bei helped Ning Shu into the boat, along with Mr. Serenity and Amina. Ehrich followed suit, under the ever-watchful eye of Zhengfu Zhe. They pushed off in their stolen craft toward the middle of the Hudson River.

The journey across the open waters of the Hudson tested

Ehrich's sea-worthiness. The boat rocked back and forth and up and down as the soldiers rowed away from the Statue of Liberty. Choppy waters batted the boat.

The craft sailed further north. Soon, they left the main shipping lanes and headed to a remote part of New York, where apartment buildings gave way to country estates. Not too far away, a low-hanging cloud appeared. Ning Shu had perched herself at the prow, carrying herself with the air of someone in charge. In the months following Hakeem's death she had gradually distanced herself from the world. In the presence of the soldiers, however, she seemed to be right back in the center of life, commanding a royal air that even her friends found daunting.

On the other hand, Amina seemed edgy as they neared their destination. She flexed her hands opened and closed as she watched the soldiers rowing. Ehrich wondered if she was thinking of the attack on her home world. Perhaps these two men had even participated in the destruction that had forced Amina and Mr. Serenity to flee their home dimension. Ehrich nudged her knee with his. She shot him a glare. He shook his head. She slowly unclenched her fists.

The cloud rapidly drew closer. Had the crimson men found a new burst of strength? Then Ehrich realized the cloud was moving toward them. Wu Bei stowed his oars and stood up. He waved to the sky, but nothing happened. Several minutes passed without a single movement from above. Then, the wisps of cloud parted and revealed the barrel of a weapon turret aimed directly at the boat.

AN OLD ACQUAINTANCE RETURNS

On the choppy water of the Hudson River, Ehrich wanted to capsize the boat to escape the weapon aimed at them, but he'd need everyone's help. A quick scan of the faraway shorelines of Manhattan and New Jersey eliminated the prospect of swimming to safety. He hoped Wu Bei would be able to keep the airship from firing on them. The flame-red man waved frantically at the cloud.

"It's all right," he yelled. "We have brought—"

The weapon's barrel hiccupped once. A barbed metal circle struck the bottom of the boat right between Ehrich's feet. Water began to seep into the boat from the puncture. A few more hits and the skiff would sink.

Ning Shu pulled Wu Bei down as she stood up and drew the jade tael from inside her emerald robes. She whipped the tael around the leather strap until it hummed. More projectiles rained down from the airship, but none hit home. The metal discs deflected harmlessly off the energy shield Ning Shu had created. The turret stopped, and Ning Shu caught her jade tael. She flashed it up at the sky to reveal the symbols around the edges and the square hole in the middle.

A bead of sweat rolled down Ehrich's cheek as he waited for the airship's response. The turret might start firing again any second. Would Ning Shu have enough time to create the shield again? Minutes passed.

Then cables began to lower from the cloud. Ning Shu lowered her tael and sat down.

"I believe they received the message," she announced smugly.

Once the metal cables were within reach, Zhengfu Zhe jumped up and grabbed them. He tapped Wu Bei on the shoulder, then jumped into the river with the line in one hand. He swam under the boat and handed the line to Wu Bei, who clipped the end to the original line. They repeated this process, creating a cradle for their stolen boat.

Once the lines were secured, Zhengfu Zhe climbed back into the craft while Wu Bei signalled the airship. The cables began to retract and tighten.

"Sit in the middle of the boat, and do not shift," Wu Bei instructed. He positioned himself at the prow. Dripping wet, Zhengfu Zhe balanced the boat at the rear.

The boat rose from the river. Water poured off the sides. As the craft ascended, Ehrich picked out the merchant ships docked at the piers on either side of the river. From this bird's eye view, he took in the Manhattan skyline and marvelled at the buildings crowded in amongst each other, almost looking as if they were jockeying for space. The skyline reminded him of the cramped travellers on Devil's Island, standing elbow to elbow, waiting for their chance to enter the city.

The cloud had obscured most of the mammoth airship, but now that they were closer, Ehrich counted several dozen taut suspension cables, wrapped around the whale-shaped envelope from bow to stern. Bright red and yellow silk panels had been stitched together to fashion the massive balloon. Fins protruded from the rear of the ship, while a massive spinning propulsor at the rear of the gondola provided forward momentum. On either side of the craft, smaller whirling blades stabilized the airship.

Unlike other gondolas Ehrich had observed, this one was fashioned almost entirely from bamboo. The control car at the gondola's head featured wide glass windows for the commander to pilot the craft. The gondola appeared to stand at least three storeys tall and extended into the envelope. Ehrich estimated the massive airship could carry at least a hundred and fifty passengers. It was much larger than any of the other gondolas Ehrich had come across, and he assumed the lighter bamboo allowed for more additions. Their boat ascended toward the open bay doors under the airship's midsection.

"This is incredible," Ehrich said. "Did your people design this, Ning Shu?"

The ruby-skinned girl pulled her black braided hair to the front, nervous. "No, this is not of my sector. How did you acquire this airship, Wu Bei?"

"We took it from the humans here."

Ehrich wrinkled his nose. "I think we would have heard about an airship being stolen."

"The craft came from the Orient. When the airship set course for China, a few of our soldiers stowed away and took over the ship. It will be two weeks before the airship is scheduled to arrive. When it doesn't arrive, people will assume the ship crashed in the ocean." Wu Bei explained.

The boat swayed as the stabilizing propulsors stirred the air around them.

Mr. Serenity's face paled. "I'm going to be sick."

"No sudden movements to the right or left," Wu Bei warned.

"If you must throw up, do it in the boat."

"You'll be fine," Amina said, rubbing her friend's back until he controlled his breathing. "Look up. It's easier."

As they neared the bottom of the gondola, Ehrich spotted a Chinese symbol on the hull of the envelope. Alongside it was the image of a pagoda. Several black boxes dangled from thick wires along the length of the envelope. The devices emitted a heavy fog that draped the craft.

As the boat neared the gondola, the whirring of a powerful winch filled the air. The cables coiled around several spools connected to a steam-powered motor that reeled in the boat. Their craft was the odd one out, compared to the sleek skiffs hanging from cables around the landing deck.

A crimson soldier wearing a bandolier of razor discs over a purple silk jacket and mauve flared trousers stood near a large control panel. He pulled a lever and the bamboo bay doors shuttered closed. Ba Tian's soldiers, wearing similar purple uniforms, surrounded the craft. Each man held a metal disc at the ready.

General Xian stepped from the crowd. She was the only one unarmed, but she seemed to need no weapon to protect herself. An amazon of a woman, she stood at least two heads taller than Ehrich. Her jet-black hair was braided into one long queue. She wore a vibrant purple robe with an embroidered golden dragon snaking around her waist and over her shoulder. She placed both hands on her hips as she glared at Zhengfu Zhe and Wu Bei.

She snapped her fingers. "Did you hear that?"

They nodded.

"Intriguing. Nothing wrong with your hearing, and yet you disobeyed my orders."

Ning Shu stepped forward. "General Xian, I can explain."

She pulled out the jade tael and the armed soldiers bowed. Only General Xian remained upright, staring impassively at the girl in the emerald robe.

"General Ning Shu. The long lost prodigal daughter returns. You've been away so long, it would appear you've forgotten the protocol about outsiders."

"I'm rather concerned about your lack of respect for the House of Qi," Ning Shu retorted.

"Of course," the amazon said, bowing slightly. "You are welcome onboard this vessel, but your companions are another matter."

"They serve me, so they serve the House of Qi."

"I'm sure you have your reasons to consort with their kind, but this is my airship and I dictate who can and cannot remain onboard. This is the protocol."

"As long as I possess this," Ning Shu held up the jade tael, "it is my airship, and the protocol is whatever I *dictate*."

"General Ning Shu, when you joined the Council of the Arch Generals, I believe it was with the understanding that you wouldn't use your stature as the daughter of Ba Tian to usurp the other generals. Are you here as a general or as your father's daughter?"

"Both."

"Then I would advise you as your father would. We do not trust anyone beyond the inner circle."

"My father is not here."

"All the more need to protect ourselves from outsiders," Xian said.

The two women faced off against each other. Ehrich began to doubt their plan to get onboard the airship. If this encounter turned sour, the only way out involved a long drop to the

Hudson River. He didn't relish the option.

General Xian waved her arm, the wide sleeves of her purple robe billowing with the sweep of her hand. "Let us retire to the offices and resume our discussions."

"Yes, that would be wise," Ning Shu said.

General Xian clapped her hands, and eight soldiers jumped up and formed ranks behind Ehrich and the others. The general turned on the heels of her black flat shoes and led the group up the bamboo steps to the catwalk. They ascended the wooden steps and entered a narrow corridor. The sounds of the engine powering the propulsors grew louder as they walked to the rear of the ship. The layers of bamboo that formed the walls had been intricately lined up with one another so that even the knuckles of wood were in line. The ship builders had demonstrated not only their skills in aerodynamics but also their artistry.

The throbbing engines were almost deafening when they reached a section of the corridor that split into stairs leading up to the engine room and down to General Xian's quarters. She walked down the bamboo steps and stopped at the second door on the right. She opened the door and ushered the group in while the soldiers stood guard outside.

Red and green silks draped along the walls, sheer enough to allow sunlight to pass through and bathe the room in a cheerful glow. A mahogany desk dominated the centre of the room. Jade trinkets of smiling Buddhas and Chinese lions adorned the desk and nearby shelves. Whoever inhabited the room before Xian's forces stole the airship was a person of wealth and taste.

Ehrich barely noticed the décor, however. He was more focussed on the individual seated on a divan in the corner of the stately room.

Ning Shu's eyes widened at the sight of the man in the raggedy black suit. "You break your own protocol by bringing this outsider onboard."

Xian shook her head. "Though his appearance is different, he is Kifo, the assassin who serves your father."

Ning Shu sized up the raggedy man in the stovetop hat. "I thought you were more thorough than this, General Xian. He doesn't appear to be anything like the boy who served my father."

"I assure you—this is Kifo."

"How can you be sure?" Ning Shu asked.

"Yes-s-s. The proof. Perhap-s-s this-s-s might ass-ss-uage your fears-s-s." Kifo reached into his pocket of his black sack jacket and retrieved a vivid purple and gold puzzle box. The intricate design of symmetrically arranged dragons ran up and down the edges of the cube.

"The enigma box," Ning Shu said.

"Yes, the gift your father gave to Kifo as a symbol of his pledge of loyalty."

"S-s-satis-s-sfied?

Ning Shu clenched her jaw so hard the muscles on her neck began to protrude. She wanted to lunge at the man who had killed Hakeem, but she would risk her friends' safety in doing so. She couldn't contradict the assassin without revealing she had been there and was responsible for sending her father into another dimension. Kifo could expose Ning Shu, but for reasons only known to him he elected to remain silent on the matter. Instead, the assassin stood up and cracked a crooked grin to reveal the yellowed teeth of the new body he possessed. The body once belonged to Ole Lukoje, an illegal Dimensional Ehrich had caught trying to steal the eyes of innocent New Yorkers. In the struggle, Ole Lukoje lost his right arm. During the attack on Devil's Island, Ehrich had enlisted Ole Lukoje's reluctant help. It appeared that the price the traveller paid was to become a puppet body for Kifo.

The assassin sported an improvement to his new body. The amputated arm had been replaced with a metallic hand. Gears and coils ran up the iron gauntlet all the way to gears at the elbow, and a copper shoulder mount stabilized the contraption. The fingers curled into talons, operated by tense wires hooked to a series of gears running along the forearm.

"General Ning S-S-Shu, it is-s-s good to s-s-see you again. And who might your companions-s-s be? I don't think I've had the plea-s-s-sure," he spoke slowly, relishing the sound of his words.

The familiar sibilant speech grated on Ehrich's nerves, reminding him of their past encounter. Surely, Kifo had not forgotten their last meeting and was feigning ignorance now.

"What is the assassin doing here, General Xian?" Ning Shu asked.

"The s-s-same as you, General Ning S-h-hu. S-s-serving Ba Tian." His metallic arm whirred and clicked as he slipped the enigma box back into his pocket.

"What happened to your other body?" she asked.

"I grew tired of it, and I finally acquired the means-s-s to adopt a new form," he said, toying with the medallion around his neck, almost taunting Ehrich with the display.

Ehrich stared at the rust-coloured Infinity Coil, so named because of the infinity symbol on the front. Nested within the twin loops of a sideways '8' was a myriad of tiny gears. Ehrich knew this device better than anyone because he had worn it for two years. He had inadvertently taken the Infinity Coil from Kifo during their first encounter in Ehrich's home world. If not for Kifo, Dash would not have been possessed and dragged into this dimension, and Ehrich would still be stealing apple pies from his mother's cupboard instead of risking his life on this enemy airship. His hands twitched as he fought the urge to lunge at Kifo, snatch the medallion, and free all the souls the assassin had trapped inside it. Amina grabbed his elbow and kept him in check.

Ning Shu raised herself to full height. "Kifo, you serve the House of Qi."

"Of cours-s-se, General. That is-s-s what I meant."

Xian stepped forward. "I believe you will want to follow your father's last wishes."

"What do you know of his last command, General Xian?"

The general pointed at Kifo.

"I was-s-s there when he gave them. I was-s-s with him on Devil's-s-s Island when we tried to take Demon Gate."

Ning Shu straightened up, wanting to refute the assassin, but she remained silent.

General Xian commented, "Ning Shu, your absence means you've not been privy to the plans in motion."

"I am remedying that now," Ning Shu said.

"I'm curious, General. Where have you been all this time?"

"I had my own mission."

"Your father did not speak of any mission," Xian said, pressing the issue.

"No one else was to know. My father knew where I was and what I was doing. I answer to him and him alone."

"Unfortunate that he is-s-s not here to s-s-settle this-s-s matter," Kifo said.

"You are not of our kind, so you might be forgiven for your ignorance, but I speak for the House of Qi in my father's absence."

General Xian replied, "And I was speaking for the House in your absence, General. I obeyed your father's wishes, and I am curious about where you intend to take the army."

Ning Shu hesitated, glancing back at Ehrich and the others. Had Kifo already exposed them to the generals? She changed tactics.

"I had not learned of your sudden meteoric rise in the ranks. When I left, General Ling Po served as the steward for the House of Qi."

"He does not understand your father's wishes as I do," Xian said.

"I want him here. He will put an end to this nonsense."

General Xian feigned a smile. "The dynamics of power have shifted, General."

"Do I need to remind you that you're speaking to the House of Qi?"

The older woman didn't back down. "I am loyal to your father."

Kifo snickered. "S-s-such an awkward moment."

The two women glared at each other.

"The House of Qi would not consort with outsiders," Xian accused.

"We are her allies," Mr. Serenity proclaimed. "Just as Kifo served her father, we serve Ning Shu."

"Why should I believe you?" General Xian asked.

"Ask your scouts," Ehrich said. "I saved them from hunters. I have kept your airship a secret. And I've given nothing away about the exoskeletons under the Hudson River."

General Xian's eyes widened at the mention of the exoskeletons. "There is much to consider here."

Ning Shu held up the jade tael. "This is the only thing you need to consider, Xian."

The general didn't blink. "You will be treated in accordance with all the trappings that symbol entitles you to, but your accomplices do not enjoy the same protection."

"What are you going to do with us?" Amina asked.

"My men will prepare quarters for you."

"Where they go, I go," Ning Shu said.

General Xian flashed a thin-lipped sneer, her first since Ning Shu had appeared on her airship. "As you wish."

The quarters Xian had in mind were the brig. Ehrich and Mr. Serenity found themselves together in a cramped cell. Ning Shu and Amina shared one farther down the corridor.

Ehrich tested the door. Bamboo shafts interlaced with one another in a criss-cross pattern. They could bend, but they wouldn't break. The only way out was to pick the lock. Ehrich reached down to his right shoe and sprang open the heel to pull out his lock pick set. He approached the lock, but as soon as he inserted the tension wrench and the hook pick, he sensed something was wrong. This lock was neither European nor American in design. The ship had been built in the Orient, and the mechanism had a completely different design that did not rely on pins within the lock. Instead, the lock required a set of long prongs to be inserted into the keyhole at the same time, but at various locations. He dug around the lock, but to no avail. He didn't carry enough picks to access the mechanism.

After several failed attempts, he stepped back from the door and sat on the hard cot beside Mr. Serenity. "So close to Kifo, and now I'm thwarted because of a lock."

Mr. Serenity patted him on the leg and consoled him. "At least we know where he is. A small victory is still a victory."

"Tell that to Dash," Ehrich mumbled. He thought of his brother, hooked up to Mr. Serenity's cryogenic chamber in Purgatory, the underground sanctuary for the survivors of Ba Tian's wars.

Two years apart had worn on Ehrich's conscience. He blamed himself for losing his brother, but when he learned that Kifo

Marty Chan

had possessed Dash and taken him to this dimension, Ehrich's guilt sharpened into a dagger of hate. He wanted his brother back, but he needed Kifo to suffer for the years he had stolen from Dash.

Mr. Serenity tapped the wall with an erratic rhythm. Three beats. Short one. Longer rap. Multiple raps.

"Is this really the time to make music?" Ehrich asked.

"Shh," Mr. Serenity said. "Listen."

Faint knocking replied to the man's tapping.

"Amina's all right," Mr. Serenity said.

"How do you know from this?"

"We devised various codes to communicate with one another. A tapping code for when we are separated. There are beats and pauses we use to spell out letters. Takes a little longer, but we have the luxury of time. If people were within earshot, we would switch to saying code words so enemies can't guess our true communications."

Ehrich raised an eyebrow. "How does it work?"

"We use certain catch phrases, so the other person knows we are sending a code. For example, 'you're the apple of my eye' means 'someone is watching us.' If I want you to pay attention to someone, I might say "dear me" for a woman or "my stars" for a man. Once you know the code words, you can string them together in a sentence that sounds innocent to the unsuspecting ear. Now, shush."

He tapped again and waited. A series of knocking replied.

"She and Ning Shu are all right, but Ning Shu is worried about what has happened to the old steward, Ling Po. Hold on."

More knocking.

"Ning Shu believes General Xian might have killed the man so she could assume the reins."

They listened to another series of taps.

"Someone is coming."

Ehrich rushed to the door and peered through the tiny window. Footsteps rang out along the corridor. A door opened. A gasp.

"General Ling Po!" Ning Shu's voice cried out.

"In the flesh, General. Let her out. The others too. All of them."

Soldiers came to Ehrich's door and swung it open. He and Mr. Serenity stepped into the corridor. General Ling Po stood as tall as General Xian, but he was a plank of a man, thin and reedy. His long yellow robe was slit open at the legs to reveal golden flared pants that bore a thigh band of throwing stars. His long black queue of hair hung to the floor. Scars cut across his wizened face, but he had a brilliant smile.

"I apologize for your treatment," he said. "This would have never happened if I were the steward."

"What happened, Ling Po?" Ning Shu asked. "How did Xian seize control of the Council of Arch Generals?"

He embraced Ning Shu. "General Ning Shu, it is good to see you again." He whispered, "There are ears everywhere."

Ning Shu pulled away from her friend. "How long has it been, Ling Po?"

"Too long. Come. You must be starving."

He led the group away from the brig. The soldiers fell in step behind Ehrich as Ling Po led them to his quarters at the rearmost part of the gondola. He closed the door, shutting out the soldiers, then he motioned everyone to sit. "I don't have much to share, but I was able to secure a few rations."

Ning Shu waved off the offer to sit. "Ling Po, what has happened here? This is madness. Why would Xian deny the seal of the House of Qi?"

"It is a long story."

"Tell me."

"Your mother was a strong woman. I see much of her in you, Ning Shu. I swear I never thought anyone would replace her in your father's heart, though some have tried."

"Xian."

"She's a devious one. She is the type who whispers in the shadows to bring down her opponents."

"Do you think she caused you to lose your stewardship?" Ning Shu asked.

"Only your father can answer this question."

"How do you explain her sudden rise to power?"

"I don't know, Ning Shu, but I do know that though she has the title of steward, she acts as a ruler. I suspect she was no fan of your return. Don't misinterpret me, Ning Shu. I'm glad you are back, but at this point we need your father to set things right again."

"Don't count on it, Ling Po. I fear the humans have captured him."

"I still don't understand why he took such a small force to take Demon Gate."

Ehrich knew the answer. Ba Tian was too ashamed to let the generals see that his own daughter had turned against him. He had gone alone with a small force because he wanted to limit the number of people who knew the truth about Ning Shu's rebellion.

"George Farrier promised Ba Tian access to Demon Gate," Ning Shu said. "As commissioner of Demon Watch, he would have been able to turn a blind eye to Ba Tian. Probably not so much to an invading force."

"Yes, the human traitor. Your father put too much trust in him. Do you think he double-crossed Ba Tian?"

"It's a possibility," she lied. "He could be in the prison right now."

"I suspect this is why Xian is leery of your allies. The optics of a member of the House of Qi consorting with outsiders might be hard for the soldiers to accept. She may use that to press her authority."

"The generals accepted Kifo," Ehrich pointed out.

Ning Shu shook her head. "My father forced the generals to accept Kifo. His ability to disguise himself and slip into other dimensions as a scout gave him a purpose. General Xian is most likely keeping Kifo alive out of fear of angering my father."

Ling Po drummed his fingers against his chest. "When Ba Tian returns, he will settle accounts, unless she is able to change the regime to eliminate the power of the House of Qi."

"The generals will not allow that to happen," Ning Shu said.

"The climate has changed much since your absence. I would not have expected to lose my stewardship to Xian either."

"She doesn't possess enough power to oppose the House of Qi directly," she said.

Ling Po glanced down at the floor, "She wouldn't stand up against Ba Tian, but she may use your friends as an opportunity to challenge you. They are your weak point."

Ehrich cleared his throat. "Actually, I think we might be her greatest advantage."

"What do you mean?" Ling Po asked.

"We have a problem with the optics, so let's change the perception. We need a meeting with Xian. Can you arrange that, Ling Po?"

"Please, General. Trust my friends," Ning Shu said.

He scratched at his chest, considering the offer. Finally, he agreed.

Hours later, the group convened in General Xian's office. She occupied the huge desk in the middle of the room while Ling Po motioned the soldiers to leave the room. Kifo perched on the divan, drumming his metal fingers against the arm of the chair and plucking at the fabric, one strand at a time.

Ling Po addressed his colleague. "I called this meeting to entertain a proposal from General Ning Shu's allies."

"General Ling Po, your allegiances are clear," she said, leaning back in her mahogany chair. "Fascinating."

Ehrich stepped forward. "We have a problem. We don't know who is in charge. You think you are, and Ning Shu believes she is. I think we can all agree that if Ba Tian were here, we wouldn't be having this debate."

"True," Ning Shu said.

"I suppose. But he isn't here. Most likely, he's rotting in a prison on Devil's Island."

"Yes, and that is where I believe I can help you. I can break Ba Tian out from the prison."

Xian leaned forward. "You have my attention."

"I once worked for Demon Watch. I can sneak you past the defences on to Devil's Island and help you break into the prison."

General Xian glanced at him, her head turned to one side. "Forgive me if I don't jump at the opportunity, but George Farrier vowed a similar promise and now Ba Tian is missing."

"I understand you might not trust me, but you trust Kifo. If I could sneak your assassin on to Devil's Island, he might be able to possess one of the hunters and open a cell door or two."

Kifo shook his head. "Your plan s-s-sounds-s-s dangerous-s-s to my health."

Ehrich smirked. "I won't let you out of my sight."

Ning Shu grabbed her jade tael, flashing it for everyone to see. "My father's return is paramount. I am surprised the steward would not think of a rescue earlier."

"Without the exoskeleton machines, we control no means to storm their fortifications."

"Now we have the means to slip past their defenses, but you still don't act," Ling Po said, pressuring Xian. "I question whether you truly care about Ba Tian's well-being."

She glared across the desk. "We have been betrayed once by an outsider, yet you would so willingly trust another."

"If it meant the return of Ba Tian, yes."

She narrowed her gaze at Ehrich as she pulled up the sleeves of her purple robes to reveal scars tracking up her arms. "Why would you risk your life for Ba Tian?"

Ehrich launched into his gambit. "Kifo. I want him. He has something that belongs to me. Or more accurately, someone. He possessed my brother, Dash, and now he has trapped my brother's consciousness in the Infinity Coil."

Kifo hissed. "S-s-still pining for the little one?"

"I want my brother back."

"And you think you can forc-c-ce the general to do your bidding. I will releas-s-se the boy when I have no us-s-se for him."

"You don't control his body anymore," Ehrich argued. "What good is he to you?"

"Possess-ss-ing his-s-s s-s-soul means-s-s I can control you."

Ehrich stiffened. The assassin was a master of extortion and manipulation. He tamped down his anger and forced a smile.

"The body you control now doesn't suit you, Kifo. The lack of an arm must hamper you. And the appearance means you can't hide among the New Yorkers. You are as much an outsider to them as anyone of Ba Tian's soldiers. What good are you in that form?"

"This-s-s body has-s-s its-s-s merits-s-s."

Ehrich turned to Xian. "Listen, I know the layout of Devil's Island. I might even help Kifo slip into the new commissioner's office. How would you like to trade for Thomas Edison? With Kifo taking control of him, you'll have the Demon Watch leader in your pocket. You can open the prison, free Ba Tian, and take control of Demon Gate in one simple tactical move. All it will cost you is the return of my brother."

Ling Po let out a low whistle. "A small price to pay, General Xian, for the return of Ba Tian and control of the portal. I like the notion of taking this sector without losing any more of our soldiers. We could order Edison to re-open the Tunnel Project so our soldiers can acquire the exoskeleton machines."

Ehrich pointed out, "The risk is all mine. I fail, you lose none of your men, except for Kifo."

General Xian shook her head. "Do you take me for a fool? Once this boy has Kifo, he will never return."

"Do you wish the Council of Arch Generals to hear your argument as to why you would not want to rescue Ba Tian from the prison?" Ling Po asked. "To be quite frank, I'm puzzled as to why you would spurn such an offer."

"I don't trust him."

Ling Po scratched at his chest, considering. "You are correct, General Xian. Perhaps it would be wise to give the boy some incentive to return. His companions?"

Ehrich shook his head. "Send me alone with Kifo? I need some backup in case he decides to betray me."

Xian shook her head. "You know the island. Kifo can take control of Edison. Anyone else on the mission is redundant."

Mr. Serenity volunteered, "I will stay behind."

"You can take General Ning Shu," Xian offered.

Ling Po cocked his head to the side. "Risk a member of the House of Qi? Your stewardship skills are slipping. Of all the people who cannot go on this mission, Ning Shu stands at the top of the list."

Ning Shu said, "I'll stay onboard to ensure you adhere to the deal, General Xian."

Ehrich argued. "You put the two of us out there on our own, he's going to slash my throat the first chance he has. I want Amina with me at the very least."

"Fine," General Xian said. "If you succeed in taking over Edison and returning with Ba Tian, Kifo will release your brother."

"What if I choos-s-e not to give up my little friend?"

Ning Shu's nostrils flared. "Whatever personal grievances you or anyone else may have, this is no time to act on them. I made a promise to Ehrich to help him and you are the only one who can fulfill that promise no matter what I think of you."

"Then it would s-s-seem you are beholden to me, Ning S-S-Shu."

Ling Po slammed his hand on the desk, a razor-sharp tael in the other. "Break your word and you will answer to me!"

Kifo stared at the floor. "I unders-s-stand, Ling Po."

Ehrich turned to Xian. "We bring you Ba Tian, you make Kifo release my brother."

"When I see Ba Tian on my airship, Kifo will do as you bid," Xian said.

"In this sector, a handshake is a promise. A commitment of honour," Ehrich said. He held out his hand to shake on the deal.

Her hand felt clammy and limp.

UNLIKELY REUNION

The airship hovered over the East River. Devil's Island awaited. Ehrich and Amina climbed into a skiff hooked to cables. A squad of soldiers pushed the boat over the closed bay doors. Already onboard, Kifo tested his metal arm, flexing the metal talons of his new hand. He smirked at Ehrich as if he were sending a message with his menacing claws.

On the deck, Xian and Ling Po flanked Ning Shu and Mr. Serenity. Xian handed Ehrich a grey metal box about the size of Ehrich's fist. On top of the box was a small tube and on the side was a gear wheel. Through the lattice panel, Ehrich could see the internal workings, which consisted of a system of gears, a nest of wires, and a bank of tiny diodes. She shouted over the wind blowing through the bay doors. "If you find Ba Tian, go to the pier farthest north along the Hudson River at night. Turn the gear on the side until the tube opens and releases an antenna. It will transmit a signal to my airship. When we pick up your signal, we will come to collect you."

"How can you send a signal without wires?"

Xian ignored his question. "Only use the radiotelegraphometer when you've completed your mission. Do you understand?"

"Yes!" Ehrich took the small box and stowed it in his satchel.

The airship floated north of the island. Ehrich gripped the sides as the boat dropped slowly through the bay doors and to the river below. The moonless night offered the perfect cover for their descent. Ehrich suspected that the hunters would never think to look up for an attack. Usually, they were more concerned about people trying to leave the island and not the other way around.

The skiff splashed in the water and rocked back and forth with the rhythm of the river current. The scent of the salt air penetrated Ehrich's nostrils. He slid to the aft and unclipped the cables while Amina worked on the lines at the prow and Kifo snapped off the cables on the side of the boat.

Once free, the craft began to drift along the current. Ehrich reached for the oars, but Kifo waved him off. He held up his metal hand. The fingers splayed out like blades. Kifo tapped a button on the forearm and the metal appendages extended, then began to whirl around like a fan. The assassin crept to the back of the boat and dipped his whirling hand into the water to propel the boat.

"S-s-show me the way," Kifo said.

"Aim for the first island. There's a blind spot on the shore where the patrols never go."

The only sounds of the night were the waves lapping against the boat and occasional sputter of Kifo's propeller hand in the water. Ehrich leaned to Amina and whispered, "Keep an eye on him."

"You're mad, Ehrich. This is a farce. Kifo knows Ba Tian isn't in the prison."

Kifo snickered. "Of cours-s-se, I know."

Amina spun on him. "Then what's your game?"

"Thomas Edis-s-son. We control him, we control Demon Gate. We can bring back Ba Tian."

"You could have given us away on the airship," Ehrich said.

"Then I wouldn't have a guide to lead me to my quarry. If you two are finish-sh-sh-ed bickering, we have matters-s-s to attend to."

Ehrich gritted his teeth.

They sat in silence as the boat puttered toward Randall's Island, the smaller of the two land masses. The island was once home to Nikola Tesla and his laboratories, but after the attack on Devil's Island, Ehrich didn't know what had become of his mentor and his facilities. He intended to learn the truth.

The skiff ran up against the rocky shore. A few hundred yards over, a watchtower lit up the night, but the light was directed on the island pathways, not on the sea. They had arrived undetected.

No hunters patrolled the shore. When Ehrich worked for Tesla, at least one patrol roved the island. Now, the shore was deserted.

The trio hauled the skiff up the island and hid the craft behind some foliage. Then they trekked toward Tesla's tower, the tallest structure on the island.

Ehrich whispered, "We can try to sneak onto Devil's Island across the bridge between the two islands, but we may have to subdue the hunters."

Kifo flexed his steel talons. "I can't wait."

"Subdue," Ehrich reiterated.

Amina crouched low and followed Ehrich as he headed toward the tower. He slowed as he neared the building.

"What is-s this-s-s s-s-tructure?" Kifo asked.

"Tesla's laboratory. He constructed the weapons the hunters use here."

"Ah, yes-s-s. Your companion. Do you think he might be there?"

"I doubt it," Ehrich said.

"Then who left the lights-s-s on?" Kifo pointed at the top of the tower. Indeed, one of the lights was on.

"We need to take a detour," Ehrich announced.

Amina turned and raised an eyebrow. "Are you sure about this?"

Ehrich pointed up at the lighted window on the sixth floor.

Kifo shrugged. "I mus-s-t admit; I, too, am curious-s-s."

They crept to the entrance of the tower and spotted the first signs of any kind of security. Four armed hunters patrolled the base of the tower. Ehrich didn't recognize any of them. Older than the regular hunters on Demon Watch, these ruffians were at least thirty. They looked as if every one of their years had been spent in a boxing ring or street fight. Ehrich crawled on his hands and knees until he was within earshot. Their conversation might offer a clue as to who was in the tower.

One of the hunters, a menacing fellow with a scar across his face, spit on the ground. "You hear the latest about the demons on the waterfront?"

The others shook their heads.

"They're turning into a mob. Heard there was a riot at the Tunnel Project."

A scrawny man with a hooked nose laughed. "Eliot, we're on the wrong detail. Would have loved to been down at the Tunnel Project to break some heads."

The others agreed.

"The week's young," Eliot said. "Edison called for more troops to be deployed to break up the mob. The situation is a powder keg ready to go off. Only a matter of time before...boom."

"What's Edison think of all this?" another hunter asked.

"Happier than a pig in mud. The more the demons squawk, the more the mayor listens to him. Edison can get anything he wants. Troops. Money. Anything."

"I'd like some of that to trickle down," the hook-nosed man said.

"Don't worry. The gravy will seep down."

The men laughed at what seemed like an inside joke. After a few more minutes spent listening to a debate on the relative merits of various professional athletes, Ehrich crawled back. The hunters weren't about to give any useful information. The once-hidden door in the smooth white stone wall had been replaced by a heavy iron door with a large metal lock. Whoever was inside the tower was a prisoner. Ehrich thought back to Wilhelm's comment about Tesla, and he worried his friend may be in trouble.

He crawled back to Amina and Kifo. "I have no idea what's up there, but it must be important enough to need four guards in front of a locked door. We need to distract the hunters and lure them away from the tower."

"What about the lock?" Amina asked.

Ehrich lifted his foot and pulled open the heel of his shoe to pull out his lock pick set. "You two need to lead the men away. Okay, Kifo? Kifo?"

But the assassin had slipped away. Amina and Ehrich searched the area. The sounds of battle caught their attention. They rushed back to the tower base just as the last of the four hunters clutched his bloodied throat and collapsed. Standing over him, Kifo brandished his metal claw and admired his handiwork. He had dispatched the men in a matter of seconds.

"What do you think you're doing?" Ehrich said. "They'll notice four bodies down here."

"All the better to bring them here while we s-s-sneak on to the main island don't you agree?"

"We could have distracted them and come up with the same results."

"Dead men make a better impact."

Amina shook her head. "No more corpses, or you can get on the island by yourself."

"S-s-suit yours-s-self. S-s-step ins-s-side or I will have to be forc-c-ced to create another dis-s-stract-t-t-ion."

Kifo operated on a level of twisted logic where bodies were a means to an end. Ehrich shuddered. He stepped over the bloodied corpses and examined the door. He slipped the tension wrench into the lock and drew it down while he inserted the hook pick into the mechanism to feel around for the pins. After a few nudges, he found the first one and gently lifted the pick, pushing the pin up. The work was intricate and required patience.

"Are you in yet?" Kifo asked.

"Shut up," Ehrich hissed. He could pick the lock when no one was looking, but under the eyes of an audience, his hands always seemed to tremble just a little more than they should.

Amina said, "Stand over there, Kifo. Let's give him some space."

Ehrich grinned. His partner read his mind. He focussed on the task at hand and poked around for the second pin.

"Or we could do this-s-s," Kifo said. The assassin kicked over the nearest corpse and searched his pockets. He crept to the second body and found what he needed: the key to the iron door. He tossed the metal key to Ehrich. "Makes-s-s for sh-sh-shorter work."

A pang of envy shot through Ehrich's cheeks. He wished he had thought of searching the fallen hunter, but he was so intent on showing off his skills as a lockpick that he forgot the obvious. Of course, simplicity was always the best solution. He inserted the key in the lock and opened the door. Then he beckoned the others to join him as he entered the tower.

Layers of dust covered the white marble tiles of the lobby, except for where footsteps headed toward the winding staircase. Ehrich followed the trail and led the group up the stairs. At each level, they checked for hunters, but the only security detail seemed to be lying dead outside the tower. As Ehrich looked around the familiar surroundings, he noted that much of the equipment had been removed from the labs. Other than the lab stations and worktables, the areas were bare as if the traces of Tesla's work had been systematically erased.

Kifo seemed particularly interested in the content, or lack of content, in each of the rooms. "What happened? I thought this-s-s was-s-s a great man of s-s-scienc-ce. What of his-s-s work?"

Ehrich shrugged. "Your guess is as good as mine."

Amina hushed them both. The faint clatter of chains echoed from above. They slipped up the steps and approached a closed door. A sliver of light emitted from the crack under the door. The sound of the chains rattling grew louder.

"Perhaps-s-s it is-s-s the ghos-s-t of Tes-s-sla," Kifo quipped.

Ehrich ignored the comment and pressed his ear against the wooden door. A metal rattle and a low groan sounded in the room.

Ehrich cracked the door open and peered inside. He was rewarded with the sight of the tall Serbian who had been his mentor and friend. The man's limbs were outstretched and chained to metal supports.

Ehrich stepped into the room. "Mr. Tesla?"

The man lifted his weary head. "Ehrich?" His eyes narrowed when he caught sight of Kifo. "Behind you!" he gasped.

Amina entered the room and raised her hands. "No. Calm down. He's with us."

Tesla's hardened gaze turned to bewilderment. "What? I don't understand."

Ehrich loosened the straps around his friend's wrists and ankles, and considered how he might strap Kifo into the restraints. He explained everything to his mentor, noting that Kifo now possessed the body of Ole Lukoje.

"Where are your gadgets-s-s?"

"Edison took them," Tesla said, rubbing his sore wrist.

"What happened to you?" Ehrich asked.

"A long story, my friend. After you escaped from the prison, I returned to my cell while the hunters ran frantically through the hallways searching for what they thought was a stray dog. By the way, Amina, I am most impressed with your device. What clever disguises the cameo can create and all by a simple means of projection."

"Thank you, sir. Do you still have it?"

"Sadly, Mr. Edison took the device away along with most of my laboratory equipment."

"Why did he put you in the laboratory?" Ehrich asked.

"My tower has become an interrogation centre. The cad had the gall to use my own AC generators to shoot electricity through my body to extract information."

"Did you tell him anything?" Amina asked.

"What was there to tell? I knew nothing of what happened to either of you."

Kifo cocked his head to the side. "He has-s-s taken everything? What of the items-s-s taken from the Dimens-s-sionals-s-s?"

"Everything has been transferred to his private laboratories.

He has been amassing all the technology he can find. I think he means to study the devices for any commercial applications."

"Where is-s-s his-s-s fac-c-cility?"

"He has two. West Orange and Menlo Park."

Ehrich stood up. "You're free."

"Ah, good work." Tesla clapped his hand on Ehrich's shoulder.

"Do you know where Edis-s-son is-s-s now?" Kifo asked.

He shrugged. "Not a clue. I only see him when he needs to ask a question about one of my inventions."

"Then this-s-s has-s-s been a was-s-te of time."

"Nothing is a waste of time when we gain another ally," Amina said.

"All I need is-s-s Edis-s-son," Kifo said.

A voice sounded from behind them. "Don't worry, you'll see him soon enough."

The trio turned to face Wilhelm, flanked by Margaret, Gino and half a dozen other hunters.

PARTING OF THE WAYS

Ehrich raised his hands and backed up between Amina and Tesla. Kifo crouched low, tensing for battle. The hunters outnumbered them. They couldn't fight their way out. The best thing to do was bide their time and wait for an opportunity to escape.

Wilhelm aimed his dynatron pistol at Kifo's head. "At this range, demon, I'm not going to miss. Hands up."

Kifo refused.

"You were right, Wilhelm. Ehrich is a traitor," Margaret spat at Ehrich. "I didn't really believe you until now. Demon lover."

Ehrich straightened up. "They're not demons. They're travellers, Margaret. You weren't always like this. What happened to you?"

Her gaze hardened but she said nothing. Gino answered for her. "What happened to Charlie—it's on your head, Ehrich."

He flinched, feeling the hard sting of the truth. Their former squad leader, Charlie, had been seriously injured at the hands of travellers, and it was all in the pursuit of a lead Ehrich had convinced him to follow. He searched Gino and Margaret's faces for any sign of the comradery they once shared as fellow squad members but whatever trace had existed now had been replaced with the bitter hate fuelled by their belief that he had betrayed the hunters. He returned their hateful glares, forging a thick skin of indifference against their hatred.

Wilhelm said, "I told Commissioner Edison about our run-in, and I said you would come to see what happened to Tesla."

"You didn't need to torture him," Ehrich said.

"No, we didn't," a new voice declared. "Although, I do tend to be thorough."

Thomas Edison entered the lab, appearing as frumpy as he did the first time Ehrich had seen him at the tenements. The man had never seen the clean side of a brush. A bit of silver in his hair gave him a distinguished air, but he was unkempt. Still, he carried the weight of authority as the hunters cleared space around him.

"Your assumptions were correct, Wilhelm," he said, clapping the German teen on the shoulder. "I owe you a hundred dollars."

"You will never receive the wager, unless you have a promise in writing," Tesla shot back.

"Still nursing the old grudge, Mr. Tesla. I told you before, you don't understand American humour. Now, is this the culprit who turned Demon Watch upside down?"

Wilhelm nodded to Ehrich.

"Ah, Mr. Weisz, I presume. And who are your companions?"

He said nothing.

"Cat got your tongue? No matter. I relish the opportunity to test my new interrogation equipment. Mr. Tesla, I imagine this invention will be your legacy. A footnote in the War of Currents."

The hunters chuckled.

"Take the one with the metal arm," Edison ordered. "He might have some useful information, but don't damage his appendage. I would like to examine the device."

"You are making a mis-s-s-take, mortal," Kifo said.

"The only mistake here is what you did to my hunters below. Strap the demon to the interrogation platform."

Kifo turned to Ehrich. "Now we proc-c-ceed my way." He opened his metal hand and whirled about as he extended his claw. Tiny darts spit out of the four metal fingers. Three hunters fell, howling in pain as the darts pierced their eyes. Margaret stepped in front of Edison and took one in her chest. She crumpled against the commissioner, driving them both back against the wall. Wilhelm ducked. One grazed Gino's cheek. At first, he seemed unfazed, but then he began to wobble on his shaky legs. Blood gurgled at the back of his mouth as he fell to his knees and keeled over. The darts were poisoned.

Kifo rushed at the group and shoved Wilhelm toward the other hunters as he bent down and hauled Edison from under Margaret's now still corpse. He pressed the claws of his metal hand against the man's exposed throat. The remaining hunters backed away. Ehrich stiffened at the sight of his former friends now dead on the floor. Just like that, their lives had been snatched away. Fury mixed with guilt and remorse flooded his chest and he had to swallow hard to keep them from spewing out.

"Take him down," Edison wheezed.

A teen raised a weapon, but Kifo flicked his wrist and a dart streaked across the room, striking the boy in the eye. He shrieked once and fell to the ground lifeless.

"Weapons-s-s down unless-s-s you want me to hurt your leader," Kifo warned.

The hunters obeyed.

"Now s-s-step away from the doorway. I leave you thos-s-se fools-s-s as a cons-s-solation priz-z-ze."

"Kifo, we had a deal," Ehrich yelled.

"I have what I need, no thanks-s-s to you." Kifo took Edison out of the room, using him as a shield as he headed out of the lab.

Amina rushed the unarmed hunters and shoved two of them away as she kicked a dynatron to Ehrich. "We can't let him escape."

Ehrich grabbed the pistol, then took Tesla's arm and pulled the Serbian out of the room. Amina scooped up a teslatron rifle and elbowed a hunter in the gut as he tried to tackle her.

Kifo shuffled down the winding stairs. Edison slowed him down. He clutched the railing and resisted every step of the way.

"Kifo," Ehrich yelled. "Far enough."

The assassin looked up but didn't stop moving down the marble steps. Ehrich tracked Kifo with his pistol, his finger itching on the trigger. The assassin was about to slip through his fingers again. Not this time. Ehrich's finger twitched on the trigger, but before he could fire, a bolt of energy seared the wall just over his head. Wilhelm rushed out with a rifle in hand. Amina whirled around, pulled Tesla behind her, and fired at the German teen. Wilhelm dropped to the floor as the bolt sizzled over his head.

"Looks-s-s like you have your hands-s-s full," Kifo taunted as he pulled Edison another step down.

Wilhelm peered over the railing and trained his rifle on Kifo. "Let him go!"

"Drop your weapon or your leader dies-s-s," Kifo threatened.

"My hunters will track you down if you do."

"They'll be too bus-s-sy accus-s-sing you for allowing your

leader to die on your watch. If you want him to live, do me the kind favour of taking out thos-s-se three on the s-s-stairs-s-s."

Wilhelm swung his weapon to Ehrich and his friends. Ehrich had no choice. He fired an electro-dart into Edison's leg. The energy danced up the man's body and rendered him unconscious.

"Damn you, Weisz!" Wilhelm yelled, squeezing off a shot at Ehrich.

Amina tackled Ehrich out of the way. The bolt seared the wall just past Tesla's head. Amina returned fire, driving Wilhelm back behind the cover of the thick marble plinths of the railing.

"He's getting away," Ehrich cried, pointing at Kifo dragging the limp body of Edison to the bottom of the stairs. He struggled to get out from under Amina, who squeezed off another round from her teslatron rifle.

"Stay down!" Tesla yelled. "I will stop him." The lanky Serb jogged down the white steps.

Kifo raised his metal hand at Tesla, but before he could fire, a bolt of energy struck his arm, lighting up the copper shoulder. He howled in pain.

Wilhelm stood up with his teslatron aimed at the assassin. "One more move and you're done."

Kifo hoisted the limp Edison higher and used him as a shield. Wilhelm hesitated, unsure of whether or not to shoot. Kifo flicked his metal hand in the air, and a dart caught Wilhelm in the throat, spinning him to the marble floor. He would be dead within seconds. Ehrich resisted the urge to run up the stairs and tend to his former squad mate. Though they had their differences now, Ehrich couldn't forget the young German boy who was fascinated with learning how his magic tricks worked. Now that boy was gone. Ehrich gritted his teeth and glared at

Kifo, trying to focus his anger in any direction but inward. He couldn't allow grief to overwhelm him.

The hunters then turned their fire on Ehrich's group. Amina provided cover fire for Ehrich and Tesla to rush down the winding stairs. Kifo shoved the unconscious man toward them and bolted away. Ehrich caught Edison and lowered him to the floor. They couldn't take him with them, not with the hunters bearing down on them.

By the time they stepped outside, Kifo was gone. They stepped over the bloodied bodies in front of the entrance and scanned the field for any sign of the assassin. He was running across the field toward the skiff. They had to catch up before he fled the island. Ehrich stopped to strip one of the dead bodies of his duster and teslatron rifle. He motioned the others to do the same. In the dark, they might be mistaken for hunters.

Shouts of the hunters echoed after them. More shouts were picked up from other hunters. Ehrich picked up the pace and stayed low, avoiding the lighted areas. They reached the shore, but not in time.

On the water, Kifo had the skiff and was propelling himself across the East River toward Manhattan. They had no means to leave the island, and the hunters had them surrounded.

"What do we do?" Amina said.

"Run along the shoreline," Ehrich ordered. "I'll lead the hunters away."

He dashed off in the opposite direction, yelling at the hunters in pursuit. They turned toward him as his friends slipped away. He sprinted across the rocky shore. The intercepting hunters drew closer. He swung his rifle around and fired into the nearest one. The girl's body lit up with blue energy as she fell twitching to the ground. Her companion stopped to check on her. The other hunters returned fire. He ducked low and ran toward the boathouse at the far end of the island.

He reached the guardhouse and spotted two teen hunters on watch. They pointed at the hunters shooting, but did not see Ehrich. He drew his duster's collar up.

"What are you standing there for!?" he cried out. "The demons are attacking again."

"Where?"

"There. They've taken my squad's weapons. They're posing as hunters."

One of the pursuing hunters fired at Ehrich. The energy singed his hair, barely missing him. The pair drew their weapons to return fire at the approaching hunters. Ehrich's ruse wouldn't last long. As energy bolts seared the air overhead, he inched toward the dock. He slipped the rope from the post and pushed off in the boat. He then fired at the other craft in the dock, setting it on fire. He started up his boat. The motor roared to life, and he sped out of range of the hunters' weapons. He piloted the boat toward the southern shore until he spotted his friends. He waved at them to swim out to his boat while he scanned the river for any sign of Kifo. The assassin was long gone.

"Lend a hand, would you?" Amina called out from the icy waters.

He hauled her into the craft. She helped Tesla climb in as Ehrich gunned the engine and pointed the boat toward Manhattan. The wet pair huddled in the boat as Ehrich piloted away from Devil's Island. He searched the river for any sign of Kifo with no luck.

"We need to find a safe place to hide," Ehrich said.

Amina shivered. "The nearest portal to Purgatory is across the city. It's too far away."

Marty Chan

Tesla beamed. "I know the perfect place. I think this evening's adventure has earned us dinner at Delmonico's."

"Are you kidding?" Ehrich asked. "A fine dining restaurant?"

Tesla beamed. "The last place Mr. Edison would search for fugitives."

"Madness," Ehrich argued.

"If they catch us, at least we'll be well fed," Tesla countered.

Amina shouted, "He's got my vote. Better than hiding in the streets."

"Fine. Tell me where to go."

Tesla clapped his hands together. "Oh goodness, it has been so long. You're in for a treat."

North of the Lower East Side and the Bowery, Manhattan's cityscape changed from dilapidated tenements where people crowded elbow to elbow to opulent buildings where entrepreneurs rubbed elbows with bankers. Fifth Avenue served as the lavish playground for New York's wealthy, and the centrepiece was Delmonico's restaurant. This legendary business catered to the wealthy with traditional French cuisine.

Decked out in a borrowed tuxedo, Tesla seemed at home among the theatregoers stopping by for a late-night dinner. Amina shifted uncomfortably in her linden green bodice and bustle. She tugged at the tight waist, trying to breathe without ripping the outfit. Even Ehrich wore a change of clothes. At Tesla's insistence, he wore a grey tweed suit jacket, so he matched his dinner party. The clothes came courtesy of the restaurant's owner, Charles Delmonico, who preferred to be called Young Charley. Tesla called in a favour with Young

Charley, who was able to offer a selection of clothes from his own wardrobe, as well as his Aunt Rosa's collection. Once dressed suitably for dinner, the trio adjourned to the smoky dining hall for a meal Ehrich would never forget.

He examined the linen tablecloth on the table. In all the eateries he had been in, he had never seen such extravagance as to cover a table with a cloth. The assortment of cutlery on the table dazzled almost as brightly as the silver chandeliers overhead. Even the well-groomed servers provided a visual treat in their crisp, long-sleeved white shirts, smart, black trousers, and ties.

"How are we going to pay for this?" Ehrich asked. "I barely have five dollars."

Tesla's eyes lit up. "Ah, the wonder of Delmonico's is the honour system. When it is time to settle my bill, I will know."

The French restaurant was the epitome of decadence. Hand painted on fine paper, the menu itself was a canvas of art. Ehrich left the parchment on the table for fear of smudging it with his sweaty hands. Though he had no need to read the offerings; Tesla ordered for them.

The svelte Serbian leaned back in the wooden chair and sighed. "Ah, it's good to be home."

Ehrich leaned forward, "But sir, we're not out of the woods. Someone is going to recognize us."

Tesla shook his head. "Thomas Edison did not make a public statement about my arrest—and when was the last time you saw a patrol on Fifth Avenue?"

Ehrich nodded, recalling how few patrols reached into the wealthier neighbourhoods of New York.

"Amina, your elbows," Tesla chided.

Tesla waved at the slouching Amina with her elbows on the table.

"Like this," he continued as he demonstrated the proper way to sit with his back against the mahogany back. She complied.

"The trap they had set for us was quite the gamble," she said. "No way the hunters could have predicted when we'd show up or where we'd go."

Ehrich shook his head. "After the run-in at the pier, I think Wilhelm knew I would come for Mr. Tesla. I'm sure he had hunters stationed near the prison entrance as well."

Amina leaned forward, resting her elbows on the table again. "Now do you want to explain yourself, Ehrich? What exactly was your plan?"

Tesla brushed her back from the table. "You mean the plan was not to rescue me?"

"Sorry, sir, but not exactly. We didn't even know that you were being held in the tower. I was going to take the Infinity Coil from Kifo and make him restore my brother."

"But Ehrich had promised General Xian that he would free Ba Tian. Of course, this isn't possible because we trapped Ba Tian in another dimension."

"An uncomfortable predicament," Tesla surmised. "What do you plan to do now?"

"We need to track down Kifo and convince him to release Dash."

"Don't you think Kifo will report back our mission's failure?"

"I have the radiotelegraphometer," Ehrich said. "Besides, I can't quite put my finger on it, but I have the feeling he's operating on his own agenda."

"Where do you propose we start searching?"

"Mr. Tesla, Kifo won't be able to sneak onto Devil's Island again. He'll try to find another location to nab Edison. If we capture Edison, however, Kifo will have to come to us."

"The commissioner travels with security at all times," Tesla pointed out. "Not the easiest target to acquire."

Amina slapped the table. A few patrons turned their heads, but Amina didn't care. "What about our friends on the airship? We can't abandon them."

Ehrich winced. The mention of friends caused his mind to wander to the loss of Wilhelm, Margaret and Gino. Even though the hunters had turned against him, they were still once his friends, and their loss left an absence in Ehrich's chest. Kifo had much to answer for, and the deaths of his former squad mates was now another on the list. Ehrich answered, "If we capture Edison, we can bargain."

"And if we don't?"

Ehrich said nothing. The tension was broken when the waiter arrived with oysters, the traditional start to any meal at Delmonico's. They ate in silence. Ehrich slurped the fresh pea soup that followed the oysters, not even glancing from his bowl. By the time the crab cakes had landed on the table, he was more inclined to speak. "I'm sorry, Amina. I haven't forgotten about Ning Shu and Mr. Serenity. We will find a way to help them. And Ning Shu volunteered to stay on the airship. I suspect she might have a plan of her own."

"Your food is getting cold. Eat," Tesla ordered. He cut into the crust of his crab cake and arranged three piles before scooping one up with his two-tined fork.

"You're banking on the fact that Kifo will go after Edison," Amina said.

"He knows as well as we do that Ba Tian isn't in prison, and he didn't protest too much about my proposal. He must want something down here. Did you remember how curious he was about Edison's labs and his whereabouts?"

"I suppose, but this is still a long shot. I don't like long—"

Tesla interrupted. "Patience, Amina. When one fishes, the chances of success increase when one takes his boat on water rather than leave it on dry land."

"But you can't be sure that's where Kifo is headed," she pointed out. "General Xian isn't going to wait forever."

"Short of amassing an army to storm the airship, this is our only option. Unless you have another plan."

Amina fell silent.

Tesla rubbed his hands together as a trio of waiters approached with steaming plates. "Ah, Lobster Newburg." The once intense scientist now seemed giddy, perhaps because he had his first taste of freedom in a few weeks.

"I've never tried lobster," Amina said.

"Then you will be spoiled for all other forms of lobster you may encounter in the future. Chefs can prepare lobster many ways, but this is the one method which puts all the rest to shame."

The trio tucked into the hearty pieces of lobster in rich cream sauce. Tesla was right. Ehrich had never tasted such a dish. The thick cream had a hint of salty brine, and the lobster was meaty and sweet. He could have eaten ten of them.

The meal did not end there. A light sherbet was served to cleanse the palate, and then a crown roast of pork followed. To end the meal, the three devoured Baked Alaska. Ehrich tapped the meringue topping and cut through to a sweet surprise of ice cream at the centre of this dessert. For a moment, he lost himself in the food and enjoyed every single bite. He hadn't had a decent meal in quite some time. Mr. Serenity was resourceful when it came to scraping together meals, but he lacked a refined palate.

After dinner, they conversed about the weather as if they were one of the posh diners, oblivious of the world beyond the walls of this cultured restaurant. Ehrich imagined himself sitting at the table with his father and mother, and he pictured Dash beside him. He imagined them all celebrating the family's reunion. The first time they had been reunited was when his mother came to America with Ehrich and Dash in tow. They met their father in New York and had a humble but celebratory meal. He believed the next reunion would be even better. He took the time to appreciate this moment because he didn't know when an opportunity like this would arise again.

Amina took a sip of wine and nearly spit the red liquid out. "What is this? It tastes like old bread."

Tesla laughed. "Stick with water, my dear. That wine is too expensive to end up on the floor."

She sat back. "Do you think we can order more of this Baked Alaska?"

Ehrich shook his head. "Where do you put it all?"

She patted her belly. "Can we order more?"

Tesla smiled. "I suggest we try the roasted figs instead."

Amina wiped the corner of her mouth with the linen napkin and glanced at Ehrich. "You have some.... Here." She used the same cloth to wipe his mouth. "I can't remember the last time I sat down and enjoyed a meal. Before the war, I think. My aunt made—I don't know how you would describe them—*grelbach*. They were like dumplings. Inside was meat and tiny dots of dried bread. The outside was soft dough. You dipped the grelbach in a spicy and sweet sauce. I ate twelve of them in one sitting once. Auntie stood over the pot and cooked as we ate. One time, she never left the pot because we couldn't stop eating."

Ehrich laughed.

Tesla added, "Family meals are the best. My mother insisted that every Sunday, no matter what we were doing or where we were, we had to all sit down together and share a meal. The food she cooked was incredible, but the conversations we had…I learned things about my father that I never knew." He raised his wine glass. "To families."

They clinked glasses.

Ehrich said. "To families and friends."

"Old and new," Amina added.

The server arrived with the roasted figs in sabayon, and Amina's eyes widened like a kid in a confectioner's shop. The delight on her face was infectious. Tesla beamed. Ehrich couldn't help but grin like a fool. The waiter must have sensed this because he set the largest serving in front of Amina.

"Enjoy," the waiter whispered, winking at her.

She picked up a spoon and bit into one of the figs. Her eyes rolled back in her head with delight, and her bodice threatened to pop at the seams.

"I could live on this," she said, her mouth still full of fig and sabayon.

"Savour the dessert," Tesla said. "We have all the time in the world." He laughed. "In fact, if we wait here long enough, Thomas Edison may eventually come to us."

Ehrich stopped mid-bite. "Would he show up here?"

"The man eats like a bird, barely enough to sustain a child. The only time he would ever come here is to be seen or to entertain clients. No, if he isn't working at Devil's Island, he would be hard at work at one of his laboratories. Most likely finding some way to make money from the devices he has taken."

"You mentioned the laboratories before," Amina said. "West Orange?"

"Yes, that's his new facility in New Jersey, but I heard rumours that he had resurrected Menlo Park after he took over Devil's Island. The only reason he would do that would be to use the laboratories to store and test the devices he has taken. There's no guarantee we'll find him here. We would be making a stab in the dark."

Ehrich shook his head and grinned. "Not if we gave him a reason to come out."

A TEST OF LOYALTY

General Ling Po rubbed his tusks as he sat behind his mahogany desk. Scattered scrolls and calligraphy brushes littered the top. He squinted the tiredness out of his eyes. He had argued long and hard with General Xian to convince her Ning Shu and Mr. Serenity did not belong in the brig. The only concession he won was the right to keep them locked in his quarters. Now he was a virtual prisoner like them, held captive in his own quarters while two soldiers stood outside. Xian had even replaced his personal retinue with her own men, adding insult to injury.

"Times have changed," he sighed.

Ning Shu paced around the room while Mr. Serenity marvelled at the calligraphy art on Ling Po's desk. "I don't know what my father admires in that woman. She's nothing like my mother."

Mr. Serenity suggested, "Maybe that's what he sees in her. In grief, there are those who want the comfort of the familiar, and there are those who want to run away from the reminders of the ones they lost."

Ling Po sorted the scrolls on his desk. He used an octagonal inkpot as a paperweight. The unfurled calligraphy scrolls gave him respite from the stress of the day. He yearned for a brush in his hand right now.

"You must still carry some sway on the Council," Ning Shu said. "There must be someone who might stand with you against Xian."

"Not many," he said. "I'm an old man running with a herd of young bucks who would rather charge in than survey the field. Xian is part of the new generation. It's evident why your father managed everyone. Without his steady hand, everyone has drawn their knives to carve out their own piece of the kingdom."

Mr. Serenity leaned back from the desk. "I'm curious, General. What exactly was Xian's plan before we arrived?"

Ling Po sighed. "She wants the exoskeletons. We can't launch an attack without them. She has been sending scouts to agitate the workers, stir them up into a protest. She believed if the strikers created a large enough fuss, we might be able to ignite a riot. Perhaps sneak a few of our soldiers into the tunnel to extricate the machines."

Ning Shu set the scroll on the desk and folded her arms over her chest. "My father would have done the same. At least she is consistent with Ba Tian's wishes. How many soldiers are on board?"

"Not nearly enough."

She weighed his words carefully, eyeing him for a second. Then she tested the waters. "All this fighting, it tires me."

"I prefer a razor disc in my hand to all the political knives Xian and her ilk wield. This type of fighting I can do without."

She backed off. "What have you been doing in my father's absence, old friend?"

"Well, the answer is simple. Now that I'm no longer the steward of the House of Qi, I have had much time to express my creativity." He swept his crimson hand over the calligraphy scrolls. A rough sketch of a chimera sat on top of other paintings of landscapes.

"Beautiful, Ling Po. A hidden talent."

"I never stopped to consider all the sectors we invaded. The beauty of some of the places...I recall a waterfall flowing from the top of a snow-capped mountain into an aquamarine pool."

"Remember the realm with the river that flowed with yellow water from all the deposits?"

Ling Po nodded. "All of them eradicated with no one to record their legacy. I suppose this is the best I can do."

"You do the sectors justice, Ling Po. I could never draw this well."

"No? Have you tried?"

"I couldn't."

Mr. Serenity leaned forward. "May I try?"

"Of course."

The bald man happily picked up a brush and began to sketch on a blank scroll. His precise movements sketched the length of the airship. "I can't remember. How many propellers are on this airship?"

"Twelve on each side and a double one at the rear of the gondola."

Mr. Serenity began to sketch in the details.

"What is this?" She picked up a scroll with the drawing of a graveyard. A small boy knelt in front of what appeared to be a floating cat's eye in the middle of the air. "A bit dour, don't you think?"

"The graveyard? Yes, I'm thinking of my ill-fated career."

"You're not done yet. One more battle to fight."

"I'm a warrior, Ning Shu. I'll gladly face my enemy on the field, but this whisper campaign, it isn't me."

"General Ling Po," Mr. Serenity interrupted. "How tall is the gondola?"

"Three storeys."

The rotund man added the details to the calligraphy drawing.

Ning Shu pressed the issue once more. "Ling Po, what if my father doesn't return? Do we continue to wage war in his name?"

"What else do we do?"

She tapped the scroll of the chimera. "There is always something else we can do."

"I can't imagine your father's soldiers laying down their arms to pick up paintbrushes."

"Yes, this is true," she said, backing away. She knew she had an ally, but military training shaped his view of the world, and she would need more than one argument to sway him. He was the most moderate of all the generals. If she couldn't win him over, she might as well give up now.

"Something bothers me, Ning Shu," Ling Po said. "Your talk of laying down arms. Would this have anything to do with your allies? No offense, Mr. Serenity."

The bald man glanced up. "None taken, sir."

Ning Shu explained, "I suppose it must sound odd to you, Ling Po. My absence and this new philosophical view. I guess if I'm to be completely honest with you, I wonder about our impact on the sectors. Your calligraphy captures the beauty that was lost. We share the same thoughts. The loss."

Ling Po straightened up. "I suppose, but I wouldn't go against

Marty Chan

your father's wishes."

"Never?"

"No. I'm loyal to the House of Qi."

"I'm relieved. I think I can trust you now to reveal the mission my father sent me on. Mr. Serenity, can you give us some space?"

"Sure," he said. He picked up the scroll and brush and lumbered to the other side of the quarters, planting himself at a round marble-topped table.

Ning Shu lowered her voice. "The worlds we conquered did not perish. Survivors have emerged from the rubble, and they banded together to form an army. We must pay attention to what is behind us now, as well as what is ahead."

"We stand strong, Ning Shu. No one has been able to stand against us."

"Not before, but now, I'm not as sure."

"Why?"

She glanced over her shoulder, then leaned in. "What do you know of the exoskeletons?"

"They are our greatest weapons."

"Yes, but what about their designer?"

Ling Po shrugged. "Not much."

"His name was Hakeem. A scientist. Brilliant—but he defected. I had to bring him back."

"That was your mission?" Ling Po asked.

"I searched for him across the sectors until I learned he had joined the survivors."

"Where is Hakeem now?"

"I killed him," she answered.

"And the survivors?"

"They are hiding someplace. I gained the trust of Mr. Serenity and the others with him. They want to help us."

"We don't need allies."

"Here we do, Ling Po. We are without our exoskeleton machines. Here is the bigger problem: the scientist could not have defected without help. I learned from my friends that the traitor had assistance from one within our ranks. This person would have to be high up."

"A general?"

"Perhaps. That is why I couldn't reveal the nature of my mission to Xian or to you until I was absolutely sure I could trust you."

"The way she has been acting after your father left... do you suspect her?"

"I don't want to jump to conclusions, but I am curious why she won't relinquish her power to me."

"This would explain her behaviour," Ling Po said. "We must confront her."

Ning Shu placed her hand on her friend's arm. "No, Ling Po. If she managed to turn the scientist, who knows who else she has influenced? I'm afraid this battle must be waged with whispers and not weapons."

"I'm ill equipped to help you."

"I need to go through the Council of Arch Generals and determine whom we can trust."

"My blood is yours, Ning Shu."

"Thank you for that, Ling Po. Who else can I approach?"

"Gu Shan. We began serving your father around the same time. There is no way he would stand against the House of Qi. He is onboard the airship."

"Can you arrange a meeting with him?"

"I will try," Ling Po said. "But the other generals are not onboard. They are on missions across the country."

"We will require a reason to call them together."

"Only a meeting of the Council of Arch Generals will bring them here," Ling Po pointed out.

"We must craft a purpose for this meeting," Ning Shu said.

"Then we had better start."

FIERY GAMBIT

Menlo Park was less a laboratory and more a small village with Edison's facility at the hub. Tesla led Ehrich and Amina through the sleepy area, past many of the cottages, toward the gated entrance.

"Menlo Park exists because of Edison's laboratory. The people who work here also live out here."

"Why the protection?" Amina asked.

"If this is where Edison sent the Dimensionals' personal effects, he may believe the items have value as either weapons or new technology. I suspect a few unscrupulous dealers might want them. The devices were much safer in my facilities. I can imagine Edison's assistants combing through the knick-knacks to find inspiration for new patents."

"What is your plan, Ehrich?" Amina asked.

"Edison might come out if his laboratory caught fire."

"Along with his hunters," Amina pointed out.

"Out in the open, one hunter might look like the next."

"You think our dusters are enough to trick him?" Amina asked.

"In the heat of battle, you always rely on the familiar. The question is which facilities should we target?"

Tesla rolled up his sleeves. "West Orange is his newest one, but Menlo Park is more remote."

"We should go to West Orange," Ehrich said. "That's the new one. The more damage we can do, the better chance he will come to investigate."

Amina shook her head. "How big a fire do you want to set?"

"Something big enough to catch his attention."

Tesla disagreed. "This facility is the better choice. Fewer people and less chance of someone getting hurt."

"We need to make sure Edison leaves Devil's Island. A fire at his new laboratory is bound to draw him out."

"I know some of his assistants," Tesla said. "They are friends and colleagues with families. We set fire to the new laboratory, and we risk their lives as well as their life's work."

Amina suggested. "Let's set the fire where we know there won't be many people."

"Only if we give the workers a chance to put out the blaze before any serious damage is done," Tesla insisted.

"We need to do enough damage to draw Edison out," Ehrich said.

"A risk to any laboratory's work is enough to draw him out. Trust me," Tesla said.

"Fine, fine," Ehrich grumbled.

The trio set to work. Amina scouted the perimeter of Menlo Park, checking for a weak point in the stonewall fence while Ehrich and Tesla prepared a device to trigger a fire. Tesla pulled apart the dynatron pistol and pieced together the circuits and coil into a new incendiary configuration.

The inventor's hands moved quickly. They reminded Ehrich of a magician's. Fluid movements all aiming for some mysterious purpose. Tesla glanced up.

"Are you sure you want to go through with this plan, Ehrich? All this risk, and we don't even know if we will succeed."

"Why are you against the plan, Mr. Tesla?"

"The people who work here depend on this place for their livelihood."

"Edison will shift them over to his other lab if the facilities are destroyed. They won't be out of work."

"You're using innocent people as part of your plan. They've done nothing to deserve this."

"We need Edison so we can deal with Kifo for Dash."

Tesla stopped working and stood up. "Ehrich, be careful with the path you are travelling. Obsession can lead to the darkest of places."

"I'm trying to save my brother and my friends, Mr. Tesla."

"When I was working on AC generators, I wanted to find a more efficient motor than the ones already in existence. I decided I could combine mechanics with electromagnetism. I created a piston that would drive up and down with the help of electromagnets. A small device would generate enough power to light up a hundred bulbs. I tried to make a bigger one. I mounted the device on a pillar in one of my laboratories. For a few hours, the results were amazing. The lights stayed on without a flicker. I wanted to push the limits of my oscillator, and I increased the power. My assistants warned me the vibrations from the new motor were causing the room to shake, but I didn't heed them. I wanted to test the limits. The resulting vibrations became so strong they triggered a small earthquake. If I had not grabbed a hammer and smashed the piston, my invention would have razed my laboratory."

"Why tell me this?"

"Ehrich, no matter how noble your purpose, there are consequences to your actions. Don't be blinded to them."

"We'll set the device off at night when no one is in the laboratories."

Tesla shook his head. "You don't know inventors. Someone will be there at all hours."

"We'll make sure to give everyone fair warning about the fire."

Tesla nodded and went back to work.

They waited until well after midnight to strike. Amina had found a section of the stonewall fence that they could vault over. Tesla carefully handed the incendiary device to Ehrich who sat straddling the fence. He passed the bomb to Amina on the other side. She slipped through the yard toward an unlit window at the far end of the compound as Ehrich hopped off and followed, leaving Tesla to keep watch at the perimeter of the yard. The rooms here were far enough away from the occupied areas that whoever was still at work would be able to flee well before the fire reached them.

Amina crouched low so that Ehrich could step on her back and reach a window. He jimmied open the window and pulled himself into the building. Then he reached down to pull Amina up. The moon above provided enough illumination to reveal they were in a storage area. A collection of devices sat upon shelves and crates—valises, shawls, notebooks, and other travelling paraphernalia.

"Try this door," Amina whispered.

Ehrich opened the door to a small room. He stepped toward a table in the centre and switched on the overhead lamp. The electric light sizzled to life, shining on a collection of metal objects. The travellers' devices filled the counters around the room. Amina began to sort through the collection.

"No time," Ehrich said. "We need to set the firebomb and go."

She shook her head. "Not until I find my cameo."

He sighed and set the makeshift incendiary device on a counter to help her search. No luck.

Ehrich picked up the firebomb and set it against a wooden wall. "Time to go, Amina."

She took one last survey of the confiscated trinkets and devices on the counter, then waved to Ehrich. He connected a red wire with a black one, just as Tesla had instructed him. The device began to glow blue. He stood up and backed out of the room. They reached the window and climbed out as a loud *whoomph* shook the air. An orange glow emitted from the doorway. The fire had started.

They sprinted across the courtyard. By the time they reached the stonewall fence, the windows glowed orange from the fire within.

Ehrich climbed up and straddled the ledge at the top of the fence. He waved down to Tesla. "The fire's started. Go warn the sentries."

The Serb ran to the main gate.

Amina started to climb, but stopped when she spotted a second figure atop the stone fence. It ran toward Ehrich. She waved at Ehrich and pointed behind.

He spun around in time to receive a face full of shoulder. Kifo knocked Ehrich off. He slid off the top, scraping his back as he tumbled back into the courtyard with Amina. Kifo flicked his metal hand at the prone teen, but Ehrich rolled quickly out of the way of the darts that imbedded the dirt. He rose to his feet as Kifo landed a few feet away from him. An orange glow emitted from the building.

"Fools-s-s!" Kifo hissed.

He charged at Amina. She vaulted into the air and unleashed

a spinning kick, but Kifo was faster, raising his metal claw to block the kick and punching Amina's solar plexus with his other hand. She fell. He towered over her, his sickle-shaped nose whistling hard. Before he could finish her off, Ehrich slammed into the back of the raggedy man and sent him tumbling across the ground.

Shouts from the other end of the yard erupted. Ehrich could hear Tesla shouting, "Fire! Fire!"

Lamplights filled the night as over a dozen men rushed toward the fire. Now flames licked the edges of the window. Kifo glanced back at the blaze, then at the approaching men. He flicked his metal hand at Ehrich, who dropped low before any of the darts found their mark. He climbed to his feet, but the assassin was gone.

"Get out of here," Amina said, grabbing his arm and hauling him to his feet. The two of them sprinted to the fence and scrambled up, but the men weren't interested in them. They were more interested in attending to the blaze.

Once clear of the courtyard, Ehrich tried to catch his breath while Amina led him toward Tesla, now coming to join them.

"What happened?" the tall man asked.

"Kifo showed up," Amina said. "I think he must have been staking out the place."

"He must not want us to locate Edison first," Tesla guessed.

"Let's clear out before anyone sees us," Ehrich said.

Amina had found the perfect vantage point to spy on Menlo Park. A small stand of trees allowed them a clear line of sight to the main road coming into the village, as well as a view of buildings around the facilities. Amina set up camp, creating a lean-to for shelter out of fallen branches while Tesla foraged for food. Ehrich stood watch on the road. He knew Edison wouldn't come immediately, but his main target wasn't the Demon Watch commissioner; he had his sights set on Kifo. The assassin was sure to be around somewhere.

The night turned to day and back to night with no activity on the road besides a few villagers heading toward the city. Ehrich whiled the time by practising palming a Morgan dollar. The silver coin slipped out of his palm several times, but he couldn't stop until he executed the palm perfectly ten times in a row. The highest he reached was seven times.

The failure to perfect the sleight triggered his thoughts of Dash. No matter how he tried, he couldn't save his brother. He was too late to stop the boy from flying through the portal into this dimension. Though he had possessed the Infinity Coil for two years, he didn't realize its true purpose until after he had lost it. He had Kifo in his grasp, and the assassin had slipped away. The more he tried, the less he succeeded. Another sunset and another day had passed with no action at all. He wondered if Kifo had moved on to Edison's other facilities or if he had intercepted the man on the way.

On the morning of the third day, Ehrich declared the plan a bust. With no sign of Edison or Kifo, he realized there was nothing more to be done.

Tesla guessed, "Perhaps Mr. Edison transferred the promising items to his facilities in West Orange."

"Then why the sentries?" Amina asked.

"A distraction," Ehrich said. "If we see someone protecting the facility, we assume there is still something inside worth protecting. Thus, we waste our time and energy trying to break in."

"Fine." Amina sighed. "Let's head to the West Orange facilities."

When they arrived at West Orange, Ehrich saw firsthand the futility of making any kind of attack. The sentries tripled the contingent at Menlo Park. Armed pairs patrolled the perimeter of the walled fence. This fortress was less a laboratory facility and more a stronghold against any and all attackers.

Amina, in a hunter's duster, approached the main entrance. Two sentries eyed her approach.

"Password," the beefy one demanded.

"What?" Amina asked.

"What's the password of the day?"

"I didn't know I needed one. I was looking for Thomas Edison."

"He ain't here."

"You sure?"

"Password," the big man ordered, raising his teslatron rifle.

She backed off and walked down the road to join Ehrich and Tesla. "There is no way we are getting near this facility. They use passwords to gain entry."

Ehrich shook his head. "Maybe we can launch one of your incendiary devices into the compound."

Tesla stood up and led the group down the road. "No. Not without hurting the people inside."

Ehrich said, "We need to find a way to lure Edison out. Lure him to a place we can control."

Amina raised an eyebrow. "How are we going to draw him away from his hunters? I'm sure he'll be protected."

"Other than Devil's Island and here, where does Edison go, Mr. Tesla?"

"Well, he is a political creature. He does mingle with the mayor and the governor. He appreciates fine restaurants and the theatre. If I remember, he was known to enjoy a show or two."

"There is no way he's going to take a risk just to catch a show," Amina said.

"You're right," Tesla said.

Ehrich rubbed his arm. "What else?"

"He's a curious man. Always wants to be at the forefront of technology. Ever since he was heralded as the Wizard of Menlo Park, I suspect he has been trying to find something that eclipses his invention of the light bulb. I believe this is why he's been so interested in the Dimensionals' technologies. He's grasping for inspiration for his next great invention."

"What could we offer that might pique his interest?" Amina asked.

"Something to do with energy?" Ehrich asked. "Maybe another weapon?"

"I don't think so," Tesla mused. "His heart is an explorer's, not a warrior's. He's always curious about the world. Sadly, his curiosity is tempered by the ugly side of his entrepreneurial desires. From what I remember, he began indulging in the field of entertainment. He dabbled in devices to record and transmit sound. And I think I heard he had an interest in recording and broadcasting images. 'Moving pictures' is what I think he called it."

"I don't suppose you can whip something up," Ehrich suggested.

Tesla shook his head. "If I had laboratory equipment, maybe I could build something I've been thinking of. Tele-automatics. Remote controlled devices. Though, I'm not sure if he would be as interested in them. He does seem fascinated with images. I suspect it probably has to do with the fact that he's going deaf."

"So all we have to do is invent something that doesn't exist yet and prove that we've done it better than Edison could," Ehrich said.

Amina beamed. "We don't have to invent this. We just have to pick it up."

MOVING PICTURES

Amina detailed her plan as the trio ran through the streets. "Do you remember the codex I brought with me to the sector?"

"The large book?"

"Not a book. A *codex*."

"The thing that looked like a book."

She sighed. "Yes. The codex can project images. You remember the ones we showed of Ba Tian's conquests?"

He shrugged.

"The images are small." She flashed a glance at Tesla. "But your friend has some expertise we can capitalize on. What do you say, Mr. Tesla?"

"I'm game."

Under the cover of night, the trio trekked across the city to one of the few remaining access points to Purgatory, the underground sanctuary for the travellers who had survived Ba Tian's invasions.

Amina led Ehrich and Tesla through the Bowery. She stopped outside a tiny clothing shop squeezed in among other shops. Pushcart vendors occupied the street, trying to catch late-night revellers to buy their wares. A headless clothes dummy displayed a chiffon bodice and frilly petticoat. Amina slipped behind a Dimensional operating a pushcart of questionable oysters. A barrel-chested vendor with green skin shucked oysters with one set of his arms while giving change to a customer with his other set of arms. The man grunted at Amina and pushed the cart ahead a few feet to reveal the cellar doors underneath his cart.

She pulled open the metal doors and jumped down. Ehrich ushered Tesla after her, then followed suit. The vendor closed the cellar doors and rolled his cart over the access point.

Ehrich landed in the clear glass pneumatic tube transport. Tesla marvelled at the velocipede while Amina prepped the controls. The sled whooshed forward through the tubes and into the depths of New York. Ehrich couldn't get used to the system of transport, which sent the vehicle careening on cushions of air. The journey was a seemingly endless spiral until the sled appeared at the top of a cavern.

Tesla let out a low whistle. "Amazing."

The system of clear tubes fed into the massive globe at the bottom of the cavern—Purgatory.

"An underground city. In my wildest imagination, I could not even begin to conceive of such a place. If only my people could witness the wonders of your world."

"They would most likely attack us," Amina said.

"Oh? You have such a low opinion of the people here."

She shrugged. "Not an opinion. More an observation based on my experiences. Your people are closer to Ba Tian's race. Eager for war."

"I would not characterize everyone that way."

"What about the way the humans treated the travellers at the Hudson River Tunnel Project?"

"An aberration brought on by the stress of the situation, I would propose," Tesla said.

"How about incarcerating all the travellers with no solid evidence of wrongdoing?"

"I'll concede your point there, but I would not go so far as to charge the entire human race with the same bloodthirsty callousness."

Ehrich wanted to help Tesla, but he found himself agreeing with Amina. Everything he had witnessed in this sector since he arrived had been the worst—from the treatment of immigrants on Devil's Island to the treatment of travellers in the streets. Worse, he found many similarities between his home world and this.

Tesla had a more optimistic view of his people. "Not everyone here is prone to war. My parents, for example. The Serbian army conscripted young men into the army when they were of age, but my father had already lost one son to an accident. He wasn't about to lose me to war. My mother gave me a bundle of books and sent me into the mountains of Croatia. I survived the winter on whatever I foraged. When I returned home in the spring, I wanted to study engineering, but my father insisted I go into the priesthood to pursue a path of peace. We argued many nights, so much so that I suspect the stress caused me to fall ill, but I did not stray from my dreams. My father saw my passion—even on what he feared might be my deathbed—and he relented. In turn, I honoured my father's hopes that I would pursue a path of peace. I only used my talents to create inventions to benefit the world, not to destroy it."

"You are the exception," Amina said. "Albeit, not enough to make a difference."

Tesla tapped his finger on his knee three times. "Amina, do not underestimate the influence one person can make. I may not appreciate his personality, but I acknowledge Thomas Edison's contributions. His electric light bulb will revolutionize the world. If not for Michael Faraday's work on electromagnetism, I would not have been inspired to construct the motors and coils that power Devil's Island."

"Do you mean the generator Edison used to torture you?"

Ehrich interjected, "You have to admit, Mr. Tesla, we have more examples of the cruelty of the people here than their kindness."

"I still believe in the capacity of people to do good before harm. Don't underestimate my species. We might surprise you."

They spoke no further of the issue as the transport descended from the top of the cavern and spiralled toward a minaret in the middle of the sphere city. The trio stepped off the transport. Amina led the two through glass tube hallways until they reached Mr. Serenity's quarters. The spacious room had been decorated with function in mind and not form. The overhead light snapped on as Amina entered, sending cockroaches skittering off the crumb-covered triangular white table at the centre of the room. Other than a couple of high-backed padded chairs, the room was bare of furnishings.

In the next room, an inventor's dream awaited. Amid the work table and shelves were all manner of gadgets in various states of progress. Tesla's eyes lit up as he surveyed the copper wires, vacuum tubes, and gear parts scattered around the room. Amina reached for a book on the worktable.

"The codex," she proclaimed.

"It's a book."

Amina sighed. She set the thick volume on the table and pressed the dial of the latch on the side. The surface blossomed open to reveal a carousel within. The wheel began to spin, and images flashed in the air of Ba Tian's soldiers in exoskeleton machines marching ahead. Tesla jumped back surprised at the sudden appearance of the glowing images.

Ehrich examined the moving pictures. "Not bad, but do we want to show battle scenes?"

"The codex can also record. I'm judging by Mr. Tesla's reaction that we might have something worth using to attract Edison."

"Mesmerizing," he said, reaching out to touch the small projection. His hand passed through the image of an exoskeleton. He put his hand behind the image and it disappeared, blocked by the apparently solid projection. He giggled.

"Ehrich, even if the codex can bring Edison to us..."

Tesla clapped his hands through the image. "Oh, it will. It will."

She rolled her eyes. "Even if Edison shows up, how are we going to snatch him away from his escorts?"

"You said this device can record as well as project, right?"

"Yes."

"What if we bring Edison on the stage to examine the projection, and record him? Then let the projection play while we grab him. By the time anyone realizes, we'll be far away."

"Not a bad idea," Amina admitted. "All we have to do is figure out where to show the projections."

Ehrich said, "One step at a time. First, let's see if we can make the codex do what we want. What do you think, Mr. Tesla?"

Tesla viewed the carousel and the gear wheels within. "Let me see about expanding the range and size. Leave me to work on this." He rolled up his sleeves and pressed the dial on the latch to shut down the projection.

In the main room, Ehrich cleared the crumbs off the table while Amina searched a tall cupboard in the corner. The shelves were bare except for a clay pot. She overturned the pot and poured out a few silver coins, which she stuffed into her pocket.

"I'll have to go to the marketplace to gather some supplies. Do you want to come?"

"Thanks, but I had better stay in case Mr. Tesla needs my help."

"Ehrich, this plan to lure Edison to us is risky and may not yield the results we want. You do know that, don't you?"

He pursed his lips. "Yes, I know, but this is our best chance. Without Ba Tian, we're not getting back on the airship, and without Edison, we're not getting Kifo."

"Promise me that we're not risking any other lives in this quest."

"What do you mean?"

"The attack on Menlo Park. Setting the fire while people were still in the building. They could have died."

"But none did."

"That doesn't absolve you of this folly."

"Amina, if we make all our decisions based on what could happen, we would be paralyzed. Trust me, I know what I'm doing."

"That's what scares me, Ehrich."

She walked out of the room, leaving the weight of her accusation to settle on Ehrich's shoulders.

He took a deep breath, then headed past the workshop and through a doorway into the cryogenic chamber. His little brother slept in suspended animation inside a glass sarcophagus attached to a large chugging machine. A thick hose ran from the back of a control panel to the containment chamber. Dials measured the temperature and dipped around the freezing mark. The device chilled Dash's body to slow down its functions. The boy seemed so serene in the glass coffin, almost as if a gentle nudge would wake him from a nap.

"Dash?" Ehrich whispered.

No response. Not even a flutter of the eyelids. The body was here, but the spirit was elsewhere. Ehrich stared at his brother's face, trying to conjure up the image of the younger boy who had cherished his big brother.

Stretched between two oak trees, a thin cable awaited Ehrich— Prince of the Air. He attempted to recreate the act he had seen at the travelling circus the previous week. Though the height of the wire and size of the crowds were not as spectacular, Ehrich didn't care because he had one admirer—Dash.

His kid brother watched with big eyes as Ehrich teetered on the cable. He pressed one hand against the tree trunk as he tried to balance himself.

"You can do it, Ehrich!"

"Of course, I can. I'm Prince of the Air."

"Better than any circus performer," Dash added.

Ehrich let go of the tree and took his first step on the cable, which vibrated from his shaking legs. He tried to calm himself, focussing on the tree on the other side, which seemed so far away. He lifted his back foot and adjusted his body in the air, using his arms as counterbalance. He nearly toppled over to the ground, but was able to hold himself in the air.

Dash's applause filled Ehrich's ears, and he took another step forward. Then another. This went on until he was halfway between the trees. The line now sagged from his weight, until it was nearly touching the ground. With the act no longer dramatic, he stepped off. The cable sprang up.

Dash rushed over and clapped his brother on the back. "Amazing."

"I only got halfway. We have to tighten the rope."

"Or make it higher," Dash suggested. "Or maybe you need to lose some weight."

"Shut up," Ehrich said, punching his brother in the arm.

"Can I try?"

The older Weisz raised an eyebrow. "You want to walk the tightrope? I'm not sure what Father would say about this."

"Just a few steps. I promise I won't tell."

Ehrich eyed the rope and then his brother. He sighed and waved.

"Yay!" Dash ran to the nearest tree and pulled himself up on the trunk. He stepped on the rope. He had no fear. He possessed the courage that sprang from innocence and ignorance.

The rope vibrated with the boy's first step, and he pulled his foot back. He tried with the other foot. The line stilled after a few breaths. Then Dash inched out. He wavered, but used his arms as he had seen his brother do. He was now on the line without the aid of anything other than his own sense of bravado.

"Ehrich! I'm doing it!"

"Keep going, Dash."

The little Weisz continued. When he reached the halfway point, Dash's overconfidence spun him off the rope. He flailed to regain his balance, but his wild swinging only made the cable bounce, and he tumbled from the line. Ehrich zipped to Dash's rescue, using his own body as a cushion. They both fell, and Ehrich smacked the back of his head on the ground. He'd nurse a goose egg for days.

"Are you all right, Dash?"

"I want to do it again!" Dash exclaimed.

Ehrich shook his head as he watched his brother rush to the tree. Dash would most likely fall again, but Ehrich couldn't help but smile at the boy's fearlessness. He brushed himself off and applauded the new Prince of the Air.

In the chamber, Ehrich stared at his brother's still form. He wasn't going to be climbing trees anytime soon. Kifo had much to answer for. He spent one final moment with his brother then walked out.

Tesla was engrossed in the diodes and gears on the table. He acted like a kid in a toy shop. His eyes were wide with glee and delight as he marvelled over every little nut and bolt on the table. He glanced up. "Ehrich, come, come. You have to see this."

"What is it, Mr. Tesla?"

"What amazing inventions I could create if I had access to a fraction of what is here. A transformer to power New York for a year, and the device would be no larger than this room. Can you imagine?"

Ehrich nodded.

"They are advanced beyond anything I have ever seen. They already have a mechanical oscillator like the one I tried to develop."

Tesla held up a small tower that appeared to have an electromagnet that powered a piston.

"That's nice."

"What is troubling you, my friend?"

"Mr. Tesla, do you believe in predestination?"

"The idea that some greater power has already laid out our lives for us? Why would you wonder that?" Tesla asked.

"Of all the people Kifo could possess, he chose my brother. Why would he need him?"

"I don't know. Perhaps the boy suited his purposes. Few people question a child's actions."

"Yes, but why my brother and why did he take him...." He stopped himself, realizing his mentor had no idea that he had come to New York from a different dimension. He weighed the consequences of telling the truth.

"Why did he take him where, Ehrich?"

The teen launched into the truth: "Sir, there is something I need to tell you. I don't quite know how to say it, but I'm not who you think I am."

Tesla lowered his tools. "And who are you really, Ehrich?"

"I'm not from this place."

"None of us are."

"I mean I came from another dimension, sir. Like Amina and the others. I'm a traveller."

Tesla said nothing.

"In my world, we knew nothing of portals to other dimensions. One day, my brother and I, we stirred up some trouble. I tried to break into an apartment. The owner chased us, and we were separated. Somehow, Kifo crossed paths with Dash and took over his body. I didn't know what had happened, but I saw my brother opening a portal into another world. I tried to stop him, but we both fell through. I'm a traveller."

Tesla said nothing.

"Sir?"

"You disappoint me, Ehrich. Why didn't you tell me before?"

"This was the first chance I had to tell you."

He shook his head. "All the times we worked together in my laboratory, those were opportunities to tell me the truth."

"I wasn't sure if you'd accept me."

"I don't care where you are from. I don't know why the others in New York feel the need to judge others based on their origins, but I am an outsider like you. I may not have come from another world, but I came from another country, and I saw firsthand how unkind people can be. How can you possibly think that I would not sympathize?"

"I'm sorry, sir. I guess I was scared."

"The only thing you need to fear is losing yourself, Ehrich. And the path to that is in hiding yourself from the ones who are your friends."

"I understand, sir. No more secrets."

"Good. Now let us focus our attention to what matters, and ascertain how to make this codex project larger images."

Ehrich assisted Tesla as the scientist tinkered with the carousel's inner gears and lenses. The oscillator throbbed in the corner of the room.

"Do you need this oscillator?" Ehrich asked. "I thought you said this thing could cause an earthquake."

"But it can also generate the power we need to charge the codex. Ah, I see now. I think all we need to do is change the distance between the light and the lenses so that the picture can expand."

Tesla pulled one of the glass circles along the length of the carousel, and the images in the air grew larger. He cracked a grin. "As Archimedes would say, 'Eureka!'"

The two men built a mount to hold the lens further away from the light. They spent a good portion of the day working on it. By the time they finished, Amina had returned with supplies.

Over a platter of exotic fruits and vegetables Amina rounded up on her shopping spree, the trio discussed how they could develop a demonstration to entice Edison to come out.

"What do you remember of him, Mr. Tesla?" Amina asked.

"He is a prankster. Always quick to joke. I think he picked that up from his days as a telegraph operator. Those gentlemen can be rather rough around the edges."

"Anything we can use?" Ehrich asked.

He stroked his chin, thinking, then: "Ah, he is a fan of the Victor Hugo novels. *Les Miserables. The Hunchback of Notre Dame.* And the *Last Days of the Condemned Man.*"

Ehrich beamed. "We can use that."

"How?" Amina asked.

"The title suggests it is about someone going to his execution, yes?"

"I believe it is the guillotine," Tesla said.

"What if we project a man about to go to the guillotine? Call the act the *Last Day of the Condemned Man.* Make it obvious to Edison that this is a recreation of a Victor Hugo novel."

Tesla folded his arms over his chest. "We play the projection and Edison will be interested."

Ehrich finished the last of the fruit. "Yes, but we need a venue to use the projector, and I suspect we won't be able to convince any of the colleges to allow a demonstration without some kind of credentials."

"Then where are we going to present the demonstration?" Amina asked.

"I was thinking we might try the theatre."

Tesla stroked his moustache. "Curious ploy. Edison is interested in the entertainment industry. This might pique his interest. It could work."

"Except we don't have access to a theatre either," Amina pointed out.

"Time to sell ourselves," Ehrich said. "A new brand of entertainment for the masses. Moving pictures."

SCRATCH MY BACK

Mr. Serenity's sketch of the airship had blossomed over the days. Unable to leave General Ling Po's quarters, he had to piece together the painting with some art direction from his host.

"Does this seem right?" Mr. Serenity asked.

"Very close."

"What about the shape of the balloon?"

"Almost. The suspension cables should be spaced farther apart."

Mr. Serenity continued to sketch, but he kept one eye on the general's closed bedroom door. On the other side, Ning Shu was preparing for her private meeting with Gu Shan. He wanted to accompany her, but that would be impossible. Instead, he busied himself with the painting of the airship, picking Ling Po's brain for the details.

Finally, the door opened. Ning Shu stepped out wearing an oversized black silk jacket with knot buttons. Her trousers had been cuffed a few times to hide the extra fabric. At first glance, she might pass for one of the soldiers posted outside the quarters.

"Perfect," Ling Po said. "Now, repeat the directions."

"Out the door and to the left. Up the stairs and run straight toward the bow of the airship. Count seven doors, then turn right and find the stairs. Go down two flights, and double back on the last flight so that I'm running toward the bow again. Find the eighth door on the left. Gu Shan will be waiting."

"Good," Ling Po said. "Mr. Serenity, are you ready?"

The big man set his brush on the desk and squeezed out of his chair. "Yes, General."

Ling Po opened the door to the corridor. Two of Xian's soldiers stood impassively across the hallway.

"Sir, how can we help you?" the tall one with a crescent-shaped scar under his eye asked.

"My guests need to stretch their legs. They are verging on cabin fever."

"General Xian's orders are clear. Everyone stays inside."

"I'm countermanding her orders," Ling Po said.

"Sorry, sir."

"No more!" Mr. Serenity shouted. "I need to get out!"

He shoved Ling Po into the two soldiers. The general flailed his arms, the golden sleeves of his robe billowing and obscuring the men's vision. The three became tangled as Mr. Serenity bolted into the hallway and veered left. He ran up the nearby stairs.

Ling Po shouted, "Stop him!"

The soldiers sprinted after him. Ling Po followed, but lagged behind. When the two men vaulted the steps, Ling Po stopped and whistled, then he ran after them. Ning Shu stepped out of the quarters and scurried down the hall.

She slipped up the stairs, reaching the next level just as Ling Po reached the top of the third level. He waved down—signalling the coast was clear—and stepped through a doorway. She followed his directions, hoping not to run into any soldiers along the way. She slowed when she reached Gu Shan's room. She checked the hall, then knocked on the door.

Gu Shan answered, and his jaw dropped. "Ning Shu?"

"Good to see you, General Gu Shan."

In a royal blue robe with an embroidered eagle on the chest, he stood half a head shorter than Ning Shu but more than made up for his lack of height with his stocky girth. He had more lines across his face than dried dirt. His black braided hair had long ago become grey.

"What are you doing here?" he cried. "Ning Shu! I can't believe you're back."

"Gu Shan, didn't anyone inform you?"

"Not a word. Xian keeps everything to herself these days."

"No matter. Urgent matters require your attention."

"Enter," he said, ushering her inside.

Outside the porthole, the cloud blocked the view below. Ning Shu wondered if they were over Manhattan, and her thoughts drifted to Ehrich and Amina. Were they safe?

"Why the cloak of secrecy, my friend?" Gu Shan had clearly been about to sit down to a meal. The general scooped a ration of steamed carrots and rice on to a plate for Ning Shu.

She recounted her experiences with Xian and lied about her mission to root out the traitor within Ba Tian's army. Gu Shan chewed on a drumstick, rapt with attention. He clucked and shook his head every time she mentioned how Xian had been behaving.

He pulled up the sleeves of his blue silk robe, revealing scars up and down his arms from countless battles. He grinned. Three of his teeth had fallen out, but he enjoyed sipping the nectar from the crystal glass goblet. He wiped his lips on the edge of his sleeve and set the goblet back on the table.

"Ning Shu, you used to tell such wild stories. I remember you once tried to convince me there were two moons—one in the sky and a spare one in Lake Xanath. A great imagination."

"Sir, don't you believe me?"

"And the trouble you caused! Your mother appointed me as your official minder. I'll wager you had no idea that I had been your minder all those years ago."

"I appreciate what you've done for me, sir, and I ask for one more thing."

"Broke my heart when your mother died. Dear, sweet woman. Brought out the best in all of us, especially you."

"Yes, sir. She was the mirror of the House of Qi. Always reflecting the truth. The beauty and the flaws."

"And you are the prism, Ning Shu. You bend the truth."

"Sir, you need to put more weight on these allegations."

Gu Shan sipped from his crystal goblet. "Ling Po has nested in your ear, hasn't he?"

"What does that matter?"

"My dear friend is not himself. I suspect the bitterness of losing his stewardship weighs heavily on his mind. I also believe he questions Xian's decision to gather all the generals in this sector. Not the best tactical manoeuvre."

"Why would she do this?"

"She claims this sector is the end game. We win here, we control the portal to all other sectors."

"And her real reason?"

"Rumours," Gu Shan said, waving his hand dismissively. "Whispers that Xian fears treason within the ranks of the generals. She wants them close by in case she needs to lop off a head or two to set an example for the rest of us."

"She's tasted power and she doesn't want to give it up," Ning Shu offered.

"Your words. Not mine. I like my head where it is."

"Gu Shan, I want an audience with the Council of Arch Generals to plead my case. Have things changed so much that the House of Qi must beg?"

"In my waning years, my vision has sharpened. Odd how things change. My body aches and my joints seize up when I walk up a flight of stairs, but my vision is sharp. All the years I served the House of Qi, and all I have to show for my efforts is a broken body and clear sight. I lay claim to nothing, Ning Shu. No legacy. No wife. No children. I'm a lonely man with a few memories and fewer friends."

His grizzled hands caressed the crystal goblet. In the arch general's cabin, Ning Shu strained to listen for the engine. Were they so far away or had the airship stopped? She couldn't tell.

"The past few weeks on this airship opened my eyes. Oh yes, as an arch general, I enjoy the spoils of victory, but nothing quite like this. I would prefer to spend my final years with some measure of comfort. Perhaps as a reward for my continued loyalty."

Ning Shu narrowed her gaze. Soldiers rose through the ranks because of their prowess on the battlefield. Generals rose to power because their ability off the field, and Gu Shan was demonstrating that skill now.

"I've always been fond of Chung Lantau Island. The waters are restorative," Gu Shan said.

"They are. You are welcome to the island."

"Of course, I might need some help moving around in my advancing years."

"The House of Qi can offer a full complement of staff."

"And concubines?"

She cringed inwardly but feigned a smile. "As soon as we gather the Council of Arch Generals."

"You can plead any case you wish, Ning Shu. You could even try to convince the generals this sector has two moons. I don't care. I'm already soaking in the waters on Chung Lantau."

"You have been ever so helpful," she replied icily.

"It will take some time to call the meeting. We must collect the other generals."

"I'm sure the waters on Chung Lantau can wait."

"I'll see what I can to expedite the meeting," Gu Shan said.

"Thank you. I will have your vote at the council, I trust."

"Of course."

"One last favour, if you don't mind. I need to return to my quarters."

Mr. Serenity had eluded the soldiers at first by ducking behind the massive cylindrical hydrogen tanks that pumped gas into the ballonets above the engine room. As the big man slipped between the giant steam engines that powered the propulsors, his eyes drank in every detail. He noted the line of hulking steam engines. These copper machines with segmented smoke stacks powered the propulsors outside the gondola through a maze of pipes that snaked overhead.

Above, huge ballonets contained the hydrogen gas that enabled the airship to fly. They hovered within the massive balloon envelope that formed the overall structure of the rigid airship.

He slipped from between the tanks and stumbled across

a bamboo ladder mounted into the floor and rising up to a platform high above the tanks and over the copper pipes. He began to climb, eluding the reach of the crimson men. As he neared the top of the platform, he noticed a cable stretching from a large spool to a seam in the balloon toward the bow.

One of the engineers cried out, "Stop him before he reaches the rip line."

The two soldiers hustled up the ladder. Mr. Serenity's larger girth slowed him down. A crimson hand grabbed his ankle before he could reach the top. He clung to the bamboo rung and refused to let go. He eyed the engine room layout, committing it to memory, and tried to give Ning Shu enough time to return to Ling Po's quarters.

Gu Shan and a retinue of two armed escorts marched through the narrow corridors of the airship back to Ling Po's quarters. By now, Xian's soldiers would have informed her of the altercation. She hoped Xian didn't toss Mr. Serenity in the brig.

The general had a hold of Ning Shu's arm. "Don't worry, Ning Shu. I'll have a few words with Xian's men. I'm sure they wouldn't want their general to learn how they let a member of the House of Qi out of their sight."

"You are too kind, sir."

"I do what I can."

They ascended the bamboo steps. One escort led them up while the other walked behind. Ning Shu stopped about halfway up the stairs, unable to shake the feeling someone was watching. She was about to say something when a barbed disc flew past her face and struck the guard behind her. He shrieked once and collapsed, tumbling down the steps. His body twitched on the floor until he expired.

The lead escort drew his razor-sharp disc from his bandolier and protected General Gu Shan with his body. The general pulled back his blue robe and drew a disc from his thigh band. Though he was old, he still had a warrior's instinct. He flicked the disc up the stairs and drew another projectile.

Ning Shu peered up the stairs for any sign of the assassin, but whoever had thrown the weapon was gone.

SHOW BUSINESS

The theatres weren't ready for moving pictures. Broadway managers slammed the door in Ehrich's face. Theatres catered to the upper class with the works of Shakespeare, or playwrights like Charles Hoyt and his hit show, *A Trip to Chinatown*. Each haughty manager informed the group they performed *live* theatre. Ehrich downgraded his pitch to the vaudeville venues around Union Square.

The Bijou's marquee had seen better days, and the loiterers outside suggested this place might be a tavern rather than an entertainment establishment. Still, the Bijou was their best chance of landing any kind of stage time. The venue was their last stop in a long line of rejections.

The husky manager eyed Ehrich as the teen adjusted his slightly oversized suit. He pressed his fake moustache against his lip and cleared his throat.

"What's your act?" asked the man who reeked of garlic.

"We project moving pictures," Ehrich said.

"What's that?"

"It's unlike anything you've ever seen."

"They all say the same thing to land the job. Impress me."

"Mr. Godfrey, this presentation is about the last day of a condemned man. He's about to face the guillotine, and he doesn't want to die. We tell the story using moving images."

"This is show business. You dance? I can sell you. Sing? Even better. Tell jokes? I might be able to squeeze you in. Anything else? The audience will egg you off the stage."

"What if the act were live? We actually witness a man putting his neck under the guillotine. He's chained up in shackles, and at the last minute, he frees himself."

"An escape act, huh? I don't know. I already have a magician."

"I tell a harrowing story. Will the condemned man free himself before the guillotine drops on his neck?"

"I like the notion, but I run a family show. What else do you have?"

"How about a transformation?" Ehrich said, grasping at straws. He thought of one of the tricks Robert Houdin wrote about in his book. The effect was the Indian Basket, in which a child was tied up in a wicker basket, but miraculously escaped. Ehrich offered it up. "I step into a trunk. The lid is closed, and when the trunk is open again, I am gone."

"So?" the manager said. If there were a contest for the most cynical venue manager, Godfrey would take home the crown. He had more interest in Amina than anything Ehrich offered.

"And in my place, my beautiful assistant appears," he added.

"She's in the act?" Godfrey asked.

"Me?" Amina's eyes were wide.

"Yes, she is," Ehrich jumped in. He was scrambling now to land the deal. They needed to get on the bill if they were to have any chance of attracting Edison. "She is part of this incredible transformation."

Godfrey chewed his bottom lip and cocked his head toward Ehrich but kept his eye on Amina's leg. She stepped beside Tesla, hiding from the lascivious man's ogling.

Ehrich stepped in front of the manager. "It's an incredible performance where the magician and the assistant switch places."

"I'm intrigued. I'll give you a half-hour to impress me. Knock my socks off, and I'll give you a week on the bill."

"Now? But I'm not ready."

"Time is money. You want the shot or not?"

"We should be able to make do with something," Tesla said.

Ehrich couldn't argue with his mentor. They stepped into the theatre.

Amina whispered, "What about the projection demonstration, Ehrich?"

"We needed a venue. Once we have the job, we can bring out the projection."

"One problem. We're not a magic act," she said.

"Then we'll have to do our best to pretend to be one," Tesla said.

They walked past the wooden chairs to the empty stage. Ehrich was trying to figure out exactly how to pull off the trick he had promised the manager without a trunk or any means to do this, but Tesla seemed confident.

They climbed on stage and began their preparations. Tesla took off his jacket. "Can we instantly project the images we record?"

"Yes."

"We need to record the images of what Ehrich promised."

She cracked a smile, catching on to the ploy. Tesla set the

codex on the floor and began to work on the device. Godfrey leered at Amina for a second, but left after she stepped into the wings. She popped back on stage after the man lumbered out.

Tesla waved at the pair on stage. "I'm set to record. What shall we show him?"

Ehrich glanced around. "Search for a curtain of some type. And a trunk."

The trio split off to the wings. Ehrich spotted the props of the other performers. Amina grabbed a curtain while he examined a large steamer trunk. He began to empty it.

"What do you think you're doing?" A tiny girl with heavy eyebrows hitched up her brown skirt and ran over. "Put those things back."

"I'm sorry. We're hoping we can borrow your steamer trunk for an audition. I meant to put everything back."

"You will put my props back now."

"I won't wreck anything."

"I don't care. Didn't your mother teach you any manners?" the girl asked, her hands on her hips.

Ehrich was struck by the girl's good looks. She seemed mature for her age. Her pale skin and tiny stature reminded him of a sprite—a churlish sprite.

"I'm sorry, miss." He began to stuff the belongings back in the trunk and noted the initials read "WB Rahner."

"Stop gawking and get stuffing," she said.

"Of course, Ms. Rahner."

"How do you know my name?"

He pointed at the nameplate on the trunk.

"Don't get fresh with me."

"Sorry." He set a cane into the box.

"Stop wrecking my things. Give me that. Next time, keep your grubby paws off what doesn't belong to you. Don't you know anything about theatre etiquette?" she scolded.

Though she was tearing a strip out of him, Ehrich couldn't deny his sense of ease around this elfish girl.

"Do you know where I could find a trunk? It's for my audition."

"What kind of performer comes in to audition with nothing?"

"An unemployed one," Ehrich quipped.

The hint of a smile started to form, but she covered her mouth. "You might find an old trunk in the green room. We use it as a table. The lid sticks."

"Thank you, Ms. Rahner." He headed off to the back and found the trunk she had mentioned. He cleared the papers and bottles from the top and dragged the black box out of the room. He feared the ancient thing would disintegrate before he reached the stage, but the trunk survived.

Amina shook out a large dusty cloth. Tesla took note of both as he set up the codex in the wings.

"What do we do?" Amina asked.

Ehrich waved to Tesla. "Ready to record?"

"Yes. Any time."

Ehrich squeezed into the musty box and ducked down as Amina closed the lid.

"Amina, climb on top of the trunk."

The thump of his partner's feet reverberated inside the trunk. They held their positions for what seemed like forever before Tesla instructed them to switch places. They did. Tesla scratched his head.

"I'd like to try one more," he said. "I'm not sure if I caught everything."

Ehrich opened the trunk and helped Amina climb out. "Okay, let's go ahead."

Godfrey's voice boomed across the theatre before they could reshoot their performance. "Time's money. Ready or not, here I come."

Amina's gaze darted from Ehrich to the trunk. "What do we do?"

"Put on a show," he said.

Godfrey plopped into a seat in the front row. He folded his arms over his chest daring the trio to entertain him.

Ehrich strode forward. "Welcome to the most amazing act you will ever witness. First, an ordinary trunk."

"Hey, that's mine," Godfrey said.

"Yes, taken from the green room of your theatre, and a painter's drop cloth from backstage. With these two found items, you will witness the impossible."

He motioned to Amina to help him push the trunk forward on stage. He pried the lid open and tilted the box over to show nothing but dust and yellowed newspapers inside. He beckoned Amina to help him pick up the cloth.

"In just a moment, I will step into the trunk, and my lovely assistant Amina will shut me in. Then she will raise the cloth in front, and what you will see will amaze you."

They spun the box around three times.

Ehrich whispered, "When I climb in the trunk, close the lid. Then stand on top of it and raise the drop cloth."

"Then what?"

"Hope."

Godfrey leaned forward in his seat, intrigued. Ehrich stopped pushing the trunk and stepped inside. "Now my assistant will close me up in the trunk."

Ehrich squeezed himself into the cramped box. As he was about to lower his head, he spotted Ms. Rahner peering at him from the wings. A thrill ran through his stomach as he curled into a ball. The lid slammed against his back. The trunk reeked of old shoes.

On stage, Amina spun the trunk around once. The scrape of the heavy trunk against the wooden floor caused her to wince. Out of the corner of her eye, she noted a dark haired girl sliding from the wings to the front row. They had gained an audience member. A good sign.

She raised the drop cloth to hide the trunk and herself. Just as the dusty material was at the height of her neck, she winked at Godfrey. Give the letch another good reason to book their act. She lifted the cloth over her head.

Behind the cloth, Amina couldn't see anything, but she heard a gasp in the audience. Even Ms. Rahner let out a low whistle. From the wings, Tesla motioned her to step down. She dropped the cloth. A projection of Ehrich stood on the trunk. The image stepped down and walked to the foot of the stage.

"Now," Amina whispered as she flipped the trunk lid open.

Like a scrim, the projection shielded the audience's view of the action behind the image of the virtual Ehrich on stage. The real Weisz climbed out of the trunk, and Amina took his place inside. He then strode up to his own projection and stepped inside his virtual doppelganger. Tesla shut off the codex, and the real Ehrich paraded around the stage. Their audience of two applauded wildly. Ehrich returned to the trunk and opened the lid to help Amina climb out. She wrinkled her nose from the stench. Ehrich grabbed her hand and bowed.

Godfrey ran on to the stage. "That act will pack the houses when word spreads. What do you call this trick?"

Ehrich answered, "Metamorphosis."

The sweaty man sidled up to Amina and wrapped his arm around her waist. He smelled of onions and beef.

"I like the name. If you're in need of a costume or two, I'm sure I might be able to scare up something from my office." He leaned in close to Amina. She squirmed out of his grasp.

Tesla saved her. "We want to start this week, and we wish to have a two-week engagement. More if we bring in big houses."

Godfrey let go of Amina and approached Tesla. "I'll pay the standard rate. Bottom billing and one week run. I can put you up in my boarding house, but I'll take room and board out of your wages. I'll give you an extra week, if houses grow by 30 percent."

"We want posters and bills to distribute," Tesla said.

"Certainly. You'll have that by tomorrow afternoon if I can contact the printer in time. What should I bill your act as?" He asked Ehrich.

"Harry Houdini," Ehrich answered instinctively. As soon as he uttered the name, a pang of regret stabbed his heart. The hunters who would have recognized his stage name were dead. The last ties to his old life were gone. "Bill me as Harry Houdini."

THE HANDCUFF KING

"**U**nacceptable!" Ling Po howled as he paced the length of his quarters.

Mr. Serenity stood in the centre of the room bound in a canvas straitjacket, his arms crossed over his chest and tied up behind his back. Xian and her escorts gathered around him while Gu Shan tended to Ning Shu.

"I'll be fine. How is your escort?" Ning Shu asked.

"He's dead," Gu Shan answered. "The razor tael was poisoned."

"How does an assassin sneak onboard the airship?" Ling Po asked.

"The same way as outsiders," Xian retorted. She wasn't about to be cowed by the old man. "None of this would have even happened if she had stayed put in your quarters. What was she doing outside anyway?"

"It's my fault," Gu Shan said. "Heard a rumour that the House of Qi had returned, and I had to see for myself. Why did you keep this from me?"

"That is not the issue," Xian said. "The issue is that there is an assassin onboard the ship."

"Yes," Ling Po said. "We must find the culprit. Shouldn't you be having your soldiers search the ship, General Xian?"

She glared at Ling Po, then growled at one of her soldiers. "Spread the word. Comb every corner of the ship. I want the assassin before the day's end."

The soldier bowed sharply and ran out of the room.

"Ling Po, you've shown the same competence in protecting Ning Shu as you did in serving as the House of Qi's steward. I'm afraid I'm going to have to relieve you of your duties again."

"She's safer with me than anyone else," Ling Po said.

"A dead soldier suggests otherwise."

Ning Shu stood up. "I take responsibility for the incident, General. Unlike others, Ling Po obeys the word of the House of Qi. I asked to step out."

"Then the soldier's death is on your head, General. I suggest we find General Ning Shu safer quarters so we can avoid any more needless deaths," Xian said. "I will personally protect you, and I believe we must start with separating you from your companion."

"Mr. Serenity travels with me," Ning Shu said. "He goes nowhere without me."

"And I wouldn't mind slipping into something less uncomfortable," Mr. Serenity added.

"He will not roam free on my airship," Xian said.

"Hold on," Gu Shan interrupted. "The last time I checked, Ning Shu is the highest ranking member of the House of Qi. Are you openly defying her wishes, General Xian? Sounded something dangerously close to treason."

Ning Shu hid her glee. Though Gu Shan's help was expensive, he was worth the price.

"I'm merely expressing my concerns," Xian said.

"Duly noted," Ning Shu said.

Ling Po jumped in. "Ning Shu may stay in my quarters as long as she wishes."

Gu Shan escalated the matter. "What? Ling Po, that is an insult to the House of Qi. If anything, Ning Shu must reside in the most spacious quarters here. I believe they would be your quarters, General Xian."

Xian gritted her teeth and flashed a thin-lipped smirk. "Gu Shan, you know as well as I do that your suite is the largest on the ship."

"Ah, the memory slips," he said.

Ning Shu urged the old man to follow through on his promise. "Gu Shan, I would do nothing to oust you from your quarters. Perhaps when we return to our sector, you may soak in the waters at Chung Lantau."

"I would appreciate that, but we are far from home and we have much to discuss, starting with why the steward still holds power when the House of Qi has returned."

Xian shook her head. "I don't know what you're talking about."

"I'm talking about why Ning Shu's arrival has been kept secret from me, a member of the Council of Arch Generals."

Ling Po added, "And when she has returned with news of a mission Ba Tian himself endorsed."

Ning Shu feigned humility. "I'm sure Xian must have her reasons to withhold this information from the Council of Arch Generals."

Gu Shan pounded his fist into his hand. "Not when you were on a mission for Ba Tian. I call for a gathering, Xian."

"General Gu Shan, calm down," she said. "If you insist on the gathering, we will do so, but you know we will have to interrupt their missions."

"Then we will inconvenience them," Gu Shan said.

"The House of Qi requires their presence," Ning Shu declared. "That is not an inconvenience. It is an order."

"Very well, daughter of Ba Tian," Xian said, with surprising speed.

Ning Shu nervously grabbed her braid, wondering if she had played into Xian's hand.

The next day, Ehrich and Amina assumed disguises and roamed the Bowery streets to shove handbills into the hands of disinterested New Yorkers. They had left Tesla at the theatre to construct the effects for the upcoming performance. Few pedestrians stopped. Ehrich and Amina were part of a swarm of gnat-like entertainers buzzing for attention.

"This is futile," Amina said. "How are we supposed to lure Thomas Edison into the theatre when we can't even wrangle people off the street?"

"We don't want these audiences. We want one audience. And we know how to contact him. Through the Demon Watch."

"You're going to risk being discovered so you can hand out flyers to hunters?"

"My disguise has worked this far."

"And how do you know they'll take any interest in our act?"

"I have a plan, but I need something back at the theatre."

A few hours later, Ehrich was now decked out in his performer's suit and top hat. He wore a fake beard and he walked with a cane. He strode toward the local police station in the Bowery. The hunters used local constabularies as their base of operations as they often collaborated on cases.

Behind the desk, a bored desk sergeant read the newspaper. With a bent-nose that appeared as if it had been broken a few times, the man seemed more comfortable in a boxing ring than behind the desk. He adjusted his navy blue top, tugging the collar away from his neck. He barely peeked from his newspaper when Ehrich entered.

"Any hunters here?" Ehrich asked.

A thug sat up on the bench nearby. The older man wore a hunter's duster, and he sported a dynatron pistol at his hip, but he didn't strike Ehrich as a hunter. Maybe it was his thinning hair or the unshaven face and the bloodshot eyes of someone who had probably spent more time in a tavern than patrolling the streets. In fact, this man reminded Ehrich of the ruffians on Randall's Island.

"What do you want? Any demon sightings?" the hunter asked.

"You're with the Demon Watch?" Ehrich asked.

"I work for Thomas Edison. On loan to the Demon Watch. What's your business?"

"I'm here to warn you that if you incarcerate any Dimensionals at this station, they will not remain for long."

"Excuse me? I have a perfectly sound jail here," the desk sergeant said.

"No, you don't, sir. You have a flaw in your cell, and I'm to expose it before the hunters lose any of their prisoners."

The thug strolled toward Ehrich. "What's your name?"

"Harry Houdini," he lied.

"And why do you think this jail cell isn't up to standards?"

"Anyone can escape from it, even an ordinary mortal like myself."

"I can accommodate you," the desk sergeant said. "Want me to lock you up?"

"You will look the fool when I escape."

"Off with you," the beefy desk sergeant barked.

Ehrich winked at the thug. "I'll wager Commissioner Edison will be curious about how hunters like you risk your lives to round up Dimensionals, only to have them slip out the back door."

"Okay, I was going to let you walk out, but now you've gone and done it," the desk sergeant said. "You want to make a big deal out of this, you can spend the night in the jail to think things over."

He walked around the desk and grabbed Ehrich's shoulder with his massive hands. The man was strong and none too kind. He frisked Ehrich before he slapped Darby handcuffs on his wrists. He pulled out his key and screwed it into the cuff, twisting the key until the latch caught. The copper slapped on leg irons around Ehrich's ankles.

"Do you think that's necessary?" Ehrich asked.

"Not at all, but I enjoyed it."

The desk sergeant frog-marched Ehrich to the cell area at the back of the station. He opened the door to the cells and directed Ehrich to the nearest one. He slammed him against the wall while he fished out the key. He opened the barred door and slammed it shut behind Ehrich.

"I'm going to buy some lunch. When I come back, I expect you'll still be here." He closed the door to the cell area, leaving the boy alone.

Ehrich grunted as he crouched low and flipped the heel of his shoe open and pulled out his lock pick. He worked first on the leg irons, raking the pick inside the lock mechanism. With no one watching, he felt totally confident and at ease.

And he was able to free himself from the irons in short order. The D-shaped Darby handcuffs were harder to pick because they were behind his back.

He angled his hand to reach the hole at the cuff's bottom. If he could dig the pick deep enough, he might spring the mechanism, but to do that he needed a better angle. He kicked off his shoes and crouched into a ball with his arms behind his back. He lowered them past his rear until the chain pressed against the back of his calves. He rolled back and used the momentum to drive his arms up and around his feet. The cuffs cleared his feet. His arms had nearly popped out of their sockets, but he had brought the shackles in front.

He slid the pick into the lock and raked the mechanism until the latch detached from the cuff's thick shaft. Within moments, the Darby handcuffs laid on the cell floor as Ehrich examined the cell door lock.

Outside, the two men chatted. They were curious about the strange man who had entered the police station, and they wagered whether Ehrich was insane or drunk. They finally decided he was insane as they walked out of the station to grab a bite.

Ehrich inserted the hook pick, probing for the pins in the mechanism. After a few attempts, the satisfying click of the lock giving way resounded in the cell. Ehrich turned the tension wrench. *Click.* The door opened. He placed the lock pick set in the heel of his right shoe, then slipped into his shoes and walked out. The station was empty.

Ehrich peeked out the door and spotted the copper and the thug strolling down the street toward an oyster vendor. Ehrich followed the pair.

He waited until the copper had picked up an oyster from the vendor's cart. Then he sidled beside the burly man and said,

Marty Chan

"I'll have what he's having. I think he'll be paying."

The copper dropped the oyster, juices still dribbling down his chin. "How? What? But—!"

Ehrich bowed low. "No jail can hold me," he announced.

"What? How? You couldn't have—" the desk sergeant sputtered.

The hunter chuckled. "You'll have to teach me that trick. Spent a few nights in a cell myself and could do with a way out. Say...who are you?"

"Harry Houdini, Master of Manacles, The Handcuff King. And I'm playing at the Bijou tomorrow night and every night for the next two weeks. If you want to witness more of my amazing feats, come to the Bijou, where I will be performing the *Last Day of the Condemned Man*...which might be your story, copper."

The big man sputtered, "This was all a part of a publicity stunt! I ought to throw you in the clinker again."

Ehrich smirked. "Then you'll have to explain how a man escaped twice from your cell."

The hunter laughed.

"Remember— the *Last Day of the Condemned Man*."

Amina joined Ehrich at the next police station to witness the repeat of his escape act, but this time the sour desk sergeant tossed him out of the station instead of into a cell. Ehrich didn't quit. With only a day before his first public performance, he had hoped to drum up an audience that included Thomas Edison.

The pair tramped around the city to play their act for different desk sergeants and demon hunters. Some were tickled by the bravado; others irritated. With every stop, Ehrich refined his patter and discovered something new about how to escape from the cells. He gained confidence every time he was thrown into another cell.

In between escapes, Amina plastered posters around the area, and Ehrich procured materials for Tesla to finish constructing their props. For the first time in weeks, Ehrich wanted to be spotted. Not as himself, but as Harry Houdini. He adopted the persona of a relentless huckster, a showman who loved the limelight. In essence, by drawing attention to himself, he was hiding in plain sight. They didn't see Ehrich Weisz; they only saw Harry Houdini, The Handcuff King.

He joined Amina as they headed to a police station near the Hudson River. He wanted to check on the mood. More Dimensionals crowded around the gate. His stomach lurched from the heavy tension in the air. These Dimensionals had lost their jobs. Many had lost their homes. A few had lost loved ones. He wasn't surprised that their anger was spilling over.

A pair of sentries broke away from the fence and split up a group of Dimensionals talking to a blonde vendor, hawking corn. She flirted with the travellers as she tried to entice them to buy her roasted corn.

"Clear off," the sentry with a pockmarked face shouted.

"We're not doing anything wrong," a Dimensional with a third eye retorted.

"Bachelor demons aren't allowed to fraternize with our women," he said, waving his hand at the predominantly male group.

"She's selling us corn," another Dimensional piped up.

The sentry waved her off. "Take your business someplace else."

She placed her hands on her hips and refused to budge. "These men haven't eaten in days."

"You're not selling to them."

"You going to stop me?" she threatened. "How?"

The sentry brought out his baton and smashed it across the face of the nearest Dimensional. "Can't eat corn with no teeth."

The other Dimensionals rushed to help their friend. More sentries converged on the scene. The corn vendor screamed at the sentries to back off, but they ignored her. More soldiers poured out from the gate to quell the disturbance. Newspaper reporters hovered around the edges of the crowd, eager for a riot to report.

Amina nudged him. "I think someone is watching us."

He spun around, scanning the faces in the crowd, but he didn't notice anyone suspicious. "Who?"

"To your left."

He craned his head until he set his gaze on a copper with a handlebar moustache and a barrel chest. The police officer stared at Ehrich. He instinctively reached up to check that his beard was still on.

"Know him?" she asked.

"No, but he seems to know me."

"We should go," Amina said.

She slipped into the mob. The mass of bodies was almost impossible to push through. Ehrich shoved one traveller out of the way, and another filled his place. Some of the people pushed back. A whistle shrieked. Ehrich glanced back.

The copper charged after him. Ehrich surged ahead, slipping through a crush of people. He scanned the faces for Amina. No sign of her. Behind him, three more coppers had joined the chase.

A hand snaked out of the crowd and grabbed his arm. Amina yanked him toward a break in the crowd.

"This way," she said.

They zigzagged around the dwindling protestors and sprinted down the cobblestone street, away from the crowd and the police officers in pursuit. Ehrich was nearly out of breath.

"Who was that?"

"I don't know," Ehrich said, panting. "I think word of our stunt has been spreading. I did embarrass a few desk sergeants. Maybe they mean to return the favour."

"Well, at least they're paying attention."

Ehrich nodded. "Now if only the hunters are talking to each other."

"I think we are done for the day," Amina said.

He shook his head. "One last one."

"I'm tired."

"Do you think Kifo is resting his feet? This is a race to find Edison, and we have to finish first."

Amina said, "All right. One more."

That same evening, outside Thomas Edison's West Orange facilities, the two sentinels patrolling the perimeter detected something suspicious outside the stonewall fence. The woman narrowed her blue eyes at footprints on the ground, leading up to the stone barrier. She motioned to her partner, who drew his teslatron. She drew her dynatron pistol and peeked over the fence. The tracks led toward the laboratory in the middle of the compound.

"Sound the alert," she whispered. Then she climbed over into the yard.

Her partner placed a whistle to his lips and blew sharply three times. His alarm was picked up across the compound. Other whistles cut through the night air and sentinels rushed from all areas of the compound, aiming their weapons and scanning the area for intruders.

The woman waved at her colleagues to follow the set of footprints to the laboratory. Nearly a dozen armed men and women converged on the building and flushed out a man in a raggedy black suit and top hat hiding in the bushes beside the building.

Kifo aimed his metal arm at the nearest sentinel and unleashed a volley of darts into the man's chest. A firefight erupted. Energy blasts lit up the night. Sentinels fell to the ground clutching darts in their chest.

Kifo rushed across the bushes, sprinting at the first sentinel. She took aim with her pistol. Her shot hit the assassin dead centre in the chest. He howled in pain as electricity coursed up and down his body, but he didn't fall. He staggered to one side, took aim with his arm, and brought down the sentinel with four darts flying out of his fingertips. He then sprinted toward the stonewall fence, scrambled up and over it, and ran off into the night.

Thomas Edison emerged from the building Kifo had been staking out. He rubbed his grimy hands off on his grey suit and signalled the sentinels to gather around. "Triple the security details around the perimeter. Whatever the demons are after must be valuable."

A few hundred yards away from the West Orange facilities, the injured Kifo staggered through the woods. Now that he knew with certainty where Thomas Edison was stationed, he vowed he wouldn't underestimate the man's defences again.

The next morning, Ehrich and Amina stood in the offices of the *New York World*—one of three newspaper outlets in the city. He had one last scheme to drum up an audience. The place hummed with activity as reporters pecked at typewriters. None of them showed any interest until Ehrich cleared his throat.

"Can I help you?" the woman asked.

"I have a story for you, Ms...." Ehrich started.

"Bly. Nellie Bly," the woman in the smart dress answered. She had a keen gaze and little patience.

"I've read about you," Ehrich said. "You've travelled around the world."

She grunted. "That's yesterday's news. I'm interested in today's."

"Uh, yes. Did you know there is a flaw in the police system? Namely, the cells they use to hold prisoners."

This caught Bly's attention. She lifted her hands from the keys of her typewriter and reached for a notepad.

"And how do you know this?"

"Might be better if I show you. Where's the nearest police station?"

She stood up, grabbed her hat, and led the pair out of the office. Ehrich grinned at Amina as they headed into the street. A few minutes later, Ehrich launched into his usual patter to goad the desk sergeant to lock him up.

This one didn't bite. "I was wondering when you'd come around to me. Everyone's talking about the man who can't be imprisoned."

Ehrich winked at Bly. "My reputation precedes me."

The desk sergeant laughed. "The huckster who will do anything to drum up an audience for his magic show."

She shook her head. "I don't have time for flams."

Amina backed up Ehrich. "He's very good."

"This is the stuff for the Herald, maybe, but at the World we do important stories. We don't give ink to hucksters."

Ehrich couldn't lose the reporter. He pleaded, "You have a story here. Harry Houdini is The King of Handcuffs. Nothing can hold me. Not even the sturdiest police cell. Not even Devil's Island. Throw me in the cell, sergeant, and you'll see for yourself."

The chubby sergeant chuckled. "Oh don't you worry about that. And I have just the cuffs for you."

The man lumbered from behind his desk and frisked Ehrich. Then he slapped a pair of Irish 8s on Ehrich's wrists.

Bly jotted notes and asked, "Have you only escaped from the standard issue handcuffs?"

"Yes," Ehrich answered.

"Nothing standard about these shackles," the copper declared.

Ehrich heard a faint squish after the copper had twisted the key to lock the cuffs. Something was afoot. Before Ehrich could inspect anything, the copper spun him around and marched him to the cell in the back of the stationhouse. Bly followed. The copper slammed the door shut, crossed his arms and watched.

"I can't do this while you're watching me," Ehrich protested.

"All the more reason for me to stay and watch," the copper said, grinning.

Bly jotted notes.

"This will take some time."

"It'll seem longer for you than it will for me, boy."

There was no getting rid of the copper or Bly. Ehrich paced back and forth in the cell, trying to concoct a scheme to retrieve his tools without anyone noticing, but the witnesses weren't leaving any time soon.

"Tell you what, give me ten minutes alone. That's half the

time it took for me to escape from the other jails. If I fail to get out in those ten minutes, I'll pay you one hundred dollars."

"Why the secrecy?" Bly asked.

"I prefer not to give away my methods in the event real criminals use your article as a manual on how to do the same."

"Fair enough," Bly replied, closing her notebook.

The chubby desk sergeant cocked his head to one side and stroked his chin. "A hundred dollars for ten minutes, eh? I like the sound of two hundred better."

"I'm afraid I don't have that kind of money."

"Then I'll give you five minutes."

Ehrich grimaced, weighing the offer. Finally, he replied. "Eight minutes."

"Five, and that's my final offer, boy."

"Fine. That should be all I need."

"I wouldn't count on it," the copper said, flashing a smug grin at Nellie Bly.

"Are all members of your force so quick to take bribes?" she asked.

"This isn't a bribe. It's a wager," the copper argued as the two stepped out.

As soon as Ehrich was alone, he retrieved the lock pick set from his shoe. He snaked his legs through his arms with great ease, having performed this move at least a dozen times. The Irish 8s were aptly named because the cuffs looked like the number 8.

He twisted his hands around so he could insert the pick into the open hole at the bottom, then he poked around for the latch. The pick jammed about halfway into the mechanism. Ehrich now realized what the copper had done behind his back. He had spiked the mechanism.

A bead of sweat rolled down his forehead as he worked at

the lock, but try as he might he couldn't dislodge whatever had gummed up the cuffs. He cursed himself for being so cocky. He had pushed too far, and now he was paying for his arrogance.

He took a deep breath and tried to calm himself. Then he worked the pick into the mechanism, carefully probing the lock to edge out whatever was inside. No luck.

The copper knocked on the door. "Two minutes left."

"Almost there," Ehrich said. "Just a bit longer. Is the reporter still here?"

"Why? You need to borrow some money off her?"

Ehrich redoubled his efforts, and they began to pay off. Whatever obstructed the lock was sliding out. He vowed the next time he would insist the cuffs be tested before he allowed himself to be locked up in them.

Finally, a wad of gum fell out. His pick was covered with grey matter. He wiped the remnants on his trousers and inserted the pick into the lock. *Click*. The cuffs opened. He rushed to the cell door and picked the lock. His cell door swung open just as the copper, Nellie, and Amina entered. "Time's up!" the copper announced, but fell silent when he saw Ehrich leaning against the open cell door with his arms crossed. The sweaty Weisz hid his lock pick set under his armpit.

The desk sergeant grumbled as Nellie Bly wrote in her notepad. "How do you spell your name, sergeant?" she asked.

"Leave my name out of this," growled the copper as he stomped into the cell to examine the open shackles on the floor.

Ehrich took Amina's hand and trotted off.

"My first performance is at the Bijou tonight," he shouted to Nellie. "I promise you will be amazed."

Then he escaped into the street with Amina in tow.

THE CONDEMNED MAN

The evening of the performance, a stream of excited audience members streamed into the Bijou. Ehrich hid in the wings while the other performers warmed up for their acts. The backstage cacophony of vocal exercises and last-minute patter rehearsals nearly deafened him. He waved across the stage at the other wing, where Tesla was stationed. He shook his head—no sign of Thomas Edison.

Ehrich headed backstage to prepare. He bumped into Ms. Rahner, who was decked out in a white satin top with a huge billowy headdress. She was a dancer. A young man in a smart jacket with tails assisted with her outfit. He possessed the manicured nails of a magician. Beside the infamous steamer trunk sat the young man's gear—a table, a box, and a cage with two pigeons cooing inside.

"Ah, Harry Houdini," Ms. Rahner said. "Seems you have a knack for getting attention. I suppose we should thank you for the house."

"Bess, is this the fellow you chirped about?" the young man asked.

She smirked. "Walter, you had better keep your eyes on your equipment. You may stumble across this man using them to make breakfast one morning."

Ehrich now knew the young woman's first name. "I assure you, Bess, I have all that I need. Pleased to meet you, Walter."

"I've not seen you around the circuit."

"This is my first performance."

The young man laughed. "You brought in this crowd for your first time, Harry? Friends or family?"

Ehrich shook his head. "Neither. Good old fashioned legwork."

Bess rolled her eyes. "He probably stole them from the nearest tavern."

He slipped past them. "I have to prepare. Good luck with your show."

The nearby performers hissed.

"Never say that," Bess said. "Break a leg. That's what you say if you want to wish a performer well."

"I'm sorry," Ehrich said. "Break a leg."

He shuffled to his corner where Amina tried to slip into the arms of her costume. "Is this costume really necessary? I feel naked."

"You look incredible," Ehrich said, taken in by the beauty of his partner. He had seen her in her battle uniforms, but never in something so delicate as the white dress, which accentuated her feminine curves. She caught him staring. He blushed.

"You're getting on with the other performers," she said.

"Who? Oh, you mean Bess. She's the one I had a run-in with the other day."

"Be careful, Ehrich. It seems she has her eyes on you."

He peeked at Bess. "Her?" he said, trying to hide his grin. "I have no interest."

"Then stop staring," Amina said. "Did Mr. Tesla spot Edison?"

"No, but the audience is still filing in. We're not on until after the intermission. He might be late."

"How are we going to lure him on stage?"

"Mr. Tesla will work the crowd when we call for volunteers. He'll bring Edison to us."

When Bess was set to perform with two other girls, Ehrich sneaked a peek. The other two danced better, but he couldn't stop staring at Bess. She had a magnetic personality. He caught her glancing toward the wings at one point in the act. He felt sheepish for staring, but thrilled that she'd noticed him. The audience whooped and hollered at the girls, enjoying the flash of a bare leg here and there.

The first act ended with Walter taking the stage to perform his magic tricks. He handled the cards with amazing dexterity. He fanned the cards, then produced one card after another, seemingly from thin air, but the audience response seemed tepid at best.

Ehrich appreciated Walter's skill. This man was a magician's magician. He had incredible technique as he made a handkerchief disappear from his hand. He didn't waste a single move. With impeccable timing and rhythm, he misdirected the audience with a simple glance. The only thing he lacked? Showmanship. The crowd sensed this.

For his finale, he made a cage of pigeons vanish. No one cared. Some polite applause from the front row, then the men headed out to grab a drink before the start of the second act.

During the intermission, Ehrich tracked down Tesla, who hovered near the front of the stage. "Any sign of Edison, sir?"

Tesla shook his head. "Not tonight, but maybe tomorrow."

Marty Chan

Ehrich headed backstage to prepare for his act. The audience had come to watch Harry Houdini. He would need to deliver a dynamite performance to lure Thomas Edison to the venue.

A few minutes later, Godfrey introduced Ehrich, "The next act of our evening brings to us the incomparable Handcuff King, Harry Houdini, and his pretty little bird. The crowd hooted. After observing Walter, Ehrich had realized the trick didn't need to be clever or amazing. He had to sell the effect. If he focussed solely on the trick, he would be lost, because his skills paled in comparison to Walter's. He had to rely on his charisma.

"Ladies and gentlemen, I'm sure some of you are here because you've heard I had a run-in with the law. A few times, in fact."

Knowing laughter rippled through the audience. A couple of coppers in the back row didn't laugh, but they elbowed each other.

"Well, don't tell the coppers, but I'm supposed to be in prison right now."

The audience exploded. Even the coppers chuckled.

He pointed to the back row. "Tell your friends I'll be back in my cell right after the show."

More laughs. He had won over the audience. He forged ahead. He wanted to create a sense of danger because laughs alone were not enough to sustain a performance.

"Prison makes me think of different things. I mean, you spend a day in prison, and it puts things into perspective."

"Yeah, gives me time away from the missus," a heckler yelled out.

Ehrich took the comment in stride. "Marriage, sir, is a prison even I couldn't escape."

The men laughed. A few women elbowed their partners into silence.

"But imagine it's your last day in prison. Imagine you were a condemned man facing the gallows or the guillotine. What might go through your mind as you count the minutes? Do you want to make peace with your maker, or do you want to fight for one more sunrise? I tell you...I would fight."

Applause.

"That's what I intend to do tonight. I'll ask my assistant to come out."

Hoots and hollers as Amina took the stage bearing shackles, cuffs, and rope.

"I'll also need a few assistants from the audience," he said. He waved at Mr. Tesla at the foot of the stage, referring to him as his alias. "Mr. Vernon, find me two strapping young men. No coppers. They can't seem to keep me in custody."

Howls of laughter. Ehrich enjoyed the adoration. He almost forgot why he was performing.

Tesla ushered the men to the stage, and Ehrich presented the task at hand. They were to truss him up with the shackles, cuffs, and rope. The men set to work immediately. One wrapped the heavy rope around Ehrich's body until it nearly cut off the circulation in his arms. The other clapped leg irons around his ankles. Then both worked on the handcuffs, cinching him in. All the while, Ehrich grunted in mock pain. Amina assisted when one of the volunteers couldn't figure how a lock worked. When the men had affixed the last lock, Amina ushered them to stand back to give the audience a clear view of Ehrich, the Christmas ham.

"No possible way I could escape," he announced. "Gentlemen, are the locks real?"

Both men agreed that they were.

"I thank you and ask you to take leave of the stage. A round of applause for my volunteers."

They jogged off to thunderous applause.

"And now the dangerous part," Ehrich announced.

He motioned to Amina to part a curtain. The audience gasped when they saw the guillotine hidden behind.

"I'm fated to meet my end," Ehrich said. "If I cannot free myself in time, then I'm afraid I will quite literally lose my head."

Not a peep from the theatre.

Ehrich hopped behind the guillotine and kneeled. He placed his head on the stocks, under the heavy blade. He popped up. "I'm going to ask for privacy. My assistant will close the curtain so I may be able to work without distraction. But the guillotine will remain visible. I'm going to ask my assistant to count down from 100. When she reaches one, she will pull the rope and release the blade. If I'm free, the guillotine will strike nothing. If I fail, well, then it has been nice to meet you."

The audience members perched on the edge of their seats. Even the hecklers were rapt. Amina closed the stocks over Ehrich's neck and locked him in.

"Please close the curtains," Ehrich said.

Amina drew the curtains closed. Ehrich shed off the rope first. He had puffed his arms out when the men wrapped the coil around him, creating the illusion of being bound. All he had to do was close his arms, and the ropes slid away.

"Ninety-two, ninety-one..." Amina said.

Next, he worked on the shackles around his arms. They were a little more complicated to shake free because they intertwined with the locks. He slid the chains against his wrists to find an opening. He began to worry he had erred in adding too many locks. He pushed his arms together and tried to squirm out. The chains did not respond the way they had in rehearsal. They seemed to bind and kink against each other. He twisted his arms, trying to gain some kind of slack.

"Seventy-seven, seventy six…" Amina's voice counted slowly and steadily.

He abandoned the chains and reached into his belt for his lock pick. He attacked the first of three handcuffs on his wrists. The ones on his forearm would easily slide off his arm once he picked the cuffs on his wrist.

The pick slipped into the mechanism. By the time Amina had counted down to forty, all three cuffs clanked on the floor. He stretched his arms open and squirmed out of the chains.

"Thirty-nine, thirty-eight," Amina said, now joined by a chorus of audience members counting down with her.

Ehrich reached around to the front of the stocks and tried to pick the lock. He had to stretch to the full length of his arm. He tried not to panic. He could spring the lock in ten seconds if he concentrated. He shifted his legs, and realized he had forgotten about the leg irons. He ignored them as he tried to insert the pick into the lock.

"Twenty-five, twenty-four…" The entire theatre reverberated with the voices of all the spectators counting down.

The pick slipped out of his moist hands. He patted the floor to locate the pick. The tool was just out of reach. If not for the leg irons, he might be able to reach the pick with his foot. He began to panic.

"Thirteen, twelve, eleven, ten…" The voices were almost deafening.

He strained with his right arm, pressing his flesh into the wooden stocks as he stretched out for the cold metal pick. He grasped the end and slid it toward himself, then he picked up the key, reached around the stocks and inserted the tool into the lock. He missed on the first try.

"Eight."

The second try, the pick went in. He probed the slender metal along the lock's internal pins. Nothing.

"Five."

He raked the lock.

"Four."

Finally, the lock opened.

"Three."

He slipped the lock off the hook.

"Two."

He lifted the wood stocks off his neck.

"One." Amina said, barely audible over the chorus of audience members counting with her. She stared at the blade and pulled the rope. The blade slid down behind the curtain with a deafening *thunk*.

Silence filled the audience. Even Amina didn't know if her partner had escaped. She leaned forward and pulled the curtains open. Standing in front, Ehrich panted, drenched in sweat but free of the shackles. The blade had bit into the wood and not flesh.

The entire theatre erupted into wild applause. Hoots and hollers filled the air as Ehrich bent over to pretend to rub feeling back into his legs but used the lock pick to free himself from the leg irons.

Then he stepped out from behind the guillotine and shouted, "The last day of the condemned man is the first day of the rest of my life."

The audience stamped their feet and cheered raucously.

"For my next trick, I would like to show you the power of transformation." The crowd drowned him out. Godfrey took the stage to usher the pair off before they could present the trick.

Backstage, Ehrich fumed. "We didn't do metamorphosis."

Tesla shook his head. "No need to worry. You hear the audience. They will be talking about this for weeks."

Bess rushed up and clapped Ehrich on the back. "Amazing act. You had them from start to finish."

"But I had another trick," Ehrich said.

"Harry, we have two more performances tonight. You want to change your act up later, you can, but one word of advice. First lesson of show business, never start your act with a closer."

"What?"

"Nothing is going to top what you did out there. Enjoy the glory and don't overstay your welcome." She pushed past him to join the rest of her troupe.

Bess had taught him the first lesson—leave the audience wanting more. If they were to reveal the projection effect, they would have to incorporate the codex into the escape act. He hoped that, when Edison showed up, he would have a tight act.

Three performers followed—a singer, a juggler and a mime— but the crowd reaction dulled after Ehrich left the stage. He witnessed firsthand that his act was as Bess called it, a closer. He enjoyed being the star of the night.

The other performers didn't share his feelings.

Walter strode over and offered curt advice. "Never call an effect a trick. You call it a trick, and they know you're up to something."

Ehrich couldn't remember using the word "trick" in his act, but apparently, he did enough times for Walter to comment. The other performers kept their distance.

He performed the escape twice more eliciting bigger reactions each time. Hoots from the new audiences. Jealous glares from his fellow performers. Only Bess seemed supportive.

"Not bad for your first night, but it'll all be downhill from here."

"Ah, one of the Floral Sisters. You weren't so bad with your dancing. Get yourself a right foot and you'll be set."

She slapped his arm and walked away.

"Are the Floral Sisters really related?" he called after her.

"Second lesson of show business: everyone lies. Love you."

She flounced away. He couldn't stop staring until he noticed Amina watching him.

"We have to find Mr. Tesla, lover boy," she said, taking his arm and leading him out of the backstage area.

As they entered the theatre, a few audience members lingered in the theatre. Tesla shook his head. The one guest they wanted had not arrived. Ehrich spotted a few familiar faces in the audience. Two female hunters pointed at the stage and whispered to each other. He pressed his fake beard against his face and approached the hunters.

"Did you enjoy the show?" he asked.

"How did you escape?"

"I'm afraid I can't reveal the secrets to my—" He cut himself off before he said "trick" and instead answered, "—my effects."

"I think I know how he did it. You weren't really chained up all along. The guys who locked you up worked for you."

He shook his head. "No. They locked me up fair and square." He mentally noted he would have to invite different people to inspect the locks. "Come back tomorrow night, and you'll see something spectacular. Something, you'll be talking about for weeks. Be sure to tell all your friends on the Demon Watch."

"How did you know where we worked?" the other hunter asked.

Ehrich flashed an enigmatic smile and tapped the side of his forehead, then pointed at their dusters.

The girls rolled their eyes.

"Tell your colleagues to come. I'll give them complimentary tickets. What I have planned tomorrow will dwarf what you witnessed tonight."

The hunters waved as they walked out the theatre. Ehrich hoped he had planted the seed to spread the word. Only time would tell, but he feared time was running out.

The next night, Ehrich's condemned man act featured a new twist. At the end, when Ehrich escaped, he declared that this was the first day of the rest of his life.

Amina stepped beside Ehrich and said, "Or is it?"

A second Ehrich—still bound—appeared on stage. The audience gasped at the sudden appearance of the other Weisz. This one knelt behind the guillotine.

"How is this possible?" Ehrich asked as he approached his double. Now they stood side by side. The audience gasped.

The Ehrich doppelganger placed his head in the stocks and the curtains closed.

"This can't be me," the real Ehrich said.

"It was you," Amina answered. "Three...two...one."

The guillotine blade dropped, followed by a thud of something falling into the basket in front of it. The audience gasped.

"Tell me how this is possible," Ehrich begged Amina.

"Your last day has come and gone as your body has. All that remains is your spirit." She waved her hand in front of Ehrich, then pushed her palm right through his ghostly body. "Now be gone!"

He howled, then leapt off the stage, but he didn't land on the ground. He floated above the audience. He ran toward the nearest wall and vanished into the wood. Audience members screeched at the sight. One woman swooned into the arms of her date. The theatre erupted into a cacophony of white noise as the audience members chattered to each other about what they had just witnessed. Then they fell silent as a figure rose from behind the guillotine.

"Behold, the condemned man on his last day," Ehrich

announced, stepping in front of the device. He raised his hands in the air and took a bow. The effect sent waves of excitement through the audience. People couldn't stop talking about the effect. The debut of the projection was a smash success.

The next two nights brought more audiences in, but Edison was not among them. Coppers had shown up, as did a few Demon Watch hunters, but the bulk of the audience were civilians. Many of the new audience members dressed better than the previous night's spectators. Word of the effect had spread from the middle class audiences to wealthier New Yorkers.

The next afternoon, Godfrey approached Ehrich. "You are doing boffo for the box office, Harry. I'm going to extend your contract by two weeks. And I'm going to give you another twenty minutes for your act."

"You're making the show longer?"

"Naw. Just lost some dead weight is all."

Ehrich feared that Godfrey had cut Bess's group from the bill. "Who did you fire?"

"No one that matters," Godfrey said as he lumbered off into the theatre to ogle a few of the women rehearsing their act.

Ehrich headed backstage. Bess's steamer trunk still sat in the wings, but Walter was packing up his gear. Ehrich guessed who the venue manager had fired.

"I'm sorry," Ehrich said. "I heard Godfrey let someone go."

"I'll land on my feet."

"I'm sure you will."

Walter glared at Ehrich. "You must be pleased for yourself. I'm sure the audiences just love that kind of performance."

"What do you mean?"

"Your technique is awful. A flash in the pan. You stumble through a top change when the spectators are burning your hands. You don't know how to distract them from looking where you don't want them to look. You'll be out of work in a month, I guarantee." Walter closed his trunk and shoved Ehrich out of the way as he dragged the heavy trunk toward the exit.

"Let me help you," Ehrich offered.

Walter stopped and laughed. "Your beard is slipping, Harry."

Ehrich pressed the fake hair against his chin. Walter stomped out of the theatre. Ehrich rushed to his dressing room where Amina and Tesla carefully stowed the codex into a box. Ehrich ran to the mirror and used spirit gum to fix his beard.

"Still no sign of Edison," Tesla said. "I think we need to hit the streets.

"I think I'm about to give up on this idea," Amina said. "At the very least, it would be great to get away from Godfrey. He keeps touching me."

"No, Edison will show up," Ehrich said. "Last night, I saw a couple of hunters in the audience. They might be doing some reconnaissance."

"We need to accelerate the process," Amina said.

Tesla raised an eyebrow. "I think I can send the right message."

"What is it?" Ehrich asked.

"Patience."

AN OLD FRIEND RETURNS

Ehrich had a few hours in the afternoon to flog the show. He claimed he needed to pack the house, but he wanted the opportunity to chat with Bess as she handed out flyers for the evening's performance.

They strolled through the Bowery streets, jamming the papers into the hands of anyone passing by. Word of Harry Houdini had spread, and a few people stopped to shake his hand. No one recognized Bess.

"Don't let the fame go to your head, Mr. Houdini, or you won't get it through the Bijou stage door," she teased.

"Won't happen. Not with you deflating it at every chance," he replied.

"Just keeping you honest."

"I thought the second lesson of show business was everyone lies."

"You're right. You're the smartest man I know." She winked.

He quipped, "And you are the cleverest woman I've ever met."

She elbowed him and scurried away, divesting the last of her handbills. Ehrich chased after her, but a young man stopped him.

"You are the Houdini everyone has been talking about, aren't you?"

"Yes, sir, I am."

"I must know. Are you a spiritualist? Do you possess a medium's power?"

"A what?"

"Do you speak with the dead?"

"I'm afraid that's not part of my act."

"You're not aware if you possess the gift?"

"I suppose not."

The man reached into the pocket of his grey jacket and pulled out a flyer for a spiritualist meeting. "Come to one of our gatherings. We'll test your latent abilities."

"Sure, but only if you come to tonight's show. Tell your spiritualist friends." He gave the young man his last few handbills.

The young man eagerly accepted them and headed off. Ehrich searched the streets for Bess and spotted her leaning against a light standard at the far end of the block. He deliberately took his time strolling toward her, not wanting to appear too eager for her company.

"Hey, I can do magic too," she announced. She placed her hands together and separated her thumb, hiding the severed joint with two fingers.

Ehrich laughed. "How did you ever do that?"

She beckoned him close and whispered in his ear, "A magician never tells."

He cracked a grin. "Third lesson of show business?"

She shrugged. "No, that's just common sense."

She headed down one of the side streets toward an area where the invalids begged for money.

"Where are you going, Bess? We're out of handbills. We should go back for more."

She swept a stray hair from her face. "Giving out the handbills is Godfrey's work. Now I can do some of my own."

He followed the frail girl into the three-storey brick boarding house. She scaled the steps two at a time and knocked on the door.

"What is this place?"

"Shh, it's a secret."

A kindly woman answered the door. Her dark hair was tied back in a bun and a soiled apron hung over her tan Mother Hubbard dress. She beamed. "Come on, Bess. They've been expecting you."

"Thank you, Mrs. Sherman. This is my friend, Harry Houdini."

"Oh my, I've heard of him. Everyone in the city is abuzz about the man who can cheat death."

"Pleasure to meet you," Ehrich said.

Mrs. Sherman led the pair into the sitting room where a half-dozen men and women sat in wheelchairs. Other than the patients of this sanatorium, the sterile room had few furnishings. A few paintings adorned the striped walls and a well-worn Oriental rug covered the hardwood floor.

None of the patients seemed to care about the condition of the room. They stared blankly, barely moving in their wheelchairs. Ehrich supposed that they were victims of strokes or brain injuries. He wondered why Bess would come here and leaned over to ask, but she had already sashayed away.

To his surprise, the girl began to dance in front of a couple of the women and finished with a flourish, garnering absolutely no response.

"Looks like the audience you had at last night's show," he quipped.

"No, these people are much kinder. No eggs."

She patted the hands of her audience members and even wrapped her arms around one of the women. Then she stood up and sought another patient in need of her entertainment.

"How often do you come here, Bess?"

"Not as often as I would like."

"Do they know you're here?"

"Deep down, I think they do." She patted the shoulder of the woman next to her. "Sometimes, I can see a flicker in her eyes. It's as if she's trying to tell me that she's glad I'm here."

"Bess, why do you come here?"

"Sometimes, you have to stop and think about those who are less fortunate. When I was born, the physician didn't hold out much hope that I would live past the year because I was so tiny. My mother wouldn't hear of this. She nursed me as she did my sister Marie. Because of my state, I often became ill. One time, I had a fever so bad the physician thought it would be the end of me. I had lost consciousness, but my mother stayed by my side and sang to me. She held my hand through the night and pressed cold compresses on my forehead until dawn and my fever broke. The doctor claimed I could not have heard her songs, but I swear her voice pulled me through. You should know this as a magician. What we can't see is often the most powerful effect."

"Can these people recover?"

"I don't know."

"Will they regain their former lives?"

"Things change. Friends move on. Children grow up. I can only imagine the horrible sensation of waking up after two years and discovering everything in your life is different."

"At least you wake up," Ehrich said, thinking of Dash.

"Yes, but as you can see, few of their family members or friends have elected to wait around. So, all these people have is what happens to them now. Why not give them something to hope for?"

He considered her words for a moment, then he reached into his pocket and pulled out a white silk handkerchief. He twirled it into a makeshift rope. Then he showed the silk to a pair of patients sitting next to him. He tied a knot in the silk. He blew on the knot as he pulled either end of the silk until the knot dissolved before their vacant eyes. He didn't know if he had connected with them, but Bess applauded, and she was the spectator he wanted to impress.

He approached a patient at the back of the room. His jaw dropped. Charlie, his former Demon Watch squad leader, slumped in a wheelchair.

The last time Ehrich had seen his friend was at the Hudson River Tunnel Project. They had narrowly escaped an attack from Dimensionals. Charlie had taken a blow to his head, and then he fell into a coma.

Ehrich lost track of his friend over the months on the run from Demon Watch, but he always wondered if the teen had recovered. The answer sat before him in a vegetative state. His blond hair had grown long. Now a scruffy beard covered his gaunt face. The boy's limbs had atrophied into limp appendages, dangling over the arms of the wheelchair. Ehrich searched Charlie's eyes for some sign of recognition or spark of life.

"Charlie?" he whispered.

Not a flicker. He wondered if any of his squad even bothered to visit. If he had known about Charlie, he would have visited; at least, he believed he would have. His thoughts wandered to Dash and how many times he had visited his brother. Other than the recent return to Purgatory, he had rarely seen Dash. He tried to convince himself he was too busy with the search for Ba Tian's army, but he doubted this was the entire reason.

Bess tapped the back of his shoulder, "What's the matter?"

"I can't do this, Bess. I'm sorry." He left the sanatorium.

That evening's performance was spectacular. Ehrich had honed his patter and Amina grew into her role as the magician's assistant. But the kicker was Tesla's addition to the projection. When the ghostly Ehrich ran over the audience, the stage erupted into a shower of electricity from coils and inductors Tesla had cobbled together during the day. The eerie blue light show stunned the audience. When the ghost version of Ehrich ran through the wall, the electricity chased after him and danced across the wooden wall, searing a message into the wood: "The War of Currents is not over."

When he reappeared on stage, Ehrich was nearly bowled over by the applause. The entire audience rose to their feet and gave him a standing ovation. He noticed a few of the hunters were talking to each other and gesturing at the message on the wall. He wondered about it himself.

At night's end, he pulled his friend aside and asked, "What did that message mean, Mr. Tesla?"

"Thomas Edison will know it well. Before Devil's Island, I had partnered with a clever entrepreneur. George Westinghouse. With my AC generators and inductors, we had planned to usurp Mr. Edison's direct current technology. The papers dubbed the battle between Westinghouse and Edison as the War of Currents. We would have won as well if not for an accident that took the life of my benefactor. The horses of his carriage were spooked during a brawl in Five Points. A few conspiracy theorists accused Mr. Edison of engineering the accident, but no one could ever prove their allegations. They claimed the War of Currents was far from over. The accusation became a sore point for Mr. Edison. He will receive the message. What he chooses to do with the information will speak much about his character."

He resumed disconnecting the equipment. Ehrich lent a hand.

"What if he doesn't come?"

"Patience. He will."

"We need to draw Edison out. He's our only bargaining chip with the general. What if Kifo reaches him first?"

"Ehrich, did I ever tell you about Macak?"

He shook his head.

"He was my cat. Black as a shadow, he never left my side. Followed me everywhere. I loved watching him roll in the grass around our farm. He loved when I stroked his back. One winter's evening, I remember petting him. His fur became a sheet of light and sparks danced across my hand, crackling loud enough for even my father to hear in the next room. I asked him what caused the sparks, and he told me it was electricity. I was fascinated with the notion that a simple stroke of my hand could create such an effect, and I tried to recreate the effect on Macak until the candles grew dim and night took over. To this day, I don't know if what I saw was a trick of my mind, but my cat was surrounded by a halo. After that, I wanted to discover the origin of electricity. I wanted the answer to 'what is electricity?' To this day, I still ask the question and still don't have the answer, but I will not give up my quest."

Ehrich chewed his bottom lip. "I suppose so, sir."

"Take solace in the fact that if we have this much trouble getting to Edison, Kifo must be experiencing the same difficulty."

The young Weisz rubbed his anchor nose. His mentor was right.

"Now go join the others. They sound as if they are celebrating. Enjoy the night. You deserve a break."

"You sure you can finish this yourself?"

Tesla shooed him away. "I know how I like my equipment organized. Go, go."

Ehrich joined the other performers backstage. The jubilant performers celebrated the end of a long week and to swap stage stories. Ehrich and Amina joined the group while Tesla took down the apparatus. Everyone buzzed about Tesla's light show.

"Is it safe?" Bess asked. "I heard you can kill a person with electricity."

"If Mr. Tesla built the device, then it's perfectly safe," Ehrich answered.

"Who is Mr. Tesla?" Bess asked.

Amina and Ehrich glanced at each other, worried. He had let slip their guise in front of the performers.

"He's a friend of our stage manager. He was the one who loaned Mr. Vernon the equipment."

"Ah," Bess said, shrugging. "I'd love to see how it works."

"A magician never tells."

"I'm sure I can find a way to loosen your tongue," she purred.

Godfrey sidled into the room and wrapped his arm around Amina. She squirmed away.

"This was the best house ever," he announced. "And after that effect, I'll need to print standing room only signs next week. You were magnificent."

Amina hooked her arm around Ehrich's. Godfrey snaked his arm around Bess and launched into a story about his life as a performer. "When I worked the Vaudeville circuit, the audiences were tough. You did what you could to get a laugh on most nights. And on some nights, you did what you could to avoid the hook."

A cold ache ran through Ehrich's chest as he watched Godfrey play with Bess's dark hair. He didn't like the letch touching her. He disguised his seething jealousy with indifference, addressing Amina. "You were amazing tonight. You're much more comfortable on stage."

"Thanks, Ehrich. This isn't a life I had ever imagined for myself, but I did enjoy tonight. Almost made me forget why we're doing this."

He shook his head. "Close, but not quite."

Though the room had a few creature comforts such as pillows and a blanket and a stock of food and drink, Ling Po's quarters still felt like a cell. Ning Shu paced back and forth, surveying her surroundings. The porthole revealed the clouds that masked the airship. The sound of the propulsors turning droned outside. Beside her, Mr. Serenity—free of the straitjacket—painted another scroll. He sketched the airship's engine room.

"Ling Po should have been back by now," she said.

"Patience, Ning Shu. He is doing the best he can."

"I should be the one to talk to the generals as they come onboard."

He shook his head. "Not so long as the assassin is still on the loose. Ling Po and Gu Shan are your best emissaries. They will bring the generals to you. Then you can convince them to side with you."

"I hate waiting."

Mr. Serenity agreed. "You need something to pass the time. Care to take a brush?"

She shook her head.

"By my count, we've rounded up at least five so far. How many sit on this Council of Arch Generals, Ning Shu?"

"Twelve in all, including me. Three more to go."

"Why are they spread across America? I thought all the exoskeletons were under the Hudson River."

"If the strategy is anything like our invasion of other sectors, my father's arch generals are coordinating scouting missions. They're reconnoitering regarding the strength of the enemy forces. They might have a few dozen soldiers to launch small attacks to test their defenses."

Mr. Serenity's shoulders sagged.

"What's the matter?"

"I had hoped when you stranded your father in the other dimension, the war would be over."

"Not even close. In our mythology, we have a yao gwai. Do you know it?"

"No. What is this creature?"

"A dragon with thirteen heads. Cut one off, and the creature still lives."

"Like a hydra from Greek mythology," Mr. Serenity said. "Except a hydra grows two heads when one is cut off."

"Sounds similar. The yao gwai is a powerful symbol in my father's army. That is why the Council of Arch Generals has twelve members. We represent each head of the yao gwai. My father is the thirteenth head."

"How can we possibly stop the invasion?" he said. He slumped to the bench. "So many heads to chop off."

Ning Shu walked over and put her hands on the man's

shoulders. "Have faith, Mr. Serenity. Once I depose Xian and her cadre, the others will listen to reason."

"Do you think you can?"

"Yes, I'm sure of it." She paused and rubbed the jade tael hanging around her neck. "I have to."

Back in New York, the group's hard work had paid off. The audience member they had hoped would show up finally did. From the wings, Tesla pointed out the man to Ehrich and Amina. The frumpy commissioner took off the top hat with the gramophone horn connected to his hearing aid.

Around him gathered an entourage of nearly a dozen hunters and six coppers, not to mention a retinue of colleagues and city officials. Some of them pointed to The War of Currents message seared into the wall.

Out of the corner of his eye, Ehrich thought he spotted Walter—the disgruntled magician—in the wings, but he couldn't concern himself with old rivals. He needed to deliver the performance of his life. In full view of the hunters tracking him and a theatre full of spectators, he had to make the commissioner of Demon Watch disappear. He tried to settle his nerves as he headed backstage to prepare for a remarkable change to the act. Tonight, they would not perform the *Last Day of the Condemned Man*; tonight, they would perform the *Last Night of Thomas Edison*.

For the first time, he skipped watching Bess perform with her fake sisters. Instead, he huddled with Amina and Tesla, preparing the metamorphosis cabinet. The trio had only one shot to pull off the effect. Tesla would record Edison, and hope to grab a captivating image of the man to replay for the audience so they wouldn't notice as Ehrich and Amina spirited the original off the stage.

Godfrey waved for silence from the spectators who were now well into their cups and acting rowdy.

"Settle down, all of you. You're in for a treat tonight. We have distinguished guests in the theatre, and we're going to give them a classy performance of what everyone has been talking about. Put your mitts together for the one and only—Harry Houdini!"

Whoops and hollers filled the theatre. Only Edison's group seemed reserved. Ehrich and Amina entered, parading around the apron of the stage while the audience applauded. In the front row, Walter stood with his arms crossed over his chest. Ehrich nodded to the man, but he only glared back.

"Tonight, something new," Ehrich announced. "You may have witnessed magicians make birds disappear, but that is too easy."

Walter's heated glare might have melted Ehrich's face, but he was too giddy to pay him much mind.

"A few can make your money disappear," Ehrich quipped. "Although, the same might be said of half the shop owners on Fifth Avenue."

The rest of the audience laughed.

"Tonight, I'm going to make one of you disappear."

Waves of titters and murmurs spread through the theatre.

"All I need is a volunteer. Raise your hands if you're interested."

Amina paraded back and forth in front of the audience, surveying the crowd. A few hands went up. Edison did not raise his.

Edison's companion had to shout in his ear. "They need a volunteer for the act."

"Why?" he said, speaking a little too loudly.

"He's going to make them disappear," Edison's companion shouted.

"But we only just arrived."

The audience laughed at the exchange. It was all the motivation Amina needed. She pointed at Edison.

"What about him, Mr. Houdini?"

He beamed. "Yes, at least then I can shout directly in his ear, and we can eliminate the echo of my explanation...tion...tion."

The audience laughed. Edison's companion fell silent. Amina reached out her hand to invite Edison to stand up.

"Sir, we want you to come on stage!" Amina shouted.

"What?"

She repeated herself, but Edison waved for silence. He donned his gramophone top hat and connected the device to his ear. "Now tell me what you want."

She asked, "Will you accompany me to the stage?"

"Should have said that the first time," Edison joked.

The people around him howled. The unkempt man strode down the aisle toward the stage. Edison appeared as if he hadn't showered or groomed himself in a month. His clothes were rumpled, and he carried himself more as a tramp than a highly placed commissioner. Ehrich encouraged the audience to applaud as the man shuffled up to the stage. From the wings, Tesla waved at Ehrich and Amina to slide to the side so he could record Edison.

"Sir, what is your name?" Ehrich asked.

"Don't you know it?" Edison asked. "I thought you were a magician." This man was a prankster with a glint in his eyes.

Ehrich laughed. "Well, then for my first act, I will discover your name." He placed a finger to his forehead and closed his eyes. "Sir, you have too much of an honest face to be a politician."

He won the audience back. They roared.

"You have a peculiar mind. One given to humour. Not an entertainer, but you could have been."

"You could have been one as well," Edison quipped.

More laughter as the audience enjoyed the banter between the two men on stage.

Ehrich tilted his head. "You possess a serious side as well, sir. One which has earned you much respect. No, wait. You earned a great deal of money, which has purchased you respect."

The audience howled with laughter. He opened an eye and gazed at Edison's entourage.

"And from the companions who accompanied you, I suspect you are a man of some importance. Hmm, Demon Watch hunters. Some coppers. You must be Thomas A. Edison, the new commissioner of the Demon Watch."

The members of Edison's entourage gasped and applauded. Edison's eyes widened, but he accepted the revelation in stride and took a bow. "Guilty as charged."

"Now, sir, have we met before today?"

"I don't think so."

"So we have not had any discussions beforehand about what is to unfold tonight. No secret communications."

"None."

Ehrich waved to the members of Edison's entourage. "And will your companions vouch for that?"

A resounding "yes" came from Edison's colleagues.

"So then, all is fair with your decision to stand up here."

Edison shouted, "All is fair in love and *war*."

"Ah, yes, it is."

Edison whispered, "Your message has caught my interest. Now that you have it, what do you want?"

Ehrich ignored the man. "Mr. Edison decided to be here of his own accord."

Walter shouted, "No! He didn't make the choice! Your assistant picked him out."

Now Ehrich understood why Walter had returned to the theatre. The disgruntled magician had intended to ruin his act. The audience murmured to each other, confused and bewildered. Ehrich tried to regain control.

"Ah, you are right, sir. My assistant did pick Mr. Edison out after he raised a racket loud enough for all of us to hear."

The audience tittered.

"I know how the trick works," Walter said. "And it's not a very good one."

"Sir, I'm trying to entertain the audience."

"Edison is doing a better job than you are," Walter shot back.

The audience roared. Ehrich was quickly losing control. He had to win back the crowd and trick Edison to enter the cabinet.

He scolded Walter. "Then you had better let me finish my act and let the audience judge for themselves. The cabinet!" he bellowed, not allowing Walter any opportunity to interject. "Ladies and gentlemen, prepare yourselves for a little entertainment I call 'Lights Out for Thomas Edison.'"

"The cabinet has a false back!" Walter shouted. "You can see light shining through."

The audience enjoyed this interaction, baiting the two to continue with their jeers and hoots. Ehrich motioned Amina to roll the cabinet out. She wheeled the thing forward, but as she did, the wheel popped off and the cabinet toppled to the floor. She tried to right the cabinet, but the false back dropped open, confirming Walter's accusation.

The audience now booed. Walter led the charge, cracking a grin at the red-faced Ehrich. Walter tossed the screws to the wheels that had fallen off the underside of the cabinet. "Ta da," Walter said.

He walked out of the theatre. "If you want to see how real magic is performed, join me at the Bailiwick Theatre down the block. Half price if you say you hated Harry Houdini."

Many of the audience members in the front section followed him. Edison's entourage advanced toward the stage, fighting past the crowds now leaving.

Ehrich grabbed Edison's arm. "Step into the cabinet now."

"Unhand me, young man."

"Get in there."

"I don't need to go anywhere with you."

The pair struggled on stage. Edison shook Ehrich's hand off and tried to push him back. His hand caught Ehrich's beard and ripped it off. The man's eyes widened with recognition.

"You!" He waved at his hunters. "It's Ehrich Weisz!"

Ehrich pressed the beard back to his face, but the damage had been done. The hunters at the back of the audience jumped into action, pushing aside audience members to storm the stage. They all drew their pistols. The audience members screamed, and chaos erupted as people scrambled for cover and tried to flee the theatre. The coppers tried to calm the situation but created a jam of anxious people.

Ehrich tried to drag Edison offstage toward the wings, but the commissioner proved to be strong. He reached up and tapped a switch on his hatband. The gramophone horn emitted a sonic wave. The screech of rending metal scraped at the inside of Ehrich's eardrums. He let go of Edison and staggered to the back of the stage.

"Ehrich Weisz!" the frumpy man shouted, shutting off the scream of his gramophone horn. "It's the traitor!"

The hunters jumped on stage. Ehrich slowly stood up grimly

as he straightened and then charged the hunters. They fired, but to their astonishment, their electro-darts passed through Ehrich's body. He leapt off the stage and into the air. His ghostly figure ran through the wall, and he was gone.

"After him!" Edison yelled.

Most of the hunters scrambled off the stage, leaving a trio to guard their leader. They flanked Edison as he descended the stairs. A spectator in a tattered leather duster blocked his way. Kifo pulled the sleeve down to reveal his metal arm.

"Mr. Edis-s-son, I pres-s-sume."

"Demon!" one of the hunters shouted.

The trio of hunters whipped out their dynatron pistols, but Kifo flicked his metal hand and unleashed a volley of darts. Two hunters fell instantly. The third stepped in front of Edison and fired at the assassin. The dart flew wide.

"You have s-s-something I want," Kifo said. He flicked his hand again, and the last of Edison's escorts crumpled to the ground.

The assassin advanced on Edison, who began to back up the stairs.

"Help!" the commissioner cried out to his remaining hunters.

A half-dozen of them raced to his aid, but they were too far away. Kifo raised his metal claw. "You have s-s-something that belongs-s-s to me."

Edison pressed his hatband and the gramophone horn screeched. The sonic wave drove Kifo back. He clutched his ears. The hunters fired at him. One dart struck his shoulder and energy sizzled across his raggedy duster. He vaulted over Edison and ran across the stage.

Another electro-dart flew past him. He ran toward the wings and fled out the stage door entrance with several hunters in pursuit. Edison's entourage rushed to his aid and helped him flee the theatre.

In the chaos, no one noticed the trio of Ehrich, Amina, and Tesla huddled in the wings, hidden behind the codex's projection of an empty stage.

A STAR FALLS

Tesla shut down the codex and disconnected it from the oscillator. Amina picked up the electromagnetic piston while Ehrich gathered his handcuffs and other props into a satchel.

"We were so close," she said. "Edison was right in our grasp."

"Forget him. We need Kifo."

Tesla shook his head. "No, we must clear out before someone spots us. Grab those hunters' uniforms. We need a disguise."

Ehrich stripped the long jacket from one of the dead hunters then grabbed the jackets from the other two. The dusters were stained with blood, but no one would spot the stains in the night. Beside the last body, Ehrich spotted Edison's top hat with the gramophone horn—dropped during the scuffle. He picked up the hat and tucked it under his arm as he intercepted Amina and Tesla. He handed each of them a jacket which they donned as they headed to the stage door exit.

A scrape of something heavy across the hardwood floor

beside him stopped Ehrich in his tracks. He spun around and came face to face with a wide-eyed Bess, who had been hiding behind her steamer trunk.

"Who are you?" she squeaked.

He clamped his hand over her mouth. "Shh. You're not going to scream if I let go, are you?"

She stared at him wide-eyed. This close, Ehrich detected the sweet fragrance of her hair and thought of peaches.

"I'm not going to hurt you," he said. "I just need your promise not to give us away."

Still no response.

"I'm going to let go," he offered. "To show you I mean no harm."

"Stop," Amina hissed. "She'll call for help."

"I know Bess. She won't, right?"

The girl glared at him.

"I'm trusting you, Bess." He let go of her mouth.

She pursed her lips but did not scream. "You're not Harry Houdini so who are you?"

"I'm nobody you want to remember, Bess."

"Yes, but you're somebody the hunters want, aren't you?"

Amina slid closer. "Ehrich, we're wasting time. We need a place to hide."

"Do you think we can reach an access point to Purgatory?" he asked.

"Might be able to, but it's far."

Tesla edged back. "I think I can program the codex to camouflage us, but the charge won't last long. Better if we find someplace close."

"I know a safe place," Bess said.

"What? Where?"

"Take me with you and I'll tell you."

"You don't want to get involved," Ehrich warned.

"I'm already involved," she said.

"Throw her in the green room and lock her up," Amina said.

Ehrich shook his head. "No." He took Bess's hand in his. "Listen, Bess. The kind of mess we are in, you don't want any part of it. Just tell us where to go and we'll leave you alone. No one will bother you after we're gone."

"I could also scream for help," she said.

"You didn't the first time."

"A girl can change her mind."

Tesla hissed, "Do something."

Finally, Ehrich decided. "Okay, show us where to go."

"I'm glad you came to your senses. Follow me."

"Hold on," Tesla said. He pressed the latch on the codex, and the air shimmered with the image of the empty stage. Tesla explained. "I adjusted the codex to record and project at the same time. There may be a slight delay in the image, but not enough to give us away. Everyone stay close to me. Hold hands so you don't stray out of the perimeter."

Amina and Bess complied. Ehrich enjoyed the warmth of Bess's hand, but flinched when Amina squeezed his fingers hard. He nodded at his partner and focussed on the task at hand, which was to evade the hunters.

Bess led the group along the side of the cobblestone lane. The projection from the codex mirrored the street with a slight hiccup, but none of the street vendors or night owls paid any heed to the group behind the image. Ehrich and his allies slinked away from the crowds to the section of the Bowery where the sanatorium was located. He recognized the destination and stopped.

"I don't think this is a good idea," he said.

"None of the patients are going to say anything, and Mrs. Sherman sleeps on the top floor."

"What choice is there?" Amina said. "We can't stay out on the street."

Tesla agreed. "Where else are we going to go?"

Ehrich had been outvoted.

"There might be an open window around the side," Bess suggested.

"Don't bother, Bess. I can get us in." Ehrich reached down to the heel of his shoe and retrieved his lock pick set. He opened the door and let in the others.

Once inside, Bess peeked up the stairs and waved back to the group. "Lights are out. They're asleep."

The group settled in the unfurnished drawing room, sitting on the floor. Tesla set the codex down. Amina hoisted the oscillator off her shoulder and rested against the striped wall.

Ehrich shook his head. "Never counted on Walter messing up our plan."

"I should have warned you about him. He's petty," Bess said.

Amina whispered, "At least Kifo didn't capture Edison."

"But he nearly did," Ehrich said. "He still might if Edison's men don't catch him tonight."

"Who is Kifo?" Bess said.

Ehrich shook his head, "You wouldn't believe me if I told you. The story's too crazy."

"I took up dancing even though everyone told me I had no rhythm and two left feet. That's crazy."

Ehrich had brought Bess this far. No turning back now. "First of all, my name's not Harry Houdini. It's Ehrich Weisz."

"Mine is Wilhelmina Rahner. We all change our names."

"I'm not from your world," he said.

Bess narrowed her gaze and crossed her arms over her chest.

He explained everything from his arrival in the dimension to the battle on Devil's Island to Kifo's possession of Dash. Her eyes never left his as he talked. When he finished, she let out a low whistle.

"Your entire magic act was a ruse to lure Thomas Edison so you could abduct him?"

Ehrich sat beside Bess. "The long and the short of it is...yes. We need him so we can make a deal with Kifo."

"Then why don't you tell him you have Edison?"

"But we don't," Ehrich said.

She rolled up the sleeves of her crinoline dress. "What's the second lesson of show business?"

He cracked a wide grin. "Everybody lies."

"He's going to need proof," Amina said, shooting down Bess's idea.

"I have Edison's hat," Ehrich said.

"That might intrigue Kifo," Tesla said, musing. "But he'll want to see the real person next."

Bess pointed at the codex in Tesla's hands. "I watched you use this contraption every night. The box has something to do with the effect of Harry...I mean Ehrich running over the audience, doesn't it? An illusion of some kind, right?"

Tesla raised a dark eyebrow. "She's rather astute."

Amina scowled, but angled away from Ehrich.

Bess continued, "Can you make this Kifo think he's looking at Thomas Edison?"

Amina's eyes widened. "Yes, we could create an illusion."

Ehrich clapped his hands. "Bess, you're right. Magic isn't about what the audience actually sees; it's about what you make them think they are seeing. Edison and his hunters are combing the street for Kifo right now. The codex has stored the images we've recorded, including the one of Edison tonight. All we have to do is project our image out there and hope Kifo spots it before he runs across the real one."

"He won't be easy to catch, even if we can spring a trap on him," Amina pointed out. "His metal arm is dangerous."

"True, but what if we can render Kifo helpless?"

"What do you mean?"

"We trick him into possessing another body. Someone we can easily control."

"Who?" Tesla asked.

"Charlie," he answered.

"Who?"

"One of the guests here."

Bess's nostrils flared. "One of the stroke patients? Have you lost your mind? You're going to use someone who can't even defend himself to trap this demon."

Ehrich explained. "Charlie's been here so long he's wasted away. His arms and legs are weak from inactivity. If Kifo possesses him, he'll be helpless."

"I don't know about this, Ehrich," Amina said.

"Well, I do," Bess huffed. "You're not doing it."

"Mr. Tesla, you agree, don't you? With Kifo in a helpless state, he'll have no choice but to give up Dash."

"And what about our friends on the airship?" Amina asked. "How does this help them?"

"We can hold Kifo as a hostage to exchange for Ning Shu and Mr. Serenity."

"You're using an innocent person, Ehrich. This makes you no better than Kifo. This boy doesn't have a say in what you're doing to him."

"Don't lecture me, Amina. Your rebels chose to fight Ba Tian's army here, but you haven't warned the people in this sector about the devastation that's about to unfold. You've given the people here no choice either."

"You're twisting things, Ehrich. We're trying to save entire races. All you're doing is using Charlie to save your brother."

Tesla pursed his lips. "She's right. The danger in obsessing over one goal, Ehrich, is that you lose yourself in the pursuit. Your friend is incapable of defending himself. Could you live with yourself if something went wrong?"

"To get Dash back, I'm willing to take the risk."

"I wish I had never shown you this place," Bess said bitterly.

"Ehrich, we have to find a different way," Tesla said.

"This is the only way," Ehrich said, raising his voice. "If we don't nab Kifo now, he will eventually find Edison and take over his body. And when he does, that means he controls Demon Gate and the Demon Watch. He can order the hunters into whatever trap Xian sets for them and wipe out everyone. If we do nothing, New York falls."

A woman's voice called down the stairs. "I warn you. I have a pistol, and I'm not afraid of using it."

"The woman who runs the sanatorium," Ehrich whispered.

"Who's down there?"

Bess answered, "Mrs. Sherman, it's me..."

Ehrich clamped his hand around Bess's mouth and cut her off. She struggled against him, biting his palm. He winced in pain, but didn't let go.

"I'm calling the coppers!" Mrs. Sherman yelled from upstairs.

Ehrich bit his lip to fight off the pain. Through gritted teeth, he delivered the ultimatum. "You want to save New York or not?"

Slowly, Tesla nodded. Amina flared her nostrils, but finally agreed. She slipped out the dynatron pistol from the back of her belt and crept toward the stairs. Ehrich hung onto Bess and hoped that she would forgive him, but he knew his star had fallen.

THE TRAP

Ehrich tied a gag around Bess's face. She tried to kick him, but Darby leg irons kept her legs bound to the foot of the bed. Her wrists were similarly shackled. She squirmed against the headboard of Mrs. Sherman's bed. Next to her, the frightened operator of the sanatorium stared bug-eyed at the ebony girl who trussed her up with torn bed sheets. Amina set a pillow behind the woman's hand, but Mrs. Sherman flinched.

"We're not going to hurt you," Amina said. "We need you to be quiet. Hopefully, this won't take more than a couple of nights."

The woman shook her head and squirmed. Her gag muffled her screams for help. On the nightstand beside her bed, the low-burning lamp illuminated the room, including Mrs. Sherman's "pistol"—a rolled up newspaper.

Once the woman was tied up, Amina left the room without a word to Ehrich. His gaze followed her out of the room. He fluffed a pillow for Bess.

"I can only imagine what you think of me right now, but you

need to understand this is the only way we can save your world. Think of all the people you love wiped out in a bloody war. That's what is coming to New York. If I don't do this now, everyone will suffer. Do you understand?"

She glared at him.

"I'm doing this to save everyone," he said. "Everyone."

She looked away.

He sighed. "No noise from either of you. When we get what we need, I'll set you both free. I'm sorry."

He headed out of the bedroom and closed the door behind him. Ehrich stepped into the main floor dormitory where the patients slept. The odour of human waste lingered in the air and the rhythmic snoring of a half dozen patients filled the room. He wheeled one of the chairs to Charlie's bed. He picked up his friend and set him into the chair. Charlie's eyes fluttered open, but his blank stare gave away nothing of his feelings. The blond teen was as light as a breeze. Afraid of breaking his friend's atrophied limbs, Ehrich gently tucked his arms inside the wheelchair and wheeled Charlie into the drawing room.

Tesla had set up the oscillator in the corner of the drawing room and connected the generator to the codex in the middle of the room. Amina stood in the corner, her arms folded over her chest. She said nothing.

"Mr. Tesla, did you find a recording that will work?"

"It's a short clip of him walking toward the stage. We can show him walking down the street and into the building. Then I can freeze the image of him standing where your friend is. The only problem is that I can aim the projection through the window, but I'll need to shift the codex over to position the image in the drawing room. Not an elegant method, but I can't think of how to hide the sudden disappearance of Edison."

Amina volunteered, "I'll shut the door when the image comes through."

"Good idea," Ehrich said.

"The primary problem will be how to convince Kifo to search here," Tesla announced.

"I have an idea," Ehrich said. "Leave it to me."

Minutes later, decked out in the hunter's uniform, Ehrich settled near an intersection about four blocks from the sanatorium. He held up Edison's top hat and pressed the hatband to trigger the sonic scream. The gramophone horn vibrated as its shrieks shred the calm night. Pedestrians scattered with their hands over their ears. There was no mistaking the shriek. If Kifo were near, he would have definitely recognized this.

Ehrich jogged two blocks over with the device and sounded it off once more. He circled around the sanatorium in a wide radius and worked his way closer to his home base.

He let loose one final blast, then popped the top hat on his head, rushed into the building, and waved at Tesla in the drawing room. The image of Edison appeared on the street outside the sanatorium and walked slowly toward the building. Amina opened the door just as he arrived and closed the door behind him.

Tesla shifted the codex, so the image of Edison was projected directly in front of Charlie in the wheelchair. He slipped to the other side of the drawing room to hide with Ehrich and Amina.

The wait began. The oscillator pumped in the corner with a quiet whir, powering the codex. Ehrich hoped the ploy worked. If not, he would have to hit the streets again, but he feared that their window of opportunity might have passed.

The hours ticked by. Ehrich measured time with the number of times he nearly dozed off. Around the twenty-third chin dip, he detected a scratching noise. He bolted awake and nudged Amina and Tesla.

The sound wasn't coming from the door. A figure stood at the window. Someone was trying to open the latch. Hidden in the shadows, beyond the dim candle burning in the room, the trio observed the raggedy man slipping into the drawing room. The air passing through his sickle nose whistled as he approached the image of Thomas Edison, who had his back to the window.

Ehrich waited, willing the assassin to take over the form of Charlie, but Kifo didn't seem to be in a hurry. He didn't even draw out the Infinity Coil. Instead, he dragged the edge of his metal talon across the wall.

"S-s-swivel around, old man."

Amina tensed, but Ehrich grabbed her arm and held her back.

"You have s-s-something that belongs-s-s to me, and I'd like it back."

What was Kifo talking about? Ehrich couldn't understand why the assassin wasn't using the Infinity Coil.

"You might not even know you have it, but when you cleared out Tesla's-s-s fac-c-cility, you took my dus-s-st."

Ehrich stiffened with realization. This wasn't Kifo. It never had been. This Dimensional was acting of his own accord under no control of the assassin.

He was Ole Lukoje.

HOODWINKED

"**I**s-s-said turn around." Ole Lukoje flashed his metal claw and reached for Edison's shoulder.

Ehrich jumped up and raised a dynatron pistol at the raggedy man. "That's enough."

Ole Lukoje hissed and whirled around, flashing his metal claw. A dart slammed into the wall just behind Ehrich's head. The teen fired the weapon into the man's chest knocking him back against the wall. He slumped down to the floor, unconscious.

Amina and Tesla rose from their hiding place. "What did you do, Ehrich?"

"That's not Kifo. It's Ole Lukoje."

"Are you sure?"

"Search for the Infinity Coil," Ehrich said.

Amina searched under the man's shirt and retrieved the Infinity Coil. The front seemed right, but the back was missing the chimera etching.

"I don't understand," she said, rotating the medallion over in her hand. "This isn't the device. It's a fake. Did Kifo give up the body?"

"Ole Lukoje must know."

Ehrich cuffed the unconscious man with a set of Darby handcuffs. He snugged the cuffs behind Ole Lukoje's back. Then they waited for the effects of the electro-dart to wear off.

Tesla shut off the codex and wheeled Charlie to one side of the room. "Have we been chasing shadows?"

Ehrich drew his pistol and spun around to scan the window. "What if he found another body and used Ole Lukoje as a decoy."

Amina and Tesla drew their weapons and stood back to back. She aimed her pistol at the doorway while Tesla trained his weapon on the man on the floor starting to wake up. He struggled against the handcuffs but couldn't shake free of the D-shaped restraints.

"Well, well, well, you are brighter than you let on, flesh-sh-sh bag," the raggedy man said.

"We need some answers," Ehrich said.

Ole Lukoje squirmed in his cuffs. "A sh-sh-shame our game has-s-s come to an end."

"Where is Kifo?" Amina asked.

"I am not my partner's-s-s keeper."

"Partner?" Tesla asked. "What do you mean by partner?"

"We sh-sh-shared thoughts-s-s for a time, and when Kifo perc-c-ceived I could s-s-serve him better as-s-s mys-s-self, we arrived at a new arrangement."

"What arrangement?" Ehrich asked.

"He wanted to be in two places-s-s at onc-c-ce. In return, he gave me the opportunity to recover what the flesh-sh-sh bags s-s-stole from me."

"Your dust," Ehrich guessed. "Or whatever you call that cloud of material you use to open portals."

The raggedy man smiled. "One cannot live without his-s-s toys-s-s."

"And what is Kifo doing while you're down here?" Amina said.

Ole Lukoje said nothing.

"What is his plan?"

"You will have to as-s-sk him yours-s-self."

"Where is he?" Ehrich demanded.

"Here and there."

Ehrich rushed at him and hauled him to his feet. "You are going to tell us everything we want to know."

"You have no power over me, flesh-sh-sh bag."

"I can turn you over to the hunters. Throw you in prison."

"I highly doubt that."

"Why?"

"Becaus-s-se you underes-s-stimated my new toy," Ole Lukoje said, flashing his freed copper hand. The Darby handcuffs dangled from the wrist, severed at the chain.

He slashed his metal talons across Ehrich's chest. Flames of pain seared across his chest as he recoiled.

Amina raised her pistol, but Ole Lukoje was faster. He flicked his claw. A dart spit out the fingertip. She threw herself to the floor, dodging the flying projectile.

"Stop!" Ehrich yelled, raising his dynatron.

Ole Lukoje backed away toward a window.

"I said stop," Ehrich said.

"S-s-shoot me and you'll never find Kifo."

Ehrich hesitated and Ole Lukoje took advantage of the pause. He leapt through the window, crashing through the glass. Ehrich chased after the man, jumping out of the window and landing in the dark street. He checked both sides of the lane. Nothing. The creature had fled. Ehrich ran to the right until he reached the end of the block. Eerie blue light from hunters' bowlers lit up the night. Ehrich backpedalled to the sanatorium and met up with Amina. She shook her head.

"He's gone."

"Get Tesla out," Ehrich said. "Hunters are coming down the street. They're going to notice the broken window. I'll meet you at the rendezvous point along the Hudson River."

"Where are you going?"

"I'm going to catch Ole Lukoje and find some answers."

Ehrich ran in the other direction, scanning the buildings for any sign of the raggedy man. The hour was late, and all the pushcart vendors had shut down for the night. He was the only one in the street.

Ehrich wondered what Kifo was up to, in the meantime. Why did he need the subterfuge? And where was he? He recalled the negotiation on the airship and the agreement to take Thomas Edison. Then he recalled how General Xian had agreed to keep his friends onboard the airship as collateral to ensure his return. She allowed Amina to leave, but not Mr. Serenity. Wait, no. He had volunteered to stay. The only one the general cared about was Ning Shu.

Ehrich skidded to a stop as the ugly truth dawned on him. He retraced his steps and veered toward the Hudson River. He needed to find his friends. Fast.

Suddenly, a heavy weight fell on his back. Pain erupted across his back as he fell forward, his pistol dropping out of his hand. He rolled to his feet and spun around to face Ole Lukoje, who plucked the shreds of Ehrich's bloodied jacket from his claw.

Ehrich fired. The electro-dart missed Ole Lukoje. The creature rolled across the road. He raised his metal claw to fire, but only puffs of air emitted from the ends of the fingertips. He was out of ammunition.

Ehrich reached for his fallen pistol, but Ole Lukoje kicked it away. It clattered across the cobblestones far out of reach.

The menacing creature advanced, flexing his metal claw. The gears whirred and powered the taut wires that operated the fingers. It was a deadly weapon. Ehrich crouched low, searching for some weakness in his adversary's defences. They circled each other.

The raggedy man lunged and slashed his talons at Ehrich's stomach, trying to open him up. Ehrich leapt back and slammed against the brick wall of the three-storey building. He used the wall as leverage to push himself off and throw his body into his opponent, but the raggedy man was faster. He slipped out of the way, and Ehrich ate pavement. He rolled over on to his back, Edison's hat flying off his head. Ole Lukoje towered over him.

"I'm going to enjoy this-s-s," the raggedy man said. "An eye for an eye. An arm for an arm."

He reached down and grabbed Ehrich's wrist. The boy tried to pull away, but Ole Lukoje had a firm grip. Out of the corner of his eye, Ehrich spotted Edison's top hat with the gramophone horn, just slightly beyond his grasp. Ole Lukoje yanked on his arm and stretched it out. He raised his metal claw and the fingers became fan blades, whirring in the air. He lowered the blades, flaying off a strip of flesh from Ehrich's forearm, near the elbow.

"No!" Ehrich howled, arching his back and angling his bloodied forearm away from the blades. He pushed against the man's legs, reached out and grabbed the hat. He pressed the hatband, and white noise blasted out of the gramophone horn like a thousand locomotive wheels screeching to a stop.

Ole Lukoje staggered back, clutching his ears. Sound hammered Ehrich's eardrums, making him dizzy, but he gritted his teeth against the pain. He slammed his feet right between the creature's legs, causing him to double over. Rising, he then brought his knee up to Ole Lukoje's nose and bloodied it. The sickening crack of bone breaking filled the night. The creature hissed and fell back.

The sound had woken up the residents and attracted nearby hunters. The blue glow of hunters' lights approached. Ole Lukoje stumbled away. Ehrich split off in the opposite direction. He dove into a pile of garbage and hid until the hunters passed. Then he climbed out. Overhead, a clothesline offered a few drying shirts. He climbed up the trash pile and yanked down a couple. His own shirt had soaked up much of the blood and stuck to the wounds. He peeled the material off and sucked in air to fight off the pain.

He ripped up one clean shirt to dress his wounds and slipped the other shirt on. He pulled the duster over everything and began the trek toward the Hudson River. One detour. He veered near the sanatorium to witness hunters combing the area. A hunter escorted Mrs. Sherman and Bess out of the building. Part of him wanted to call out to her, but he remained in the shadows. He slipped away, sure he'd never see Bess again.

When he arrived at the Hudson River, dawn was breaking. Tesla and Amina awaited near the pier. They waved him over.

"Did you find Ole Lukoje?"

"He got away."

Tesla glanced over the river. "I still don't understand the ruse. Why bother sending Ole Lukoje down here if they knew there was no way to capture Edison? We are back to the beginning in the search for Kifo."

Ehrich shook his head. "I know exactly where he is."

"Where?" Amina asked.

"On the airship. Ning Shu has the seal of the House of Qi. She's the only thing that stands between Kifo and complete control of Ba Tian's army. Where else would he want to be?"

The rays of the rising sun illuminated Amina's face.

"We need to get onboard that airship."

COUNCIL OF ARCH GENERALS

Outside the porthole window, Ning Shu tried to peer through the false cloud to determine her bearings, but the mist was impenetrable. A few hours earlier, Ling Po had told her that the last general had arrived, and he would arrange the meeting. The Council of Arch Generals couldn't begin soon enough for her.

She stepped away from the window to join Mr. Serenity at Ling Po's desk. He hunched over his calligraphy painting of the engine room.

"Impressive memory, Mr. Serenity."

"Thank you, Ning Shu. The brief time I spent in the engine room proved to be quite illuminating."

She paced the room.

"Are you ready to talk to the generals, Ning Shu?"

"Hardly."

"Relax. You have allies on the council."

"Too much rests on my shoulders. How can I relax?"

Mr. Serenity set down his brush. "My wife showed me this trick. Sit."

She obeyed. He cracked his knuckles and rubbed his hands together.

"Are you trying to relax yourself or me?" she asked.

"One minute." He finished rubbing his hands, then placed two fingers on either side of her temples. Warmth spread across her forehead as he massaged the sides of her head from the temples to the top of her head.

"Oh, this feels amazing," she said. "Where did your wife learn this technique?"

"I owned a small shop where I built clocks for the people in my village. Many people had a fascination with time, but piecing together the gears and stems took a toll on my body. Hunched over for hours and squinting at tiny pieces bent my body into a question mark. My wife, she developed a means to help me uncoil from my position. I was her living experiment. She eventually became so gifted that she took on the role of the village healer. People came for her treatments from three villages away. She accepted all patients..." His voice drifted off and he stopped rubbing her head.

Ning Shu took his hands. "I will not fail your wife."

He squeezed her hands. "Thank you, Ning Shu."

Ling Po entered. "The Council of Arch Generals will now meet. Ning Shu, you must come."

She stood up, her shoulders relaxed and her mind clear. "I'm ready."

Mr. Serenity took a step toward Ling Po.

"Not you," Ling Po said. "Ning Shu, you recall the protocol of the Council of Arch Generals."

"The House of Qi demands an exception."

Ling Po shook his head. "I'm sorry, General Ning Shu, but

Marty Chan

you know as well as I do that the council will not allow this exception. His presence will undermine your case. He's a liability."

Mr. Serenity agreed. "General Ling Po is right. We can't afford to give Xian any ammunition against you. I'll be all right here."

"I'll leave my personal escorts with him," Ling Po offered.

Mr. Serenity shook his head. "Protect Ning Shu. She is Xian's target."

"Don't worry, sir. She will be safe." He pulled open his robe to reveal his thigh strap of razor-sharp discs. "It's time."

She followed Ling Po out of the room. The soldiers closed the door, leaving Mr. Serenity alone. He returned to the artwork splayed across the desk.

The Council of Arch Generals brought together the twelve leaders of Ba Tian's army. In theory, their ranks were equal, but they had their own fiefdoms, and their seating arrangement at the oval table hinted at the power structure. The thirteenth seat—Ba Tian's—remained empty, but Xian had ensconced herself in the seat beside his. Two younger generals sat to her left. One absently traced his long finger over the dragon design along the edge of the table.

At the opposite end sat Ling Po and Gu Shan. The rest of the generals filled in the spaces along the table. Ning Shu included herself among those in between.

Xian called the meeting to order, "Close the chambers."

The dozen escorts filed out of the room. The last warrior closed the door, and the generals settled in for the meeting. Ning Shu placed her hands on the mahogany table and scanned the faces of the generals. So few veterans of her father's army remained; so many lives had been lost.

Xian banged a jade gavel on the table. "This meeting will come to order."

"Why call the Council?" asked a grizzled crimson general.

"General Kwok, as you can see, one of our own has returned."

"The House of Qi thanks you for your courteous reception," Ning Shu said.

"It is the *least* we can do for the prodigal daughter."

"And I'm sure my father will recognize your efforts."

The generals glanced at one another. The air crackled with tension as the two women glared at each other.

Gu Shan spoke, "I called this meeting. A serious issue is before us. Ning Shu's return means the steward of the House of Qi must step down. What troubles me is the fact that Xian has not ceded her authority."

The generals near Xian shifted uncomfortably on their high-backed chairs. She sat impassively, barely registering Gu Shan's accusation with even a raised eyebrow.

Gu Shan continued. "Ning Shu now speaks for the House of Qi."

Xian leaned forward in her chair, drew up the wide sleeves of her purple robe, and rested her elbows on the table, hunching over like a wolf about to pounce. She flashed a thin-lipped smile at the group. "And yet, General Gu Shan seems to speak for her. Perhaps he has something to gain by challenging my stewardship."

"I am more than able to speak for the House of Qi," Ning Shu said, "but I'm concerned the steward doesn't want to listen."

"I serve Ba Tian. He and he alone is the House of Qi," Xian declared. "I will step down when he returns."

Gu Shan sputtered, "The House of Qi is the family: the ancestors and the progeny."

Three of the older generals agreed. The five younger ones did not react. Ning Shu noted them all and mentally counted the votes. Not enough. "General Xian, as the House of Qi, I'm at a loss as to why you would not step down as steward."

Ling Po backed her up. "Surely, as the council, our duty is to uphold the laws of the House of Qi. To disobey them would be tantamount to sedition."

The young generals squirmed in their chairs. The veterans leaned forward, eager to see how this would play out. But Xian seemed nonplussed by the ploy. "General Ling Po, you would be more than happy to return to your position of power as the steward of the House of Qi. In fact, I can almost see you salivating over the prospect, but I hate to disappoint you. Today is not that day. As for Gu Shan, it seems that without Ba Tian, our Council degenerates into petty squabbles and posturing for power. In fact, even his own daughter plays politics."

Ning Shu stiffened at the accusation. "Why do I need to usurp your power? I am the House of Qi."

"Unless your father deems otherwise. I'm sure the Council is curious about your absence. While we were serving the House of Qi, where were you?"

"I was on a secret mission for my father."

"Ba Tian wouldn't keep your mission secret from the Council," Xian said.

General Kwok and another veteran general nodded. The balance of power shifted toward the steward.

Ning Shu cleared her throat. "If you must know, there were survivors of realms we invaded. They are plotting against us in secret. My father wanted me to infiltrate their forces to discover their numbers and strengths."

Xian betrayed not even a hint of surprise at this news. "It is odd your father would inform me of every action in the event he might be incapacitated, yet he neglected to inform me of this. He led me to believe you had no mission and that you left for personal reasons. Something to do with a man named Hakeem."

General Kwok narrowed a suspicious gaze at Ning Shu.

"That's what my father wanted Xian to believe. No one could know my true mission, which was to find the traitor among us."

The room burst into chatter.

"Silence," Xian barked, banging her gavel. "This is a serious allegation, Ning Shu. What proof do you have?"

"Hakeem, the man you accuse me of consorting with is the designer of the exoskeleton machines we have been using. My father suspected someone was whispering in Hakeem's ear, trying to lure him away. I was to get close to Hakeem and learn who, but he defected before I could get him to talk. My mission was to track him down and learn the name of the traitor."

General Kwok sputtered, "Who?! Who would dare go against the House of Qi?"

Ning Shu explained, "Only someone on the Council of Arch Generals wields the type of power required to help Hakeem defect. That's why my father didn't tell you the truth, Xian."

The room exploded with angry accusations and questions.

Xian pounded the gavel on the table. "Enough I can almost see Ling Po's hand in this. He wants his stewardship back."

Ling Po raised an eyebrow. "Are you accusing the House of Qi of lying, General Xian?"

"Ba Tian told me everything, Ning Shu," Xian said. "How you broke his heart when you chose Hakeem over the House of Qi. Why should we believe your story?"

Ning Shu drew out the jade tael that represented the seal

of the House of Qi. "Do you know why this became the seal of the House of Qi? My great-great-grandfather gave it to his wife when they wed. He said the tael was a symbol of the trust they had in each other. This symbol could only be given to one they truly trusted. Whoever bore this symbol was loyal to the House of Qi. That is why it has been passed down only by blood. Do you question this tradition?"

No one contradicted her.

"When my mother died, my father's heart was gone. He told me this in secret, but I feel the need to share it with you now. He said he would not trust another with this seal because he knew that any man or woman who would try to befriend him would only be after the power he wielded." She fixed her gaze on Xian.

The red amazon seethed.

Ning Shu continued, "Since I have returned, an attempt has been made on my life. Only one person in this room has the most to gain from my death. General Xian."

"How dare you accuse me!"

"How dare you try to usurp the House of Qi!"

"I protect the House of Qi in the manner I see fit."

"You've overstepped your bounds as the steward!"

"I am more than steward. I am..." She reached into her purple robe.

Ling Po yelled, "Ning Shu, get down! Weapon!"

A flurry of confusion erupted as the generals pushed back from the table. Xian scanned the room, bewildered. Ling Po drew a razor-sharp disc and flung the spinning weapon into Xian's neck. Blood gushed from the wound. She clutched at her neck and fell back over her chair. She landed on the ground, her eyes open and lifeless.

Gu Shan and two other generals tackled Ling Po to the floor while the other generals ran to check on Xian. The armed escorts burst into the room. Chaos overtook the room as people shoved one another.

Ning Shu stood over Xian. She gasped when she saw what Xian was trying to pull out from inside her robe: a jade tael identical to Ning Shu's, the symbol of the House of Qi.

METAMORPHOSIS

Ehrich and his exhausted companions trudged to the northern most pier along the Hudson River. He scanned the dark streets for any sign of people. No one. He pulled out the radiotelegraphometer and turned the gear on the side of the box. The tube popped open and a thin metal pole telescoped out to a foot long. The diodes inside the box began to flash intermittently.

Tesla took the box from Ehrich. "Fascinating. A radiotelegraphometer, you say."

He nodded. "They say it can transmit radio signals without wires."

"What wonders I could create if I could patent such technology. Wireless transmissions. The possibilities are limitless."

Ehrich left Tesla with the device as he walked to the riverbank to search the skies for the airship. The night passed without any sign of Xian's craft. When morning came, Ehrich and his friends moved down the street to avoid rousing suspicion. They couldn't return to Godfrey's boarding house, so they were forced to sleep on the street.

Two more nights passed with no sign of Xian's soldiers. On the third day, Ehrich led the group to the Hudson River Project, hoping to catch a glimpse of one of the crimson soldiers. Ehrich, Amina, and Tesla dressed like the poor travellers, waiting for a chance to work and blending in with the masses.

Unlike Ehrich's previous visit to the project, the Dimensionals seemed more docile. It seemed as if the fight had been drained out of them. Perhaps the constant sentry patrols through the crowd had something to do with the meeker attitudes. The sentries brandished heavy batons and rifles. Though older than teenage hunters, the military men appeared less mature and more willing to showboat for their friends. They shoved the Dimensionals around with little pity for the starving people.

Ehrich seethed at the sight of this badgering. No one stood up to the soldiers. They had lost the will to fight. The crowd seemed smaller by a third. He hoped the travellers had found other employment, but he suspected the missing people were most likely new guests of Thomas Edison in the prison on Devil's Island.

He leaned against the brick wall of a nearby warehouse where Tesla had befriended a pigeon. The tall man stooped over and fed the grey and white bird a few crumbs. Beside him, Amina closed her eyes and tried to sleep. Ehrich pushed off the wall and searched the sky.

"Patience, Ehrich," Tesla advised. "They will come."

"What if they don't?"

The Serbian stroked his moustache. "We might be able to fly up there."

"Can you manufacture something?" Amina asked, opening one eye.

"I once played around with the idea of spinning rotors that could lift a machine into the air. Unfortunately, all of it is up here." He tapped the side of his head.

"Then why bother telling us?" Ehrich said.

"Ehrich, he's trying to help," Amina scolded.

"Trying doesn't get us to Kifo. Unless someone thinks of a real plan, I suggest we keep our thoughts to ourselves."

Tesla placed his hand on Ehrich's shoulder. "I understand your urgency, but we are doing the best we can."

Ehrich glared at his mentor. "Not good enough. We've wasted all this time on a stupid wild-goose chase, and now we're stranded down here while Kifo is up there."

Amina pointed out, "So are our friends."

"If Kifo succeeds, Demon Gate is wide open for Ba Tian's forces."

"You gave him the idea in the first place," Amina accused.

"If I didn't do something, we'd all be prisoners on the airship and Mr. Tesla would be stuck in that torture room Edison set up."

"You put everyone at risk just so you could get what you want."

"Amina, I could have left you all and hunted for Kifo on my own, but I didn't. I know what's at stake. For all of us. How could you doubt me?"

"Tell me one thing, Ehrich. Would you have even returned to the airship if you caught Kifo?"

"Of course I would have," he answered.

She glared at Ehrich, then walked away.

"Amina," Ehrich called out and started after her, but Tesla stepped in front of him.

"She isn't ready to listen," Tesla said. "Let her be."

"You believe me, don't you?" Ehrich asked.

Tesla smiled then turned his attention to a pigeon walking along the street.

Alone, Ehrich wrestled with Amina's question. He would have done the right thing when the time came, he thought. He was sure of it, but the more he tried to convince himself the less he believed.

They returned to the pier at nightfall. Ehrich searched the sky for any sign of an errant cloud, but he spotted only the stars. The twinkling lights dotted the sky—a thousand possible worlds. Right now, he wished he stood on any one of them. He let his quest for Kifo consume him. His friends had warned him when he set the fire at Edison's laboratory and risked innocent lives. Bess had chastised him for using Charlie, his best friend, as bait to lure Kifo. But he ignored them all because he believed he was acting selflessly. What could be nobler than to rescue the soul of his brother?

Everything he had done was far from honourable. He risked lives and friendships in the name of saving his brother. He used people. Ehrich was essentially the same as Kifo—a ruthless manipulator with no thought or care toward others.

He stewed for the rest of the night. The thought gnawed at him, robbing him of his sleep. A few hours later, he confronted the truth, and his face burned with shame. He stood up and walked along the cobblestone street until he found Amina. She feigned sleep.

"Can we talk, Amina?"

"What do you want, Ehrich? I'm tired."

"What you said hurt."

"The truth often does."

"You're right. I'm sorry, Amina. I've been deluding myself

into thinking that I'm doing the right thing. I didn't realize it until now."

"We want the same thing, Ehrich."

"I know, and I appreciate everything you've done. I won't leave you in the lurch. We're not going to leave our friends to suffer up there."

"What about Kifo?"

"He's not going anywhere. Our first priority is our friends."

She nodded.

"Can you forgive me, Amina?"

She opened both eyes. "I look forward to storming the airship with you at my side."

"At your side? I thought I would lead the charge."

She elbowed him. "If you fight as well as you pick locks, we're in trouble."

He laughed.

She glanced at the sky. "I hope we're not too late."

Ning Shu reeled from the recent events. In the aftermath of the assassination of General Xian, the Council of Arch Generals had been dissolved, and Ling Po had been locked up in the brig. Though Ehrich's signal had been spotted, the generals were more concerned with why Xian possessed a seal of the House of Qi. No one knew what to make of the jade tael she had been wearing. By the customs of their people, Ba Tian was to have been in a seven-year period of mourning. He was not allowed to take another wife during this period. By the protocol of the Council of Arch Generals, no general could fraternize with another for fear of consolidating power. Yet, the jade tael was proof Ba Tian had contravened the laws of the people, and it was proof that he had put his love and trust in General Xian.

Now Ning Shu understood why the woman refused to relinquish her power because—as another member of the House of Qi—she had equal say in matters.

The generals fell back on protocol. With a member of the House of Qi back, there was no need for a steward. No one even considered a vote on the issue; although, Xian's cohorts had raised the idea of voting for a new steward. Gu Shan reminded them the House of Qi appointed the steward and was entirely up to Ning Shu. This seemed to silence the haughty generals.

In the meantime, Ning Shu had ordered the airship back to the Hudson River rendezvous point to collect Ehrich's group. In Ling Po's quarters, she sat behind the desk as Mr. Serenity gathered the scrolls and placed them to one side.

"The Council of Arch Generals is in upheaval. No one knows what to make of Xian's position. They are arguing about whether Ba Tian gave her the jade tael as a promise or if they were secretly married."

"How does this matter?" Mr. Serenity asked. "Either way she is dead."

"If she is my father's wife, then Ling Po is guilty of assassinating a member of the House of Qi and should be executed immediately without trial."

"And if she is not?"

"Then he is entitled to plead his case before the Council of Arch Generals."

"Do you think he believed Xian was pulling a weapon on you? Or do you think he wished she was? I mean her death did clear the path for you to be restored as the sole authority in your father's absence."

"I don't know."

"Either way, you have the reins, Ning Shu, and for that I'm grateful. We can finally put an end to the invasions."

She agreed, but Mr. Serenity's words nagged at the back of her mind. A knock at the door distracted her. She answered it. Gu Shan flanked with his escorts stood in the hallway. He bowed to her.

"General Ning Shu, I have a message. Ling Po would like to speak with you. In private."

"How is he?"

"As well as can be expected, given the circumstances. He is aware that he may be facing execution."

"I owe him an audience. Tell him I will see him shortly."

Gu Shan bowed. She closed the door. "Mr. Serenity, will you be all right here?"

"Yes, but be careful. Xian may still have allies."

"I suspect that, without the hand of Xian guiding them, they won't be causing anymore trouble."

She left Mr. Serenity in the quarters and took a personal guard to the brig. She instructed everyone to wait outside the entrance, which was the only way to Ling Po's cell.

"But we need to protect you against Ling Po," the lead escort claimed.

"He's a dear friend, and he's in the brig. I will be safe as long as you make sure no one gets past you. I'm assuming you are capable of defending this door."

The escort snapped to attention. "Yes."

She then stepped into the hallway and closed the door. At the far end of the corridor, two red hands peeked out through the bars of the bamboo cell. She pieced together what to say to her friend and mentor as she slipped toward the cell. The man had sacrificed his career to save her from what he believed was Xian's attack. His actions resulted in her regaining power over the army. A twinge of guilt fluttered in her chest as she realized she was going to use her newly restored authority to tear down the very army Ling Po had helped to build up. Still, she owed it to her mentor to at least express gratitude for saving her life.

She stopped in front of the cell. Ling Po looked bruised from the battle that erupted after he shot Xian. Some of the younger generals had been overzealous in tackling him. He beamed when he saw Ning Shu.

"Thank you for agreeing to meet me," he said. "I wasn't sure if you would come."

"It's the least I could do, Ling Po. I'm sorry for your treatment."

He shook his head. "This is for the best. I could have sworn Xian was drawing a weapon on you. Curse my old eyes and my overly cautious nature. If I had known otherwise, I would not have shot her."

"Although you did give a solution to our problem."

The old man rubbed his red hands together. "Yes, I suppose there is some small comfort that we achieved our end, even if the means were not ideal."

"And with Xian out of the way, I'm sure the young generals are scrambling to find a foothold in the council. They must be quaking at the thought that they may be accused of colluding against me."

Ling Po clapped his hands. "They will fall in line. They are followers. In the absence of Ba Tian, they were only too happy to fall in march step behind Xian. Now that she is dead, and the rightful heir has been restored, they will obey your every command."

"I'm curious about one thing, Ling Po. Was this your plan all along?"

"You are the House of Qi, Ning Shu. You are our leader. I

would give my life to protect you. This was my single driving thought in the chamber." He reached out and took her hand, patting it.

"I wish I could open this cell door, Ling Po."

The old man smiled. "All I need is your hand."

"I need you at my side. Governing without your guidance will be difficult."

Ling Po shook his head. "The only one who can challenge you is your father."

"Yes...I suppose."

"And he will not be returning to this dimension any time soon," he said.

Ning Shu stiffened. "My father is in prison."

"Please, your friends stranded him in the other dimension."

Ning Shu shook her head. "You're mistaken, sir."

Ling Po tightened his grip on her hand, refusing to let go. "I saw the whole thing with my own eyes."

"Let go."

He refused, drawing her closer to the cell. The scent of sulphur filled the air and Ning Shu felt herself separating from her body. The last thing she saw was the medallion around the neck of her mentor. The gears of the Infinity Coil stared back at her. The gears within the loops began to whir. The stench of sulphur choked out all the air in her lungs. Then blackness.

BETRAYAL

Wu Bei and Zhengfu Zhe rowed the craft to the Hudson River pier. Like many of the other soldiers, Wu Bei hated the airship and yearned for the chance to step on solid ground again. He had heard rumours of some kind of upheaval among the generals. No one had seen General Xian in some time, and now Ning Shu was giving the orders, including the one to retrieve her friends. As a soldier, Wu Bei knew to keep his head down and keep questions to himself.

He glanced at the approaching shore and spotted Ehrich and Amina pacing around the pier. Behind the pair stood a tall man he did not recognize.

"I don't see Ba Tian," Zhengfu Zhe declared. "They must have failed."

When they neared the pier, Wu Bei tossed out a line. Ehrich snatched the rope and tied it off around the mooring post.

"You promised to free Ba Tian," Zhengfu Zhe accused. "Where is he?"

Tesla pushed past the two and announced, "It's about time you picked up the radiotelegraphometer's signal. We have narrowed his location, but we'll need the airship to sneak into the premises."

Zhengfu Zhe tilted his head. "Who are you?"

Tesla smiled without missing a beat. "I had to assume a new body. It's me. Kifo."

Wu Bei sighed. "Orders are orders, Zhengfu Zhe. Get them into the skiff."

An hour later, the group rowed along the Hudson River. Ehrich and Amina sat together in the middle of the boat. Tesla perched on a bench at the stern, his hand resting on the codex.

As Zhengfu Zhe rowed, he glanced at the device, raising an eyebrow and trying to get his partner's attention. Wu Bei was too busy rowing to notice Zhengfu Zhe pretending to clear his throat. Tesla noticed. He picked up the codex and clutched it protectively. Ehrich joined his mentor at the back of the boat. He flashed a disarming smile at Zhengfu Zhe.

"Not yet," Ehrich whispered to Tesla.

His plan had been fashioned after his act at the Bijou. When they neared the bay doors, Tesla was to transmit an image of Edison walking away on the deck of the airship. If the plan succeeded, the soldiers would scramble after the apparition while Ehrich and the others slipped out of the skiff. They would leave the deck and search the ship for Ning Shu and Mr. Serenity. The only kink in the plan was the two scouts in the boat, who were the key to getting on to the airship.

Zhengfu Zhe asked, "What's that book for?"

"It's something we took from Edison," Ehrich lied. "It's what we need to get into the prison where they are holding Ba Tian."

The red scout nodded, but his gaze lingered on the codex.

When the cables lowered from the airship to the skiff, Wu

Bei and Zhengfu Zhe grabbed them and attached them to the craft's mooring rings. Now all they had to do was wait for the airship crew to reel them up. Ehrich had no more need of the scouts.

At the rear of the craft, he shifted closer to Tesla as Zhengfu Zhe settled onto a bench in the middle. Ehrich nodded to Amina. She slid behind Wu Bei at the bow of the boat. He scrunched his face, suspicious.

"What's going on?" he asked.

Amina drew her pistol from behind her back and aimed it at Wu Bei. Ehrich trained his weapon on Zhengfu Zhe's back.

"Take off your weapons and drop them overboard," Ehrich instructed.

The pair reluctantly obeyed. Ehrich pulled out his Darby handcuffs and Irish 8s as the boat rose in the air.

"Hands behind your back," Ehrich ordered.

Zhengfu Zhe hesitated until Ehrich jabbed the barrel of the pistol in his back. He complied. His thick wrists were too wide for the Irish 8s. Ehrich slapped the Darby cuffs on the man's arms and screwed the key to engage the lock. The scout wasn't going anywhere.

Now the skiff was high over the water and about halfway up to the cloud. He reached into his satchel for a pair of leg irons to snap around Wu Bei's huge wrists. He waved at Amina sitting behind the behemoth and held up the cuffs.

"I have you covered, Wu Bei," she said. "Try anything, and I'll fry you in the back. Understood?"

He nodded as Ehrich moved around Zhengfu Zhe. The boat started to rock from the movement. Wu Bei grabbed the sides of the boat and shifted his weight to one side, throwing Ehrich off balance. The skiff listed. The cuffs slipped out of his hands and plummeted to the river below. Zhengfu Zhe lashed out with a kick into Ehrich's back, sending him reeling toward the side of the boat.

Amina fired an electro-dart at Zhengfu Zhe, but Wu Bei shifted in front of her. The dart grazed the back of his arm discharging energy into his flesh. Howling in pain, he swung backwards and clipped Amina's gun, sending it to the floor.

She wrapped her arms around the man's neck and tried to hold him down. He lashed out with his legs and connected with the off-balanced Ehrich, sending him overboard. He grabbed the side just in time, but the wet sides didn't give him enough traction and his forearm was still weakened from his fight with Ole Lukoje. He began to slip.

Tesla shouted, "Hold on." He started to stand. Zhengfu Zhe slammed the back of his head into the scientist's midriff and the codex.

Ehrich's hand began to slip. Zhengfu Zhe raised a foot to step on his fingers. Amina snagged the pistol with her foot, pulling it closer to herself. She tried to reach down with one hand while she clung to Wu Bei with her other arm. He thrashed in the boat, causing it to rock wildly.

Finally, Amina grabbed the pistol and aimed it at Zhengfu Zhe. The electro-dart struck him square in the back and ignited into a shower of sparks. He slumped down in the boat unconscious.

Wu Bei elbowed her in the ribs with his good hand, knocking the wind out of her. Then he grabbed her arm, slamming it against the side of the boat. She gritted her teeth to shut out the pain.

Ehrich hauled himself halfway into the boat, just enough to reach the pistol on the floor. He picked it up and fired. A dart struck Wu Bei in the midsection and lit up his body. The charge even shocked Amina, who now lay flattened under the big man. Ehrich hauled himself into the boat and helped pull the unconscious scout off her.

"You okay?"

"I'll be all right." Her wrist started to swell.

He glanced up at the cloud. "Hold on. We're almost there. Mr. Tesla, hit the projection. Mr. Tesla?"

He whirled around. Tesla knelt on the boat floor, trying to piece together the shattered codex.

Too late. The cables reeled the boat through the bay doors and into the deck, where a dozen armed crimson soldiers waited for them. The bay doors closed underneath them. They were trapped.

"No," Ning Shu said, stepping out from behind the retinue of crimson soldiers. "They are not to be harmed."

The soldiers lowered their throwing discs. Ehrich glanced at his companions, bewildered. Mr. Serenity stepped forward to help the group climb out of the boat. They left the unconscious scouts behind.

"What's going on?" Amina asked.

"Ning Shu is in charge," Mr. Serenity whispered.

"How?" she asked.

"I'll explain later."

Ning Shu approached the group. "Are you all right?" she asked. "What happened to Kifo?"

"Ning Shu, we have to warn you. Kifo never left the airship."

"Nonsense. He left with you. Where is he?"

"Ole Lukoje was pretending to be possessed. The real Kifo is here," Ehrich said. "You're in danger."

"What do you mean he's here?"

"Ole Lukoje and Kifo conspired to trick you to stay so that you'd be open to an attack."

Ning Shu shook her head. "You did not succeed in abducting Thomas Edison?"

"No, but what does that—"

"Is Ole Lukoje still alive?"

"Yes, but it doesn't matter. Kifo is here. Are you even listening to what I'm saying?"

She stepped back behind her soldiers.

"Ehrich's telling the truth," Amina said, backing up her friend.

Ning Shu addressed her soldiers. "Surround them. They are enemies of the House of Qi."

The crimson escorts shifted to form a ring around the trio.

"What are you doing, Ning Shu?" Mr. Serenity said. "They are your allies."

She pushed the rotund man toward Ehrich and the others. "Take them into custody."

"Have you lost your mind, Ning Shu?" Ehrich stammered.

She laughed. "An apt choice of words. These intruders on the ship have given me the information I needed to know. Kifo is still on his mission. These four are of no use to us. Bind them."

The veins in Mr. Serenity's forehead throbbed. "What are you doing? Ning Shu, this is madness."

She grinned. "You didn't think the House of Qi would ever side with you, did you?"

"You betrayed us," Mr. Serenity said. "Why?"

Ehrich stifled a gasp. Ning Shu hadn't betrayed their group. She had been taken by Kifo. In control of her body, the assassin now commanded Ba Tian's entire army. The armed escorts grabbed him and trussed him up in a canvas straitjacket. Two men bound the straps tight behind his back. Another two crossed Ehrich's arms over his chest and lashed him inside the restraint. They completed the trussing with a leather strap between his legs so he couldn't squirm out the bottom. The others were also trussed in the restraints. Amina struggled but to no avail. They were prisoners.

"That's not Ning Shu," Ehrich protested. "Don't listen to her. Kifo's compromised her."

None of the soldiers listened. They herded Ehrich's group together.

"Open the bay doors and push them out," Ning Shu said. "Then we need scouts to assist Kifo."

She exited with her armed escort. Four soldiers remained behind to finish the job at hand, but they were reluctant to move, whispering among themselves around the control panel for the bay doors.

"General Ning Shu couldn't care less about Wu Bei and Zhengfu Zhe," the tallest one in the bunch griped.

A stocky one shushed him. "Yu, don't let her hear you say that. She'll throw you off the ship with this sad lot."

"General Xian cared about the soldiers. She once told me we were the true progeny of the House of Qi."

"Orders are orders," another soldier said.

Another one piped up. "I heard there was dissension in the Council of Arch Generals. Chaos reigns in Ba Tian's absence. What should we do, Yu?"

"I'm a soldier of the House of Qi. I will obey Ning Shu's orders, but I'll be damned if I ignore my comrades in arms. Wu Bei and Zhengfu Zhe need medical attention first. Let's get them out of the skiff."

As Ehrich struggled against his restraints, a twinge of guilt seeped into his marrow as he saw the reflection of Wilhelm,

Margaret, and Gino in this crimson soldier looking out for his comrades. Yu climbed into the boat while his companions glanced around nervously.

"Are you going to help me or not?"

They shuffled to the skiff. Yu rolled Wu Bei out of the ship and into their outstretched arms.

Ehrich didn't have much time. He had to escape, but the restraint had no locks to pick. If he could reach the buckles, he could loosen them, but he was bound up within the canvas jacket with no way to reach the back buckles. His arms had been pinned against his body and tied up. He began to squirm in the straitjacket, trying to find a way to loosen the straps and gain some slack.

Beside him, the others struggled as well with no luck. Ehrich felt some give in the sleeve. He hoped to create enough slack so he could stick his head under the sleeve and unwind his arms, but to do so would require him to dislocate his shoulder. He heaved and thrashed on the ground.

"Don't knock yourself," one of the soldiers taunted. "No one's ever escaped from the straitjacket."

Yu growled. "Hurry up with Wu Bei, Zhengfu Zhe's heavy."

The three men laid Wu Bei just beyond the bay doors, then headed back to the skiff to receive the other injured warrior.

Ehrich felt his arm start to give. He felt a stab of pain as he dislocated his shoulder. The right sleeve gave a little. He worked the canvas sleeve over his head, but the pain fired up. He gritted his teeth until he looped the canvas sleeve over his head. He pushed his face into the small opening and squeezed through until his head poked through. His arm burned from the pain, but he was free.

He used his left hand to undo the buckle between his legs. Then he reached up to the collar and yanked the jacket over his head. His right arm felt numb. Two of the soldiers were taking Zhengfu Zhe from Yu and lowering him out of the skiff.

"Grab the other prisoners and haul them to the bay doors," Yu ordered the third guard.

"Time to see if they have wings," the soldier said, grinning as he turned to Amina and the others.

Ehrich had only one chance to save his friends. He rushed to the control panel and with his one good arm pulled the lever that controlled the opening. The bamboo bay doors fell away and the three crimson soldiers plunged to their deaths along with Zhengfu Zhe. Only Wu Bei's body remained on the floor.

The skiff remained attached to the cables and Yu remained inside the craft, glaring at Ehrich. He prepared to leap out of the skiff, but hesitated at the sight of the drop. Instead, he swung the suspended boat side to side to build enough momentum so he could clear the opening when he jumped out.

Tesla, Amina, and Mr. Serenity squirmed and kicked on the floor, trying to get free of their restraints and get further away from the windy opening.

Ehrich slammed his right shoulder into the control panel and set his shoulder back right. The pain was excruciating, but he gritted his teeth and shut out the searing pain in his arm. He turned the crank on the controls and started to lower the skiff. Yu nearly lost his grip but was able to hang on to one of the cables. Finally, he jumped out of the swaying skiff and landed on the floor, missing the opening by inches.

The giant approached Ehrich, drawing his razor-sharp discs from his bandolier. He licked his lips, relishing the impending drubbing he planned to give the boy. He unleashed one disc after the other, forcing Ehrich to fall back and dodge the deadly projectiles.

Ehrich ran to the left, scooped up the straitjacket and

jumped up into one of the skiffs hanging from the cables. A disc slammed into the wood inches from Ehrich's leg. He stayed low in the boat, forcing the armed man to switch tactics. Yu climbed into the skiff, but Ehrich vaulted into another one before the man could grab him. The giant chased him to the next boat. The game of cat and mouse took the pair across the deck and away from his friends.

"You're running out of space," Yu yelled.

He was right. Ehrich was now at the far wall. Only one skiff left to hide in. He jumped out and doubled back across the deck. Then he hopped into a skiff near the bay doors. He unbuckled the back of the straitjacket as Yu sprinted toward him. Ehrich leapt out of the boat and wrapped the canvas jacket around Yu's head, blinding him. The giant struggled to pull off the jacket, opening his midsection to attack, which Ehrich took advantage of with a well-placed knee. Yu doubled over and Ehrich jumped on his back. He grabbed the sleeves of the straitjacket and twisted them around Yu's neck, trying to steer him like a wild horse.

Yu thrashed his arms around. Ehrich pulled hard on the right sleeve, turning the man's head and causing him to step to the side. Yu tried to straighten up, but Ehrich shifted his weight forward to keep the crimson giant bent over. He pulled again on the right sleeve until Yu staggered over and faced the opened bay doors.

"Get off me," Yu shouted, his voice muffled by the jacket.

"You want me? You're going to have to fight harder than that."

Ehrich pulled back on both sleeves. Yu responded by jerking himself forward. Ehrich let go at the same time. The sudden momentum propelled Yu forward to the edge of the bay doors. He tripped over Wu Bei and tumbled headfirst through the opening.

Ehrich tried to shut out Yu's screams, but he knew another person had died because of him. He moved to the control panel and pulled the lever to close the bay doors. He rushed to his friends' aid and freed them from their straitjackets, taking care with Amina's sore wrist. Once she was out, he helped Mr. Serenity.

"I thought Kifo was Xian," Amina said. "How did he possess Ning Shu?"

"Ling Po shot Xian at a meeting of the generals. He killed her."

"Then how did he possess Ning Shu?" Tesla asked.

Mr. Serenity slipped the canvas top off his arms. "Kifo must have been controlling Ling Po all the while. He asked for a private meeting with Ning Shu after the shooting. I'll wager my life that's when he took over her body."

"Why did Kifo kill Xian?" Amina asked.

"She fought for control of the House of Qi. With her out of the way, Ning Shu could claim all the power."

Ehrich freed his mentor. "Mr. Tesla, the only way to save you was to kill those soldiers. I wish there was another way."

Mr. Tesla rubbed his arms. "Ehrich, we are alive because of you. I'm sure if you could have found another way you would have, but the soldiers left you no choice. Sometimes, life gives you no alternatives and you must make the most of what you've been given."

"What do we do about Ning Shu?" Amina asked Mr. Serenity.

"I'm afraid she is a prisoner of the Infinity Coil now. Kifo has the power to release her, and I doubt he will want to do that anytime soon."

Tesla scratched his head. "What if we just destroy the Infinity Coil? Wouldn't that send all the souls back to their bodies?"

Mr. Serenity shrugged. "I don't know. The coil is a storage facility for the souls of all the people Kifo has taken. You destroy the coil, and you wipe out the only thing that was holding everyone together. They may just wink out of existence."

"Or they may find their bodies again," Ehrich said, grasping for any kind of hope.

"I don't know enough about the device to say for certain, but you would be making the assumption that there's a tether between consciousness and form. I can't tell you one way or the other."

"Then if we're going to save Ning Shu, we have to take Kifo alive," Ehrich said.

"What do you propose?" Amina asked.

"Find a weapon." Ehrich searched the deck. He decided against the bandolier of discs on Wu Bei and Zhengfu Zhe. A user had to be skilled to hurl the projectiles with any kind of accuracy.

After rummaging around the room, he soon found a locker filled with weapons used by the previous crew of the airship.

"Over here," he announced.

The others rushed over and equipped themselves with crossbows and quivers of bolts. The handheld weapons were sleek and wooden. They were light enough to carry and aim, but the bowstring was taut and powerful enough to fire barbed arrows a fair distance. The double bowstrings allowed the wielder to fire twice before reloading. Ehrich wasn't sure about the weapon's overall effectiveness—he would have preferred to have a dynatron or a teslatron—but he wasn't about to get choosy.

The group slipped out of the deck into a narrow hallway that led to the back section of the gondola. Mr. Serenity led the way.

"Are you sure this is the way, Mr. Serenity?" Amina asked.

"Positive." He reached under his shirt and pulled out a paper scroll. He unrolled the parchment to reveal his calligraphy artwork—a crude map of the ship he had pieced together.

"Remarkable," Tesla said. "I could have employed you to draft the schematics for my induction motor."

"This corridor will take us back to General Xian's office and quarters. I'll bet we'll find Kifo there," Mr. Serenity said.

Tesla questioned their strategy. "What do we do once we capture him? He's not likely to confess to the soldiers."

Ehrich armed his crossbow. "We're taking Kifo and leaving. Then we'll force him to release Ning Shu and everyone else he's ever possessed."

They skulked along the bamboo hallways and headed toward the rear of the airship. The narrow corridors offered little space to manoeuvre. The lighter weight of the bamboo allowed the designers to distribute more weight across the ship, but space was at a premium. Outside the porthole windows, the propulsors jutted out of the gondola and stabilized the airship.

Mr. Serenity slowed down. "We're getting close. Down these stairs."

"What about the other stairs?" Tesla asked, motioning at a set of bamboo steps leading up.

"They'll take you to the engine room!" Mr. Serenity shouted over the roar of the engines.

"Intriguing," Tesla said. "I wonder what type of engines the airship employs."

Mr. Serenity pointed out. "Steam-powered rotors that spin the propulsors. I'm not sure how efficient they are. "

"Nothing an electromagnetic oscillator couldn't fix."

"You know of such technology?"

Tesla cocked his head to the side. "I saw yours. Impressive."

"If you two are done admiring each other, we have work to do," Ehrich said.

"My apologies," Mr. Serenity said. "Xian's quarters are the

second door to the right."

Ehrich advanced down the steps, followed by Amina. Tesla and Mr. Serenity remained on the landing. Ehrich stopped before descending further and peeked ahead. Three warriors were stationed in the hallway.

Amina shouted, "The tight space gives us an advantage. They can only come at us two at a time."

"If one of us stays on the stairs, we should be able to pick them off. Amina, you're a better shot than I am."

"I don't suppose you have a magic trick that can make the soldiers disappear."

Ehrich shook his head.

"What if there are more inside the quarters?" Amina asked.

"Then we'd better reload fast."

Ehrich raised his crossbow and continued his descent. A soldier spotted Ehrich creeping down the steps. Before he could reach for his throwing disc, Ehrich leapt at him and kneed him in the groin, then grabbed the man's tunic and drove his forehead into the man's nose. Blood squirted out.

The other two soldiers reached for their weapons, but the lanky one at the rear dropped to the floor, clutching Amina's crossbow bolt in his neck. Blood spurted from the wound, and he wheezed for breath, unable to catch air. He died on his knees. The other one took aim at Ehrich, who used his stunned opponent as a shield. The disc struck the soldier in the back, and the man howled in pain. Ehrich fired from under the man's arm and grazed the other soldier in the leg.

The soldier with the bloody nose pushed Ehrich back against the wall and staggered to one side. Ehrich was now open to attack. The soldier with the injured leg drew a razor tael from his bandolier, but before he could throw it, a bolt imbedded into his chest. He wheezed, clutching the arrow, then slumped against the wall.

The remaining soldier slid along the wall, leaving a bloody smear from the tael that had pierced his back. He reached for his weapon, but Amina was faster. A crossbow bolt pierced the man's eye and he collapsed, dead. She rushed down the steps as she and Ehrich reloaded.

"Good job, Amina," he said, clapping his hand on her back.

But their celebration was short-lived. A klaxon alarm blared.

"Kifo must have heard us!" Ehrich shouted. He kicked the door once, twice. The door cracked. A third time. Another crack.

Amina reloaded her crossbow. Tesla and Mr. Serenity descended the stairs as Ehrich finally kicked the door open. In the chambers, Kifo hid behind the mahogany desk with a crossbow aimed at Ehrich. Though the body belonged to Ning Shu, its murderous gaze was all Kifo. She fired.

Ehrich angled his body into the bolt, and his shoulder lit up from the pain of the projectile striking home. He dropped his weapon and staggered back against the wall. Kifo adjusted her aim.

Amina slipped into the room and took cover behind a divan. She aimed her crossbow at the assassin. "Lower your weapon," she ordered.

Kifo refused. "Would you destroy the body of your friend?"

Amina hesitated. Though she knew this was Kifo, she could only see Ning Shu standing before her.

"Would you lose the only chance of saving Ehrich's brother from the Infinity Coil?" Kifo asked.

Ehrich gripped the bloody bolt in his shoulder and gritted his teeth. Killing Kifo would cut off his best chance to save Ning Shu or recover Dash. As much as he hated to admit it, the assassin was right.

"Lower your weapon, Amina."

A PERILOUS CHOICE

The trio was at a standoff. Kifo only had one bolt in his weapon. He couldn't take out both Ehrich and Amina, but they couldn't kill the assassin while he possessed Ning Shu's body.

"You're leaving the airship with us, Kifo," Ehrich said, applying pressure to his wound to stop the bleeding.

"You're in no position to make any demands. The more time we stand here, the more time my soldiers will have to come to my rescue."

Ehrich yelled, "Mr. Serenity, Mr. Tesla. Go to the top of the stairs. Shoot anyone who comes."

"On our way," Tesla shouted back.

"Those old men aren't going to be any match for Ba Tian's soldiers," Kifo said. "Now lower your crossbow, or I will shoot your friend."

Amina hesitated, but she finally obeyed and placed the crossbow on the ground.

"Now kick it away."

She obeyed. The crossbow slid across the floor.

"That's better." Kifo rose from behind the mahogany desk. "Now lie down on the floor."

She began to kneel.

"Both of you."

The soldiers would be upon them soon. Ehrich had one chance. He snapped the crossbow bolt in his shoulder off—igniting a new wave of pain—then hurled the shaft at Kifo, who ducked under it. Ehrich kicked his crossbow on the floor to Amina as he stumbled toward the desk. Kifo fired, but Ehrich dove to the floor and the bolt missed him.

Amina stood up with Ehrich's crossbow aimed at Kifo's chest. "You're not fast enough to reload and shoot. Drop the weapon."

"Go ahead. Snuff out the lives of your friends," the assassin taunted.

Amina didn't pull the trigger. "You okay, Ehrich?"

He grunted. "I'll live."

He ripped a part of his shirt to tie off his wound. He'd have to dig out the remnants of the bolt, but not now. There was no time.

"Kifo, drop the weapon," Amina ordered.

The assassin finally complied.

"Let's go up," Ehrich said. "This is no place to defend ourselves." With his good hand, he picked up Amina's crossbow.

"Move, Kifo," Amina said, herding her quarry to the doorway.

They ushered Kifo up the stairs to join Tesla and Mr. Serenity. The two men exchanged fire with soldiers at the other end of the corridor, keeping Ba Tian's men from getting any closer. Ehrich motioned the pair to head up the stairs to join their friends.

"You might as well give up," Kifo said. "There's no escape."

Mr. Serenity took another shot and reloaded his crossbow.

"The engine room. We can fortify ourselves in there. And then we can bring the bird out of the sky."

Amina's eyes widened. "Are you insane? We'll perish."

The big man beamed. "I'm insane, but not suicidal. Not crash the ship. Bring it down."

"How?" Ehrich asked.

"I'll show you, but first we have to get them to stop shooting at us." He fired down the corridor twice.

Amina pushed Kifo in front of her, using the assassin as a shield. The soldiers stopped throwing taels. Mr. Serenity led Tesla and Ehrich up the stairs to the engine room. Amina followed, moving backwards with Kifo as her shield against the soldiers. "Stay back or your general dies!" she cried.

They squeezed through the doorway and slammed the door shut. Amina spotted a large tool kit near the door. She grabbed a tapered punch—used to start holes for drills—and a hammer. She pounded the punch into the floor at the base of the door then pounded several more of the metal rods into the floor as makeshift doorstops.

"Whatever you have planned, Mr. Serenity, you'd better be fast," she said. "I think I've attracted some attention."

Two engineers who stood near the segmented hydrogen tanks looked up at the noise.

Kifo shouted, "Help! The intruders have taken me hostage."

The scarlet engineers were technicians, not warriors, but they weren't helpless. The two men grabbed heavy tools and chains and advanced on the group, joined by another two who approached from further down the engine room.

Ehrich fired at the nearest engineer and brought him down. The remaining three scattered behind the tanks.

"Watch Kifo," Ehrich yelled back as he headed toward the giant copper tanks.

As he slipped around one of them, a chain slammed down on his weapon and knocked it out of his hand. He came face to face with a burly engineer in overalls. The man twirled the length of chain as he advanced.

Amina pushed Kifo down on the floor and signalled Mr. Serenity and Tesla to watch the assassin. She rushed to Ehrich's aid, but another engineer appeared from behind a tank. He brandished a giant wrench. She spun and fired. He fell with a bolt in his chest. His partner emerged. She took aim and fired, but her weapon was empty. He flashed a gap-toothed grin and charged. In the tight space between the hydrogen tanks and steam engines, Amina couldn't manoeuvre and had to confront the engineer head on. He rained punches on her head and forced her back.

Mr. Serenity took aim at the gap-toothed engineer, but Kifo struck him with a well-placed kick to the groin. "Storm the engine room," she shouted as she ran through a lane between steam engines.

Tesla tried to catch the assassin, but a heavy slam against the door caused him to stop. The metal punches began to bend under the pressure. He rushed to the door and braced himself against the wood to keep the soldiers from entering.

Amina elbowed her gap-toothed opponent. He staggered back. She advanced for another blow, but Kifo kicked the back of her knee, knocking her down. The engineer clipped her chin with an uppercut, dazing her. Kifo turned her attention to Ehrich.

Across the engine room, Ehrich ducked under the whirling chain and rushed at his assailant, slamming his good shoulder into the man's midsection. The impact sent shockwaves of pain into his throbbing wound. He clenched his jaw and drove the engineer against the hydrogen tank, knocking the wind out of the man. Then Ehrich lifted his head and connected with the man's jaw, knocking him out cold.

The door cracked loudly as the soldiers smashed into it. "I can't hold the door much longer," Tesla screamed.

Ehrich started toward the door.

Mr. Serenity groaned, "No. Ehrich...up the ladder. The rip line."

"What?" Ehrich asked.

The injured man pointed up. "There's an emergency device for rapid descent. It's a rip line in the balloon. The winch at the top of ladder. Crank it until the rip opens.... I'll help Mr. Tesla."

Ehrich ran to the ladder and began to climb. About halfway up, he spotted a thick cable running from the winch at the top of the platform to what appeared to be a seam in the balloon near the bow. He scaled the bamboo rungs.

Suddenly, a hand grabbed his ankle. Below, Kifo had a hold of Ehrich's leg. He kicked free of the assassin and swung around to the other side of the ladder to climb. His adversary followed and snaked her hand out again, but Ehrich kicked it away. He lost his grip and slid down the ladder, slamming into Kifo, stunning her. The pain in his shoulder and forearm throbbed and he bit his lip to keep from screaming. Ehrich then redoubled his efforts and climbed up until he reached the platform. He searched the engine room for Amina and spotted her fighting the gap-toothed engineer at the base of the ladder. He turned his attention back to the device on the platform.

The cylindrical winch had to be operated by hand. A heavy rope was already wrapped around one end of the spool, and the rest of the line ran up to the seam in the balloon skin. Ehrich lifted the safety stop and cranked the wooden handle around once to gather the line. His muscles strained from the effort, and his wounds throbbed. He turned the crank a second time.

Before he could crank a third time, Kifo grabbed the back of his jacket and hauled him back.

Ehrich's hand snaked out and grabbed the bamboo railing in time to keep from flying off the platform. Kifo punched the wound in his other arm, causing a fresh spurt of blood. He screamed and staggered back. Kifo pressed the advantage and shoved Ehrich back against the railing. The bamboo bent but did not break. He tipped over the edge. One more good shove and he was done for.

Before Kifo could finish the job, Amina grabbed the assassin's leg from the ladder. Her face was bruised and bloodied, but she had an intense determination in her grey eyes. Kifo drove her boot into Amina's face. She slipped down the ladder but clung to one of the bamboo rungs. Kifo raised her boot for another blow.

Ehrich covered his wound with one hand and threw his body into Kifo, driving her off the platform. The assassin grabbed a rung just in time and slammed against the ladder beside Amina, who slipped down a rung below the assassin.

Below, a loud crash resounded as the door splintered to pieces. Tesla and Mr. Serenity scrambled for cover as a dozen soldiers rushed through the doorway. They spread out across the engine room.

Ehrich reached out to grab Amina, but she was out of reach.

"Forget me," Amina cried. "Take the ship down."

The soldiers would swarm the engine room in seconds. This was their only opportunity. Ehrich pulled back from the platform's edge and cranked the winch. The rip line coiled around the spool. The tear in the balloon opened up wider, and air rushed in. The ship began to take a nosedive.

Mr. Serenity grabbed Tesla, and the two braced themselves between the steam engines. The sudden pitch of the airship sent the soldiers skidding across the floor. One smacked his head on an overhanging copper pipe and fell down unconscious. Others reached out to grab anything to stop their sliding. A few scrambled to climb up the incline to the safety boats at the far end of the engine room.

"Get out before the ship goes down!" one of the soldiers shouted.

Panic overcame discipline as the men pushed each other out of the way to get to the safety boats.

The airship yawed to an even sharper angle. Ehrich grabbed the railing and peered over. Kifo and Amina struggled to hang on. A fall from this height would be fatal. Kifo's grip started to slip. Ehrich reached over the platform and grabbed the assassin's wrist. His crossbow wound pulsed with pain, but he gritted his teeth and hung on to Kifo with his good hand.

Amina began to lose her grip. "Ehrich! I can't hang on any longer."

"You have to hang on," he shouted.

"I can't!"

"Don't let go of me," Kifo yelled.

"Help!" Amina said.

Ehrich tried to shift himself over so he could help Amina, but his grip on Kifo slipped and he knew he had to stay put.

"If you let go of me, you lose Ning Shu," Kifo yelled.

"Shut up," Ehrich yelled.

Amina tried to shift her grip, but she slipped. Now she hung on to the bamboo ladder by one hand. Ehrich had to make a choice.

"Let her die," Kifo said. "Save me, and you will have what you want. I'm the only chance your brother has."

Ehrich stared into the assassin's eyes, and knew there was no other choice. He let go of Kifo. Her arms flailed as she plummeted to the angled floor below. Her body landed on one of the pipes leading from the ballonet to the copper pipes. There was a loud crack as Kifo's back broke on the impact. Her limp corpse fell to the network of pipes just over the hydrogen tanks.

Ehrich grabbed Amina, the pain in his shoulder erupting again. He hauled her up.

"Why?" she gasped. "Kifo was the key to everything."

"I couldn't let you die, Amina."

The airship began to level off. The pair could climb down the ladder. Only Tesla and Mr. Serenity remained below with the bodies of the dead soldiers on the floor. The other soldiers had cleared the engine room to climb into the safety boats. Ning Shu's twisted body lay on the overhead pipes. Her eyes were open, but blank and lifeless.

The ship splashed down in the Hudson River. The gondola listed heavily to one side. Water poured in through the giant tear in the envelope. They had to flee.

"Can everyone swim?" Ehrich asked.

"I can't," Mr. Serenity said, eyes wide with panic.

Tesla patted his colleague on the shoulder. "Don't worry. We'll help you."

Amina said, "Mr. Serenity, I'll carry you out if I have to."

They waited until the water filled up the engine room. They waded through the briny water until they had to swim. Tesla and Amina bracketed Mr. Serenity and towed him with them as they swam out the opening.

Ehrich lingered behind, watching the water wash over Ning Shu's body. He gritted his teeth and floated toward the body. He wrapped his good arm around one of the copper pipes and reached out to pull the Infinity Coil from around his friend's neck. Then he gently caressed her pale face in a silent farewell, before he kicked off and swam to join the others. His injured shoulder forced him to turn to his side so he could paddle with his good arm and kick with both his legs.

Once outside the airship, Ehrich surveyed the damage. Parts of the gondola had snapped off from the impact in the water. The airship started to sink. All around, soldiers were floating on escape rafts.

He noticed some floating bamboo rods a few feet away and grabbed one of them, propping up his injured arm. The water rushing into the balloon threatened to carry him back into the sinking ship but he flutter-kicked with vigour until he surged forward. He retrieved another bamboo rod and swam to his companions struggling with the panicking Mr. Serenity.

Ehrich slid the bamboo between Tesla and Mr. Serenity and ordered, "Grab hold."

The big man lashed out and hooked the rod with his elbows.

"Now kick," he said.

Mr. Serenity obeyed. He stayed afloat, barely keeping his mouth above the lapping river. Tesla and Amina took either ends of the rod and stabilized the big man in the water. They pushed away from the sinking craft and aimed for the Manhattan shoreline.

In the distance, merchant ships sailed toward the downed craft. The people of New York were coming to save the very people who were bent on destroying them. Ehrich couldn't help but note the irony of this. The soldiers were in no condition to fight, and they would welcome the help.

Tesla grinned. "I told you my people would show their best side when it mattered."

By the time Ehrich's group reached shore, merchant sailors were hauling up the crimson soldiers. In short time, the generals would be rounded up, leaving no heads to rule the

House of Qi. Ehrich wanted to celebrate, but he couldn't. All he could think about was the image of the limp body of Ning Shu. Ehrich clutched the Infinity Coil to his chest. Once, this device was a prison for his brother. Now the medallion was a symbol of Ehrich's failure to save his friend, Ning Shu.

DASH

Ehrich's group arrived on shore without anyone noticing them. Too many people were rushing to the aid of the airship evacuees. The rescuers would be surprised to discover the people in the water were not luxury airship passengers, but Ba Tian's soldiers.

The quartet navigated the New York streets to the nearest access point to Purgatory without incident. Hunters had been diverted to the airship disaster. Almost everyone in the city was curious about the dirigible in the Hudson River.

Mr. Serenity tossed Ehrich a peach-coloured towel. "I'm sure Edison will be busy for weeks. His interrogation room will be filled to the brim."

"We need to shut down the room," Tesla pointed out. "I can't abide my AC generators being used for his dark purposes."

Amina agreed. "One step at a time. The good news is there is no army to invade this sector."

"The day is ours," Mr. Serenity said.

"Not quite," Ehrich mumbled.

The bald man glanced at the medallion in the teen's hands. "Ah yes, one last thing to do. May I, Ehrich?"

He reluctantly handed the Infinity Coil to Mr. Serenity.

"I will find a way to free Dash."

"What about Ning Shu? Can you set her free?"

Mr. Serenity shook his head. "Her body was broken."

Ehrich chewed his bottom lip. "I was hoping you might save her as well."

"I will lend my expertise," Tesla said. "I'm sure we'll deduce how the mechanism works."

"Thank you, sir."

The two men brought the Infinity Coil to the workshop table to begin their examination. Amina walked over with a towel to dry off Ehrich. She scrubbed his scalp with vigour, but her gaze lingered on his face.

"What you did back on the ship, I won't forget."

"I don't think I will either. I let Ning Shu drop."

"She isn't lost to us."

"Without her body, she's trapped."

"The person you let fall wasn't Ning Shu. It was Kifo. A body is a vessel. The mind or the soul is the person."

"I can't help thinking I let Ning Shu die. I want to believe Kifo fell, but I only see Ning Shu's face."

"Ehrich, you had no choice. You gave us all a chance to survive. As for Ning Shu and Dash...we can't lose hope. Life finds a way. Every survivor in Purgatory is proof of this."

Amina's words rang hollow in Ehrich's ears. He excused himself and walked into the cryogenic chamber where Dash slept. The boy seemed serene in the suspended state, but Ehrich noted how his face had changed over the two years they had been apart. His body had grown. Ehrich wondered if his mind had grown as well.

The next morning, Mr. Serenity gathered everyone around the worktable. Amina wiped the sleep from her eyes. Ehrich had not slept at all.

"The technology is ancient, but I think I understand. At first, I believed the gears were nothing important, but then I noticed how many of them were within the loop. When I examined them closer, I realized they were portals, like Demon Gate, except they open to pocket dimensions. Each one contains a consciousness or soul—whatever you want to call them. Open the right one, and the soul within is released."

"How did Kifo know the right one to open?" Ehrich asked.

"I believe he possessed a psychic link to the Infinity Coil so he could recognize the souls. Without him, the next best connection is the soul's original body. Maybe the body can draw out your brother."

"I think I understand."

"I must warn you. The process may simply release all the souls at once and banish them into the ether. We don't know for sure if this will work or not, but if it fails, we may lose your brother forever. I leave you to decide what to do."

"Let me think about it," Ehrich said. He wondered about Ning Shu and all the other hundreds of innocents Kifo had trapped within. Could he callously risk throwing away their lives for the sake of his brother?

He agonized over the decision through the day and into the night. Finally, he approached Amina. "What would you do?"

She offered an answer he didn't expect.

"What is life, Ehrich?"

"What do you mean?"

"What do you define as living?"

"I never thought of it. I guess it means the ability to enjoy the world. To be with family and friends."

"Life is the freedom to make your decisions and to shape the world as you see fit. Even when I lost my people to Ba Tian's army, I appreciated my life despite the grief. I knew I could reshape my life. I could have surrendered to grief, but Mr. Serenity and I clung together as the sole survivors of our race. We reshaped our lives so we would try to give meaning to the deaths of so many. That's why we chose to rebel against Ba Tian, fully aware this act may cost us our lives. The freedom to control your own destiny is what makes you alive."

"Kifo took away this choice from my brother and the others inside the Infinity Coil," Ehrich said.

"Now you can give it back to them," Amina said.

"How?"

"We don't know how the Infinity Coil will work. Maybe the medallion will release the souls into the ether and dissolve them into nothing. Who knows? What we do know is they are trapped without form. If they want to remain in the Infinity Coil, I believe they will linger. If they want to be released, they will surge forward, even if this means the end of their existence. No matter what the result is, remaining trapped in the prison of the Infinity Coil isn't being alive, either."

"What if they don't have a choice? What if reversing the Infinity Coil will jettison them out? What if Kifo kept them from winking out of existence? What if my one decision changes everyone else's lives?"

"Ehrich, you've just described life. Everything we do has an impact on someone else. If you had not been on Demon Watch, you would have never found me to begin with, and I might not be here now. Whatever decision you make, Ehrich, it will have an impact on the souls inside the Infinity Coil. But you can't make their decisions for them. You can only make your own choice."

"What do you think Ning Shu would do?"

Amina tilted her head. "She risked her life to stop Ba Tian. I can't imagine she launched into this ploy without understanding the consequences. She didn't ask to be the daughter of a warlord tyrant, but she chose to stand against him. She acted so no one else would ever suffer because of her father or his emissaries. You forget, Ehrich—you are one of his victims."

The weight of her words rested on his conscience. "I think I'm ready to decide."

They gathered around the cryogenic chamber. Mr. Serenity placed the Infinity Coil on Dash's chest, then he powered down the bed so that the chamber began to warm up. Tesla and Amina gathered on one side of the chamber, leaving Ehrich alone at the other side. He took his brother's hand and squeezed it tight.

Mr. Serenity then reached down and pressed the gears on the Infinity Coil. Slowly, the tiny wheels began to spin, each one connected to the other, spinning a universe of souls. There was no sound, but the reek of sulphur filled the room. Ehrich winced at the smell, but he kept a hold of his brother's hand. To his surprise, the hand began to feel warm.

"Dash? Dash?"

The younger Weisz brother opened his eyes. "Am I really here?" he croaked.

Tears welled up in Ehrich's eyes. "Yes, you're here. It's real."

Dash coughed. "I'm cold."

Ehrich pulled his brother up out of the cryogenic chamber and hugged him, refusing to let him go even when Amina tried to place a blanket over the young boy's shoulders.

"Do you know anything that happened in there?" Mr. Serenity asked.

"One moment I was in this...place...with everyone else. Ehrich, do you remember when you used to tell me about the ghost in our room? How you told me to stay in the light? I tried to do that in the weird place, but I couldn't find any light until now. I ran toward the light until I found myself here. I could feel the others around me, pushing to reach the light. I had to fight them off. They wanted to come with me, but I wouldn't let them come."

"Do you think they are still there now, Dash?" Tesla asked.

"I think so."

Ehrich squeezed his brother once more. He was glad to have his brother back. He was relieved to know Ning Shu might still be in the Infinity Coil. He had hope that she too could be free.

"You're crushing me, Ehrich."

"Dash, I'm going to take us home. Back to mother and father. That's a promise."

The younger Weisz beamed and returned his brother's hug. "Home would be perfect."

THE PURPOSE OF DUST

Outside the fence surrounding Thomas Edison's West Orange facilities, two sentinels walked their nightly patrol. A whistling caught the attention of the blond sentinel. She reached for her weapon, a dynatron pistol. Her companion did as well. The whistling came from behind an oak tree a few dozen yards beyond the fence.

The pair approached the base of the massive tree. She pointed her weapon up, letting the glow of her bowler hat light illuminate the foliage overhead. "You see anything, Bernard?"

There was a short hiss of air.

"Bernard!"

Bernard clutched his throat as he fell to the ground. His partner rushed to his side, but he was dead. The whistling grew louder. The woman came face-to-face with Ole Lukoje.

"Been s-s-so long s-s-sinc-c-e I had some tas-s-sty peepers-s-s," the raggedy man rasped.

Before the woman could scream, he was on her. She fell to

his iron claw, and he gleefully inserted his talons to scoop out her eyes.

A few minutes later, Ole Lukoje dragged the eyeless bodies to the main gate where a quartet of sentinels was stationed. He let out a low groan, loud enough to attract the men, then backed away into the safety of some nearby bushes. Two of gatekeepers emerged from their station with pistols drawn. Upon discovering the corpses of their fellow sentinels, they sounded the alarm. Soon, more men rushed through the iron gate.

Ole Lukoje slipped along the fence away from the commotion until the clamouring was a dull roar. He scaled the barrier and scoped the courtyard. No sentinels. He jumped down and scurried across the grassy area to the laboratory building.

Inside, two scientists in white lab coats tested a cameo that projected three-dimensional images in the air. They were so absorbed in the image of an ebony girl, they didn't hear Ole Lukoje sidle behind them. With a few quick slashes of his iron claw, the scientists were no longer a problem.

The raggedy man searched the room. The array of items confiscated from Dimensionals was a junk peddler's dream, but Ole Lukoje didn't care about the clothing, baubles or books the humans had pored over. He needed to find what the hunters had taken from him. He stopped when he noticed a green glow from the back of the room. As he inched toward it, the glow grew brighter. On a shelf, a glass jar emitted an eerie green light. The fireflies within had woken up in his presence.

"Dus-s-st," Ole Lukoje wheezed. "My friends-s-s, I have miss-ss-ssed you."

He smashed the jar on the floor and the green fireflies swirled upward and around him. He laughed as he waved his hands as if he were the conductor of an invisible orchestra, and the dust danced in the air. A loud rending sound resonated as a hole ripped in the fabric of the space.

Like a cat's eye opening, a portal formed to a barren dimension. On the other side of the gateway was a realm that had been blackened and devastated by war. No signs of life could be seen on the ground or in the air. The raggedy man twirled his copper hand, making a beckoning motion. He stepped back from the glowing portal.

A red hand began to emerge from the portal.

The raggedy man bowed with an exaggerated flourish.

"Welcome back, Ba Tian."

THE EHRICH WEISZ

CHRONICLES

METAMORPHOSIS

The adventure concludes
IN 2016